Liquid Fear

Originally published, in a slightly different form, by Haunted Computer Books in 2011.

Printed in the United States of America.

Published by Thomas & Mercer
P.O. Box 400818
Las Vegas, NV 89140

ISBN-13: 9781612182070
ISBN-10: 1612182070

Liquid Fear

SCOTT NICHOLSON

THOMAS & MERCER

CHAPTER ONE

The rain fell like bullets.

David Underwood blinked against the drops. Darkness pressed against both sides of his eyelids and the air smelled of burnt motor oil. The salvo of rain swept over the expanse of a lighted billboard.

"Need a lawyer?" read the emblazoned pitch, followed by an alphabet soup of advertising copy that swam in David's vision. The sign was upside down.

He was flat on his back, looking up, his clothes soaked. He couldn't lift his head. The rain beat tiny tattoos on his face and crawled along his skin in sinuous trickles. The surface beneath him was hard and cold. He let his head tilt toward the right and he saw a cluster of distant lights.

Buildings. A town.

But which town?

And, the bigger question: who was he this time?

He tested his fingers. None were broken, though the knuckles were sore. Maybe he'd been in a fight. Or mugged and left to leak fluids onto the pavement.

Underwood. David Underwood.

That was his name. The one he'd been born with, not the name they'd given him. Whoever "they" were.

He focused on the billboard. It featured a bland, stern face. No doubt the attorney, desperate to cash in on the misfortunes of others.

Injured in a car crash? Worker compensation claims? Product liability lawsuit? The bottom of the ad heralded a toll-free number.

David wondered if he owned a cell phone. He usually didn't, but sometimes they gave him one, slipped it into his jacket pocket with prepaid minutes.

Prepaid minutes. That was a laugh. "Pay as you go" was the name of this game.

The rain must have been pounding him for a while, because he lay in a puddle. And it was summer because he wasn't shivering. A car horn blared, probably fifty feet away, and tires spat white noise across the wet asphalt.

They were coming for him again. They were always coming for him. Or else they already had him.

He moved his lips, mouthing the words "Need a lawyer?"

The car hissed onward, weaving in the gloom, its twin taillights like the eyes of a retreating dragon.

With a groan, he rolled onto his side, cheek chafing against crumbled tar. He wore no hat. A wristwatch adorned his left wrist and he snaked his arm near his face. The LED numerals flickered red.

11:37. Nearly noon or nearly midnight, it was all the same. Constant darkness.

Unless it was time for the next dose.

The rain spattered and drummed around him in staccato fusillade. Constant war, the earth versus the sky. Us versus them. David Underwood against himself.

A nudge to his back.

He didn't have the strength to fight them this time. No running left in those freighted legs. No direction safe. All avenues took him back to the Research Triangle Park in the heart of North Carolina.

Home—the place of no escape.

He closed his eyes and flopped to one side, hoping they would make it quick this time.

"Home, home on the range," he sang.

The nudge again, this time to his shoulder. "Hey, get up."

Swim, swim, swim. His head went nowhere. He tried to smile, his last act of will, his final defiance. But his lips were useless clay.

"Are you okay?"

A woman. But which one?

"I think I need a lawyer," he said, though he wasn't sure his mouth moved.

Hands explored him, angled his head from side to side. The fingers were strong and sure.

"Can you move your arms and legs?" the woman said.

He nodded, or at least dipped his chin.

"We have to get out of here."

Here. Out. She must be new to the program. There was no "out" and everywhere was here. The universe was their lab, the world their maze, and the cheese was the disease.

The cheese was the disease. Probably a nursery rhyme in there somewhere, a modern retelling of "Hickory Dickory Dock." Maybe he had a new song.

David licked his lips and they tasted of chemicals. Rain in the city got scarier every day. Why did they even bother with the program anymore?

Civilization would accomplish the mission, given time. But time was money and money was energy and energy was power. Maze opening onto maze, forever and ever, amen.

She tugged at the collar of his jacket, sopping his head into the puddle like a biscuit into weak gravy. "Sit up, David."

She knew his name. They were getting smarter, all right. Changing the flavor of the cheese. He dared not open his eyes, but he couldn't resist.

He could never resist.

He blinked water from his lashes. Her face was a fuzzy pale moon and her naked body was glistening. He blinked again. Squinted. Focused. Which one would it be?

Her. Who else?

He clawed at the concrete, digging to bury himself alive in the wet, filthy soil of the city. Back to the nothingness of the womb. A tomb of cool, welcoming clay, not of hot, harboring flesh.

He had rolled and scrabbled about five feet across the abrasive surface when she called again. "David."

The word was an echo of childhood scolding. He wanted to cover his ears, but that would slow his crawling escape. The buildings slid into focus now, the lawyer gazing down from the billboard with poisonous solicitude.

Against the foggy sheen of silver-gray that lay across the night air, the windows of a waffle house projected a beacon of cigarette smoke, cholesterol, and safety in numbers. His soaked jacket pressed against his back, water streaming from his hair. It was long, past his collar, in a style and length he hadn't worn in years. Not since college, which was the last stretch of his life he clearly recalled.

He crawled toward the smell of fryer oil and coffee. A bare foot appeared beneath his chin, the burgundy nail polish chipped, a raw scar along the arch.

"David, it's me."

Craning the cinder-block weight of his head, his gaze went up the plump calf and higher. Did he know that skin? Or was all skin a stranger, even the skin he now wore as David Underwood?

"You don't remember me, do you?" The words fell from above, as brittle and bracing as the rain.

Of course he remembered her. His eyes traveled higher, up her young, plump legs to the dark patch of hair between her legs, then up to her belly where the blood ran in a thick rivulet.

He couldn't bear to see her face, which was haunted by the ghost of all abandoned fears. Traffic hissed in the distance, like rows of long reptiles entwining in venomous ecstasy.

He raised himself to his knees, head spinning, distant buildings the ancient cliffs of an alien planet.

Waffle house. Its squares of smeared yellow light promised some sort of security. Normality. Greasy reality. But first he had to get past her.

"They're coming for us." She reached her hand toward him, fingers pale and slick as maggots.

His stomach lurched. Dry, acidic air rushed up and abraded his throat. He had nothing to vomit. The hand touched his shoulder, and David found himself reaching up to her, surrendering. His arm was like a roll of sodden newspapers.

They'll get you anyway. They always get you.

Or maybe they had you from the start.

She helped him to his feet and he swayed, blinking against the rain. Car headlights swept over them. Two giant shadows loomed on the brick wall at his back.

Eyes everywhere.

He jerked free of the woman's grasp and ran blindly away from the swollen and indistinct shapes. His legs were limp, disobedient ropes but still he fled.

Rubber squealed on pavement, the shriek of a hungry leopard. Car doors opened, rain ticked off the metal roof, and the engine mewled.

"David!" the woman screamed.

They had her, but David didn't care. That was exactly what they would expect: for him to play hero again.

He hadn't saved her last time, and Susan was going to die again, but it wasn't his fault.

He plunged toward the dark, wet wedge between buildings, willing his legs forward. His heart knocked mallets against his temples. Sharp-toothed things would be waiting in the darkness, but they would be the lesser of two thousand evils.

A kinder, gentler evisceration, because those monsters would do it from the outside in.

Not from the inside out, like the people from the car would.

Her shriek rose against the oppressive sky and shoe soles spanked the asphalt.

"Stop!" someone shouted. Were they really dumb enough to think he'd obey them at this point? After all they'd done to him, all they had taught him?

After what they had made him *become*?

He ran into the alley, assaulted by the odors of rot, bum piss, and motor oil. A chain-link fence, ripped and curling away from its support posts, blocked his escape.

David clutched the links, praying for the strength to climb. He dug the tip of one shoe into the fence and launched himself up. He slipped and hung as though crucified for a few seconds, time enough for one deep breath before collapsing.

He lay with his face against the fence, the links imprinting blue geometry against his cheek. He listened, waiting.

Rain, *tick tick tick*.

No footsteps, no shouts. No car engine.

They had taken her. And spared him.

No. That's just what they wanted him to think. That he was safe, so the next game would be even more disturbing.

Or maybe they wanted him to cower, to doubt, to face his monsters alone.

With them, you could never be sure.

Fear was their tool and his drug.

He whimpered for his next pill and the blissful fog of amnesia.

This was who he was.

Whoever he was.

And he was home, home on the range.

He kissed the fence, and it kissed back.

CHAPTER TWO

Dr. Sebastian Briggs turned away from the monitor, content that David Underwood was sufficiently broken for the moment. The subject would be ready for his next dose of Halcyon shortly.

David let out a tired wail from behind the metal door in the back of the factory.

"Home on the range," Briggs whispered.

David was the good soldier, the one who had offered himself for the chronic, ongoing experiment, whether he knew it or not. The other subjects had finished—or at least survived—the clinical trials, unaware of their contribution to science, their crime forgotten.

But Briggs hadn't forgotten. Roland Doyle, Anita Molkesky, Wendy Leng, and Alexis Morgan had gone on to lead regular lives. Briggs hadn't let them escape completely, though, because the world was merely a larger Monkey House, and the experiment had never ended, because they carried it inside them.

He'd watched them and tracked them. Wendy, especially.

The girl, Susan, hadn't been his fault, although he'd been stuck with the blame. It had taken a decade for him to restore his reputation, but luckily his backers were less interested in publishing in peer journals and more interested in tangible results.

Soon, though, his colleagues would understand who among them had achieved an evolutionary leap in emotional engineering.

He meandered through the maze of cells until he reached the main section of the Monkey House. It had changed little since the original trials, and the rows of conveyor belts, metal storage canisters, steel tables, drill presses, rusty farming implements, and thermoforming machinery added to that sense of a frenzied inner city. Alleys and crevices broke off from the main boulevards, where the scarred vinyl flooring marked years of industrial traffic. Here and there, broken sorting machines and hydraulic arms were stacked in schizophrenic sculptures, hoses and wires dangling.

His backers had kept the property, a former tractor factory that had been haphazardly renovated for the original trials. The limited-liability company listed in the Register of Deeds office had been dummied up until it was four layers removed from the true owners—CRO Pharmaceuticals.

Briggs appreciated the seclusion, and although the Research Triangle had grown rapidly in the meantime, twenty acres of pine forest and a chain-link fence separated the massive brick building from the surrounding parcels.

Instead of the cornfields and soybean fields that once sprawled in the Piedmont belt between Chapel Hill, Raleigh, and Durham, high-tech companies and research firms like IBM, GlaxoSmith-Kline, and Cisco Systems had placed labs or headquarters here.

While a complex body of world-changing research and development was underway in a sixty-mile radius, Briggs considered himself the heart of the beast, a man who held the keys that would unlock the human mind's potential.

A pager buzzed on Briggs's belt. The metal framing, high flat ceiling, and thick block walls inhibited cell-phone signals, and neither Briggs nor his backers wanted to be vulnerable to wiretapping or signal hijacking. The pager meant someone was ringing in on the satellite phone, and Briggs hurried to his office to plug the phone into an antenna that snaked its way up the side of the building and into the North Carolina humidity.

"Hello," Briggs said.

"It's done," the voice said.

"Good. He's the farthest away, so it was important to start with him. How is he?"

"Out like a light. Whatever this stuff is, you ought to get a patent for it."

Briggs didn't appreciate the humor. Life and death were serious matters. "Do you have the identification?"

An exasperated chuff came from the other end. "Everything just like you said. I even wrote those initials on the mirror. You ask me, this is a whole lot of trouble for nothing. I could roll him in the trunk and have him on your doorstep in eight hours."

"Nobody asked you," Briggs said. His backers insisted on using this particular operative, but Briggs planned to remove all witnesses eventually. He just wasn't sure he could tolerate the man until that happy day.

"Okay, they told me to do it your way."

"No fingerprints, nothing to connect you back here?" Briggs asked.

More exasperation. "You and me, Doc. We got to have a talk soon."

"Take two aspirin and call me in the morning."

"Is that some kind of code or something?"

The man could dish out humor but couldn't appreciate it. "Can I ask you something, Mr. Drummond?" Briggs said, using the fake name Martin Kleingarten had given him in a clumsy attempt at subterfuge.

"I'm on the clock," Kleingarten/Drummond said.

"What are you afraid of?"

Silence. Briggs thought of those hundreds of miles of electromagnetic radiation beaming between him and the low-orbit satellite before bouncing to Kleingarten/Drummond in Cincinnati. Silence took just as much energy to broadcast as words did.

"I'm not afraid of nothing," came the answer a few seconds later.

"Every intelligent man has a deepest fear. Think."

"Right now, I'm afraid I won't get paid, because you guys are playing a weird game. The things you've asked me to do, it don't sound like business to me."

"I assure you, Mr. Drummond, your work is critical to a major scientific discovery. The 'game,' as you call it, is part of the work."

The man answered, but Briggs's attention had been diverted to the monitor, where David Underwood sat on his cot, peering between his fingers at the images flickering on his walls. Briggs had gone with the Susan Sharpe tape, an oldie but a goodie, to complement the footage from David's collegiate surroundings in Chapel Hill. The montage of images kept David trapped ten years in the past.

As usual, David couldn't quite look away, because Briggs had conditioned him to crave the psychological trauma. But Briggs couldn't take all the credit. Most of it belonged to Seethe, but the world would find that out soon enough. The hard way.

Kleingarten/Drummond spoke again and snapped Briggs back to the conversation. "What was that?"

"What's *your* greatest fear, Doc?"

"Easy. Not being feared."

Briggs clicked off without another word and turned his attention to his computer. Most of his records were on a removable hard drive that could be erased in the event of an emergency. Years of meticulous notes, copies of journal articles, and chemical formulas were stored on a system that an Internet connection had never touched. He'd never trust off-site storage, and he knew they were watching.

In the Monkey House trials, though, he was a traditionalist, making personal notes on a sheet of paper pinned to a clipboard. Such entries brought back so many memories, and memories were his passion.

Beside the date, he scrawled "No change in subject" in the same bad handwriting for which he had been scolded as a child.

He glanced at Wendy's self-portrait hanging on the wall, a gift from a happier era. So close.

In an uncharacteristic bout of giddiness, he drew a leering smiley face and devil horns on the chart. In the days ahead, he would relive some wonderful memories.

And destroy a few others.

CHAPTER THREE

Morning arrived with bloody rags in the sky and sputtering fire in Roland Doyle's heart.

He squinted at the pink light penetrating the window. His head hurt, but that was nothing new. In Roland's life, a headache was as reliable as the sun, the moon, and the next drink.

He didn't believe in predestination, but he had come to accept inevitability, even to embrace it. Whether those repetitive choices were made on his own or through the whim of some puckish and bemused God, the end result was the same.

Let's go with you, God. You're a fine fucking fall guy. Never around when I need you, but never around to bitch, either.

The Blame Game was one of Roland's favorite pastimes. It wasn't whether you won or lost, succeeded or failed, lived or died, so long as you found someone or something to blame. Wendy had served the most often, but he'd filled her up and moved on.

And despite his secret hope that he'd beaten alcoholism on his own, through willpower and courage, the simple truth was the craving had been lifted by the very God he was now cursing. That God wasn't a bearded white geezer in the sky, but something large and mysterious, and Roland actually hadn't probed too deeply for fear that it would prove to be nothing but vapor.

And maybe this was the proof that God had been an elaborate fantasy.

His fingers trailed between the cool sheets to the other side of the bed. The pillow smelled of a woman's shampoo, but his olfactory sense was as unreliable as the other four. She might have left in the night, or even months ago.

No, she would be there, she *had* to be there, and he would use her as a temporary painkiller, the latest contestant in the Blame Game. Whoever she was.

"Asleep?" he whispered, but the syllables still scratched his raw throat. Roland rolled toward her side of the bed and opened one eye. The blankets were smooth, his hand naked and alone.

The walls were cheap pine paneling, the curtains the deep mottled beige of unbleached linen. The gypsum whorls in the ceiling were cracked, long strands of dusty cobwebs dangling and swaying.

He drew a deep breath and the air tasted of Febreze and Lysol, the sprays fighting a losing battle with cigarettes, beer, and urine. Another motel room, although Roland had no idea of its city.

Indy? Last I remember, I was tooling through the Crossroads of America, the land of Peyton Manning and chili cheese fries.

He sat up with a groan, and the blood increased its sluggish course around his brain. His skull felt as if it were gripped in the mouth of a hungry *T. rex*. His tongue was a carpet that had been stomped on and then vacuumed dry. His heartbeat staggered and pounded in a familiar arrhythmia.

The bedside table would reveal a suicidal potion. Socrates cheerfully chose poison over the admission of defeat. When logic failed the Athenian philosopher, death seemed a reasonable alternative to putting up with more bullshit. Hemlock was his vehicle, but Roland preferred a slower-acting brand.

He'd always been a goddamned coward.

The headache suggested a white wine, something cheap from Southern California. Wine could have chased vodka or, if he'd felt sufficiently masochistic, Everclear.

Unlike many alcoholics, Roland had never suffered from denial. From the first sip on, he always knew exactly what he was doing.

Except, of course, for anything that happened during the blackouts.

The nightstand contained no empty bottles. An alarm clock blazed red numerals that said 9:35. Above it loomed a lamp, its battered beige shade held together by a strip of masking tape. An empty ashtray was the only other item on the table.

"Honey?" he croaked, going for the generic, because no specific name floated up from the mist in his skull.

Cincinnati.

The room felt like Ohio. Maybe it was an underlying muddy-river stench to the air, or perhaps it was the taint of coal-fired power plants. As a salesman for a company that made supplies for advertising signs, Roland might be in town to service major clients like AK Steel, the Kroger Company, or Proctor & Gamble.

Whether it was neon, adhesives, banners, or 3-D lettering, Carolina Sign Supply could meet every outdoor advertising need, no matter how garish. The slogans swam together like eels in his gut.

Roland swung his legs over the side of the bed. He wore a pair of black boxers that featured a clown face on the front, the bulbous red nose marking the fly. Roland slept naked when a woman was with him, so he could be pretty sure he'd been flying solo the night before.

Of course, he might have ended up at one of the local watering holes or topless joints. In that case, all bets were off. He wasn't the type who paid for companionship.

At least not in cash. For the rest, he'd trade his fucking soul and not bat an eye.

But the other side of the bed was unruffled. He had definitely slept by himself. His battered leather briefcase, which held his sample notebooks, was parked by the nightstand, his pants tossed on the floor.

A few coins had leaked from his pants pockets and glinted like dirty ice on the gray industrial carpet. He had undressed carelessly, his shirt tossed over the arm of a vinyl chair.

The bathroom door was ajar, a bar of light leaking from the opening. He wondered if he had vomited, bent in homage to the porcelain idol. His stomach fluttered up a wave of acid, though no nausea lingered.

Headache isn't too bad, either. Must be getting back in the groove.

And blackouts are a good thing, when you get right down to it, because who wants to remember shit like that? Maybe God has a little mercy in Him after all.

The air was cold on his bare chest, shrinking his nipples to red points. The air-conditioning must have been set on "igloo," because spring had been pushing hard to get winter the hell out of the way.

His face itched and he put a hand to his chin. Stubble, three days' worth, at least.

Roland wondered how many appointments he'd missed, how many clients had called the home office asking about the sales rep who had scheduled a visit. Sometimes the benders went on for a week or more, but since taking the job with Carolina Sign, he'd been dependable.

The company had known of his past. The background check had turned up the DWI, two drunk and disorderly charges, the vandalism, and the court judgment against him in the civil suit brought by his estranged wife.

In a bit of undeserved serendipity, the company's general manager was a recovering alcoholic who had shepherded Roland into a twelve-step program. "White chips and second chances," Harry Grimes, the GM, had said.

What do you think about third chances, Harry? Or is this the fourth?

He bent to pick up his pants, blood rushing to his temples. He wondered if he'd spent all his money. Once, while living with Wendy, he had maxed out his credit card in a two-day stretch, $10,000 flushed.

The worst part had been the waiting, knowing Wendy would open the envelope, pull out the bill, and see the itemized stupidity. Wendy was past waiting, though, exhausted from serial second chances, and the separation agreement showed up in the mailbox before the credit card bill.

His pants looked relatively clean, so he probably had avoided crawling on his hands and knees, at least on the sidewalk. Keys jingled in his pocket. He fished the wallet out and flipped it open, thumbing through the leather folds. A couple of hundreds and some twenties.

Maybe he'd made a late-hour cash withdrawal from an ATM. He couldn't imagine giving up a drinking bout while he still had some green.

The phone rang, its brittle bleat like a spear to his skull. The home office? A client? Escort service? Newfound-and-already-forgotten drinking buddy? The choices were endless and all were terrible.

Maybe it was Harry. As Roland reached for the phone, he realized there wasn't a single person left in the world whose voice would cheer him, who would dispense kind and supportive words, who wouldn't bring suspicion and disapproval to bear.

The phone was cold against his ear. "Hello?"

"Mr. Underwood, you requested a wake-up call at eight," said a tired, smoke-strained female voice. "We tried three times but received no answer, so we assumed you had checked out."

"Sorry, you must have the wrong room."

"My apologies," she said, though her tone suggested the exact opposite. "Is this room one-oh-one?"

Roland retrieved the rubber-flagged keychain that lay beside the alarm clock. "Right number, wrong person."

"Sir, all check-ins require photo ID. The night clerk has 'David Underwood' in room one-oh-one."

"Sorry, there's no David here that I know of." Unless he'd brought home a drinking buddy by that name. In which case, pitiful, hungover David was sleeping either under the bed or in the bathtub.

The clerk's voice grew sour. "Either way, Mr. Underwood, checkout is ten o'clock."

"Hold on a second," Roland said, before the clerk could hang up. "What time did I…what time did David check in?"

He actually wanted to ask what *day*, but he didn't want to arouse additional suspicion.

"We have it at seven ten. There's a surcharge for having additional people in the room, Mr. Underwood. If you'd care to stop by the desk on your way out—"

"Never mind." He had checked in last night, apparently, although the idiots had gotten his name wrong.

His barebones expense account covered a rental car, meals, and lodging. Extra charges would draw the attention of Carolina Sign's purse-handlers, who, as in every other American business, were tasked with extracting nickels from the worker bees while shoving stacks of Hamiltons toward management.

Actually, the confusion might benefit him in the long run. Let "David Underwood" foot the charge and let the bitchy desk clerk deal with the inaccurate billing. One problem, though: his twelve-step program was built on rigorous honesty, both with himself and others.

But the twelve steps had apparently failed him. He had a roiling stomach and jangling head to prove it. The only steps he had taken were those that led down the basement to hell.

Funny, though, his mouth didn't taste of liquor. Maybe he'd burned away his taste buds.

As he got up to shower, the wallet tumbled to the floor. Some of the plastic cards slid free of an inner sleeve. His driver's license portrait glared at him, eyes startled wide by the examiner's flash.

Roland had been dismayed when the examiner listed his hair as "gray." The gray was there, sure, but he still thought of it as dark brown. He was only thirty-four, after all, even if half of them had been hard years.

He was sliding the license back into place when he paused. The license was the wrong color, issued in North Carolina. He'd registered in Tennessee to avoid excessive auto insurance.

Yet there was his face. His height was listed at five feet ten, just as he'd fudged it by an inch, and his weight, 205, was lower than his actual weight at the time. That was before the twelve-step surrender, back when dishonesty was a second skin. Now, healthier and without the boozy bloat, he weighed 185, but it had taken two years to bounce back into shape from the decade of hard drinking.

It was possible he'd updated his driver's license after he'd settled near Raleigh. But he would have remembered something like that. He had been abusive, but he couldn't have killed *all* of his brain cells.

And if he'd wandered into a driver's license office during a blackout, chances were good he would have been denied a license and escorted to the nearest drunk tank.

One other problem with the license bearing his face: the name listed on it was David Wayne Underwood.

CHAPTER FOUR

"My psychiatrist is dead."

As she considered her friend's words, Wendy Leng sipped her coffee and ducked beneath the thin layer of cigarette smoke that hung about five feet above the waffle-house floor. The coffee tasted as if it had been dipped from the rolling mop bucket that stood in the corner.

Eggs, scrambled, had somehow managed to take on the dirty gray of the gravy. At nearby tables, newspapers flapped, people fidgeted with their cell phones as they ate, and lonely old men gazed out the window in the land of bottomless refills. They'd taken a back booth because of Anita's sensitivity to light and her aversion to being recognized by adoring fans.

Wendy looked from the congealing grease rimming the plate to her twin reflections in Anita's sunglasses. "Mind taking those off? I can't tell when you're kidding."

Anita slid the glasses down her nose and peered over the lenses with her stunning blue eyes. "Like you could anyway?"

"The sun's out, the fluorescents in here are bright enough to fry bacon, and you have absolutely nothing left to hide from me."

"My eyes are bloodshot."

"That goes without saying. Thursday is a day that ends in *y*, isn't it?"

Anita readjusted her shades and sat back in the vinyl-upholstered booth seat. "You just have this thing about faces. 'Eyes are the window to the soul,' and all that jazz."

"I teach art. If you get the eyes right, the rest is easy."

"Well, life isn't art, and doesn't even imitate it. Especially when your psychiatrist is dead."

Wendy started to ask the logical and expected follow-up question when the jukebox cut in, drowning out the banging of pots and the clatter of silverware. "Hey, I haven't heard 'Achy Breaky Heart' in nearly a decade," Anita said, smiling and swaying her head in time to the four-beat twang.

"You always did go for atmosphere." The room's cigarette smoke burned Wendy's nostrils. She'd kicked that habit last year and had become overly sensitive to it ever since. She gave Anita a hurried "bring-it-to-me" motion with her hand.

"About my psychiatrist."

"Let me guess," Wendy said. "She couldn't handle your depressed-bitch act any longer, so she slit her wrists."

"Wow, that would be poignant." Anita, who'd had the good sense to order a waffle instead of the Long-Haul Breakfast, pushed syrup around with her fork. "I'm sure if she got you on the couch, Freud would roll over in his grave."

"Only if I seduced her. Otherwise, Freud would be bored with simple old me."

"Oh, you're finally coming around to the Sapphic way, huh? Every intelligent woman visits the island sooner or later."

"If I was after women, you couldn't handle the competition, sweetie," Wendy said, dabbing the endearment with sarcasm as gooey as the waffle-house syrup. "As it is, I don't need anybody in my life, male or female."

"Methinks the lady doth protest too much," Anita said, misquoting Shakespeare. As a catalog model, Anita had quickly learned she was more at home in front of a camera than on a live stage.

Despite the drama of her past, or perhaps because of it, she still clung to a delusion of eventual A-list movie stardom.

One delusion of many, Wendy thought. *Hence the psychiatrist.*

Wendy jumped in before Anita could harmonize with Billy Ray Cyrus's addictive yet mind-numbing chorus. "So who killed her?"

Anita forked waffle in her mouth and flashed a wad of soggy dough. She had the appetite of a wrestler, but genetics and an obsessive fitness regimen held her at a firm 118 pounds despite her generous bosom. "Nobody killed her. Cardiac arrest. People die all the time."

"Then why did you bring it up?"

"Because I figured you'd assume the worst. You're always assuming the worst."

"No, I'm not." She sipped her coffee, confirming it was terrible. "Besides, sometimes the worst blindsides you and you don't get a chance to assume anything. Take my marriage, for instance."

"Well, enough about you." Anita flashed a smile that always earned instant absolution, no matter the degree of rudeness. "Anyway, it took me six months to start trusting her, and then she has the nerve to go and die on me."

"She died on her other patients, too."

"And that's my problem how?"

"Never mind." Wendy glanced at the clock. Ten was fast approaching, and she had to prep for her nooner. "I've got to get to class."

"Some people never leave college. And at your age—"

"I know, but college was God's way of bringing us together. The School of Hard Knocks."

"Or Fuck U. That's *U* like in *university*."

The sarcasm, like most, contained a good bit of truth. Anita had served as a model in one of Wendy's graduate studio art classes, stripping off her clothes for a dozen people without batting a luscious eyelash.

After the session, Anita had remarked that Wendy's rendering, though obviously exaggerated and not all that flattering, had captured her personality better than any of the more technically exact illustrations. Perhaps because Wendy instinctively appreciated the sensual radiance Anita projected.

An uneasy friendship was formed, and it had lasted through a shared apartment, a traumatic clinical trial, different sexual attitudes, and now one hell of a heart-clogging breakfast.

"Don't you want to hear what my psychiatrist's psychiatrist told me?" Anita said.

"Shrink a shrink and pretty soon you get down to nothing." Wendy put her pinky to her lips and thumb to her ear in the international sign language for "Call me." She reached for the bill, which was stuck to the table by a dot of syrup.

"No, really. I need to say this."

"Okay. But make it fast. The next generation of Pablo Picassos and Frida Kahlos are waiting."

"The pills I was on, the samples my psychiatrist gave me for free so the diagnosis would stay off my insurance?"

The topic bugged Wendy, but she couldn't pinpoint the cause. "Yeah. New class of antidepressants. I thought we'd learned our lesson about untested drugs."

Anita lowered her voice and became guarded. "We need to talk about that, because I'm starting to remember."

Wendy squeezed her fork until the metal cut into her palm. "That was a different lifetime, Nita. That wasn't us. That couldn't have been us."

"I know we're supposed to remember it that one way, but what if it happened the other way?"

"It could have happened a million ways," Wendy said. "The lesson is not to play around with drugs."

"Oh, so *now* we get all moral?"

Wendy was about to explode, to tell Anita to shut the hell up, and the rage was a warning sign. You could bury the past, but the stench had a way of rising through the cracks. But the best way to forget was to change the subject. "So tell me about this new drug they gave you."

Anita nodded. "Supposed to treat my stress, anxiety, depression, and all the rest of it. I've been on it for two weeks."

"And it seems to be working." Wendy eyed the half-full cup of coffee and weighed the need for an extra boost of caffeine against the additional destruction of taste buds.

"Sure. I've even gained a few pounds." Anita slapped at her lean thighs under the table. "But dig this—my new psychiatrist said she can't find any record of a written prescription. She has no idea what it is."

Billy Ray Cyrus's cornfield yodel faded and the late breakfast crowd filled the void with chatter and rattling tableware. "Maybe it's a generic," Wendy said, alarm bells clanging in her head. "Drug companies sometimes give their cheaper versions names that make them sound fancy. I'll bet the records just got screwed up."

With the volume in the room dropping, Anita hunched forward and lowered her voice. "The pills may not be legit."

"This doesn't have anything to do with the Monkey House trials." Wendy used the term despite her promise to never utter it again, upon pain of death or madness. "So stop getting paranoid. Briggs is finished and none of that ever happened."

"I know." Anita chopped at her waffle, scooting piles of limp whipped cream and strawberry sauce across the grid. "Well, anyway, the new shrink told me to stop taking them and to bring her a sample so she could turn it in to the authorities."

"Yeah, like we could ever trust 'authority' again."

"I told her I'd run out the day my shrink died. Seemed sort of fitting."

"So you have some left?"

"Sure. Six pills."

"A shrink was giving you illegal drugs?"

"Well, she'd been acting weird for the last few weeks. A couple of times she said stuff that sounded fatalistic. You know, like, 'Live in the moment, because the past lives forever.'"

It sounded like the kind of crap Briggs used to say. "Sounds like generic shop talk to me. If a shrink can't dish out the feel-good platitudes, then who can?"

Anita looked around the restaurant. Her sunglasses flashed in the greasy fluorescent light. The entire breakfast, Anita had been acting shifty, as if fearing someone would approach her table and ask for an autograph.

Not that the consumers of her films would have much chance of recognizing her. Her hair was now its natural light brown instead of blonde, and she'd had her boobs deflated down a cup size from their heyday.

Besides, Chapel Hill was a sophisticated university town, not a place where people expected to encounter a porn queen in a bacon-and-eggs joint.

Wendy followed Anita's gaze. An unkempt man sat at the counter near the register, talking loudly to himself while the wait staff aggressively ignored him.

"I'm kind of worried," Anita said. "The pills worked great, but I stopped them. They reminded me of the stuff we took during the trials."

"Did the new psychiatrist give you something else?"

"Effexor. Started Saturday. She said it might take a month before the effect kicks in. I could go nuts before then."

"I don't want to talk about this anymore." Wendy's eyelid twitched. A dark shadow crept from the corner of her memory, but it vanished when she turned her mind's eye toward it.

"We talked about it yesterday."

"No, we didn't."

"You don't remember?" Anita's grin was frozen in the mask of one who wasn't sure if she was the butt of a joke. "Jeez, maybe you're the one who needs drugs. You're getting senile."

"I plead post-traumatic stress disorder," Wendy said, disturbed by Anita's delusions.

"Well, I get crazy when I don't take it. Almost like the monsters are waiting in the dark, and when the medicine goes away, they all come crawling out of their holes."

Wendy noted a crease had formed in Anita's forehead, the only vivid mark of time or distress on her perfect skin. Wendy had first drawn Anita's caricature after the long-ago modeling session, when the two had roomed together for a semester.

Anita Molkesky, or "Anita Mann" as she had been known in the trade, had experienced little change to her most prominent facial features. The full lips, rounded chin, and thin nose made her face bottom-heavy, and though she was attractive in every measure, Wendy's exaggerating black marker had helped shape

Anita's self-image, and she was forever complaining about her "micro-nose."

"You're not going to take my advice anyway," Wendy said.

"Sure I will, if I happen to agree with it."

Sassy country rock erupted, Shania Twain's "That Don't Impress Me Much." Wendy tested the coffee once more. Still awful. "Okay, then—"

"Holy fucking salami," Anita said, staring through the plate-glass window.

While mired in the lurid straight-to-video world of Los Angeles, Anita claimed to have seen everything twice, including midgets copulating with canines. But the shock in her voice was enough to cause Wendy to follow her friend's gaze.

A blue sedan streaked toward the restaurant across the parking lot as if shot from a monstrous cannon, tires throwing smoke. Its roaring engine and squealing wheels drowned out the jukebox, and conversation in the waffle house died except for the monologue of the self-absorbed schizophrenic.

The sedan was gathering speed, aimed straight for the front window. It miraculously dodged a parked SUV and closed the gap, now less than thirty feet away.

Someone screamed, and Wendy grabbed Anita's buckskin jacket by its elbow fringe and pulled her from the booth.

Their waitress, a mousy-looking chain-smoker, screamed out, "Bobby!"

The cook came bounding over the counter, his mottled apron flapping across the schizophrenic's face. Anita's retreat splashed cold coffee on Wendy's leg.

She wondered which of her fellow instructors would cover her noon class, because she had a feeling she was going to be late. Then the plate glass exploded.

CHAPTER FIVE

The fog lifted, though Roland's eyeballs still felt like wads of cotton. His heartbeat galloped.

He thumbed other cards from the stack. A Visa, with "David Underwood" in raised print, sporting an approval date from two years earlier. A card from AAA promising lodging discounts and emergency roadside assistance for David Underwood. A donor card from the American Red Cross, B positive.

At least we both have the same blood type in case I need a transfusion from myself.

A Blockbuster membership card and a Higher Grounds coffee club card, with three more cup images to be punched before he received a free refill, completed the stack.

Vertigo weaved its gossamer threads around him, and he sat on the bed before his legs turned to sand. He examined his driver's license again.

No, not MY driver's license. David's. And why does that name sound familiar?

The listed address was a place Roland had lived in while enrolled at the University of North Carolina over a decade ago. The crummy off-campus apartment had been beset by cockroaches, rats, and a refrigerator that didn't adequately chill the beer, and Roland had broken his lease after three months.

If the license was a fake, it was convincing. With the advent of the Department of Homeland Security and increased scrutiny of illegal aliens, the fake-ID business was booming, the cash flow allowing forgers to stay on the cutting edge of technology. Assuming someone knew the right people, a bogus driver's license could be turned around in less than an hour.

The only problem with that scenario was that Roland had no close friends, much less one who would go to such lengths for a practical joke. Maybe Dick the Jarhead, his first twelve-step sponsor, who had traded in the bottle for a brand of aggressive humor that constantly bordered on violence.

But Dick had died last year from a cerebral hemorrhage. His wacky mind ended up doing him in after all.

A glance at the clock showed fifteen minutes before checkout.

Screw it. Won't be the first unsolved mystery of my life.

He crammed the cards back in the wallet and wobbled across the room to the chair that held his jacket.

A search of the pockets turned up nothing but lint and a set of car keys. The keys, at least, looked familiar, belonging to the Ford Escort he remembered renting in Louisville, Kentucky. Nearly a week ago.

A week? Without a calendar, he couldn't be sure of anything. Even the alarm clock might be lying. After all, in a world where your name could change, or someone with a different name could steal your face while you slept, nothing was certain.

Too bad I can't do a switcheroo with my debt. Wonder if David has a hot girlfriend?

He wobbled to the window by the door and looked out. He was on the ground floor of a three-story building. The skyline might have been Cincinnati's, but it was too generically midtown

American to tell it from that of Huntington, Muncie, Plattsburgh, or Roanoke.

A beauty salon across the street was in need of new vinyl letters. Its sign read "air Empor um."

Maybe I should drop off a business card. Score some points with Harry Grimes. Show I'm the go-getter type, even on a hangover.

A Marathon gas station, gray-walled warehouses, a chemical silo of some sort, and several urban condominium complexes lined the block. A blue Escort sat out front, presumably his ride.

So where the hell is MY license?

He dug into the wallet again, searching the opposite fold. He turned up a business card bearing David Underwood's name and a cell phone number from an area code he didn't recognize. The card bore a conservative but elegant C placed within a bordered rectangle. It was the logo for Carolina Sign Supply.

So "David" had the same employer as Roland, which made a practical joke easier to rig. Except that theory had no legs because no one knew Roland was in Cincinnati, much less which motel room he'd be staying in.

Aside from Harry and his deep-seated need to be of service to a fellow addict, Roland had remained aloof from his coworkers. Because he traveled and serviced his own regional accounts, he wasn't part of a "team," and he only checked in at headquarters for the monthly sales meetings. Most of his employer contact was via phone and e-mail.

Laptop?

He looked under the bed. Nothing but dust bunnies big enough to mate.

"Maybe David has it," he said, thinking it would be funnier if he said it aloud. Instead, utterance gave the words a palpability and weight that made the statement not only plausible but menacing.

Six minutes until checkout and his head was still throbbing, mouth still dry, tongue like a dirty sock. He was thrusting the fabricated business card back into its sleeve when he saw glossy paper beneath. He shuffled through the few cards, looking for photographs that would give David Underwood context or maybe clarify the faint tingle of familiarity the name evoked.

Did David have a family? Roland had never had time for children, though Wendy had once gone off the pill, back when she still held out hope that she could cure him solely through the power of love.

Fortunately, considering the ultimate outcome, the seed hadn't taken root, and the separation agreement had been nothing more than dollars and cents instead of a Solomon-like cleaving of flesh.

Stop it right there. You can't even remember your own name, and you're wishing you could BREED? More little Roland Doyles or David Underwoods or whoever the fuck I am, running around playing their own brands of the Blame Game?

Three minutes to dress, pound on the front desk, and get to the bottom of this mess. The anger lit its pissed-off-villager torches inside his chest, ready to storm the castle of his head and build a bonfire.

Self-righteous indignation was an emotion that alcoholics could not afford to acknowledge, let alone embrace.

Anger, hell. In a few minutes, he'd be in a *rage*. And damned if it wasn't going to feel good. The Blame Game had a new contestant.

He grabbed his jacket on the way to the bathroom, hoping he'd brought his shaving kit. He was eager to brush his teeth and rid his taste buds of the horrible, sticky residue of last night's indulgence.

He could worry about contrition and guilt later. The twelve-steppers had stacks and stacks of white chips for that. God was built of forgiveness, and God probably knew the difference between Roland and David. He could start the day with a clean face, if not a clear head.

He nudged the bathroom door the rest of the way open.

A woman lay sprawled on the ceramic-tiled floor. She wore a peach fleece bathrobe, parted to reveal the snowy flesh of her thighs. One arm dangled over the rim of the tub, its hand smooth, graceful, and young. Raven hair splayed across her shoulders, obscuring her face.

Judging from the angle of her neck and the coagulating pool of blood beneath her, she was quite dead.

CHAPTER SIX

The collision was much more dramatic than Martin Kleingarten had planned.

The clatter of the broken glass cascading along the sidewalk and the length of the sedan was satisfying, and the snapping of a steel mullion reminded him of the time he'd been forced to break a bookie's fingers for dipping into the till.

That was small-time mob work, steady pay but little chance for career development, and Kleingarten's new employers had a flair for the creative. That suited Kleingarten, although the risks were a little higher. What was life without a few risks?

The sedan plowed through the interior of the restaurant and smashed the counter, breaking it from the floor and slamming it against the grill. Hot fryer oil, which had leaped in rancid arcs with the impact, rained down on the screaming customers, and those who hadn't been lacerated with glass shards had suffered nickel-sized burns on their flesh.

One old lady, hair tinted with blue rinse, tried to raise herself on her walker, but one of its legs had been twisted in the wreck and the walker collapsed, sending her sprawling with a shriek that stood out even in the cacophony that erupted in the moments after the "accident."

The short-order cook in the filthy apron yanked open the crumpled door of the sedan. Kleingarten smiled, the swell of his cheeks pushing up on the lenses of the binoculars. The cook's mouth stopped in mid tirade and dropped in surprise.

No driver.

Kleingarten, who had boosted his first car at the age of eleven, could easily have started the sedan with the key, aimed the steering wheel, and let the good times roll. The American Disabilities Act required three handicapped parking spaces near the front door, none of which were currently occupied, so he'd had a large window of opportunity. To make it more of a challenge, he'd hot-wired the vehicle and left the key in his pocket, leaning a brick on the accelerator.

He swung his binoculars to the left. The Chinese woman appeared to be unhurt and was busy helping up the blue-haired lady. Good. His instructions had been to leave both women scared, and they'd been sitting far enough from the window that they were out of danger.

Kleingarten twisted the lenses to focus on the Slant. *Wendy Leng. Why are my friends so interested in you?*

Her eyes had the classic Oriental shape, but her hair was brown instead of raven-black. Her teeth were small and she had a mole on her right cheek. Her eyes were light brown, unusual for an Asian, so Kleingarten figured her for a half-breed. As if "breed" meant anything these days, the way everybody fucked outside their own kind.

The Slant was cute, if you liked that sort of thing, with a rounded, flat face and mouth-sized knockers. The one who had been sitting with her, though, deserved a closer look.

She seemed a little familiar, but with her trendy haircut, big sunglasses, and bright red lipstick she was hardly distinguishable from all the other scrawny thirty-somethings who watched *Sex and the City* and took Internet tests to determine whether they were more like the slutty character or the quirky character.

"Hey, babe, what you doing after the tragedy?" Kleingarten whispered to himself.

Her forehead was bleeding from a cut, but the wound didn't appear serious. She was also to remain unharmed, according to orders, and he was pretty sure that as long as the two targets walked out alive, he'd played by the rules.

One person, though, was not going to be walking anywhere. The man in the greasy army jacket had picked the wrong counter stool. The car's grill had chewed him up like a piece of toast and then spat him back out.

Most of him, anyway. One khaki-clad arm still pointed in the air, a fork gripped in the bloody fist.

If Kleingarten had calculated wrong, the car might have swerved, hit a pothole, or even struck another car, which might have caused it to veer into the back booth where the Slant and the Looker had sat with their coffee cups.

He wasn't sure his employers would appreciate the serendipity, but if they wanted it done a certain way, they should have given better instructions. And paid better.

"Inducing a state of panic" could have been interpreted in any number of ways. The Looker's dose had been administered last week, in a bottle of Perrier. The Slant had got hers, appropriately enough, in an order of General Tso's chicken three days ago. But they'd needed the adrenalin boost, apparently, for the stuff to take effect. Briggs had called the accident a "trigger," the same as Roland Doyle's trigger had been to mess with his identity and play on his guilt.

The first siren arose from the east end of town, toward Durham. Kleingarten tightened his gaze on Wendy Leng and the trendy chick one last time. The Slant had helped the blue-haired woman to the sidewalk and now rejoined her friend, who was dabbing at her wound with a napkin.

No plastic surgery would be required, but Kleingarten suspected she'd wear a little extra powder while the wound healed over the next few weeks. A looker like that was bound to be a vain bitch.

Anger flared through him, the type of anger that was riskier than any crime he could commit. He could have scared them the old-fashioned way, stalked them from a distance, figured out their patterns, then jumped them one at a time in some dark alley or parking garage, get a little action as he—

No. With DNA tests, you couldn't do hands-on work anymore. Why, just squirting a little harmless sperm in a stranger was enough to get you two dimes in Raleigh's Central Prison, and if she happened to stop breathing on you in the middle of getting acquainted, you'd find yourself on the skinny end of the needle.

Risks were one thing, but fatal consequences were another. No snatch on Earth was worth a death sentence.

Of course, after the number he'd done on that hooker in Cincinnati last night, any other charge at this point would be a bonus prize. And it's not like she'd taken his kill cherry, either.

More people emerged from the carnage: a stooped-over man with a baseball cap pulled down over his eyes, a fat woman in a "Git 'r Done" T-shirt far too small for her wobbling breasts, a boy in camo hunter's pants with what appeared to be ketchup staining the front of his gray sweat jacket.

The cook, having overcome his shock at finding an empty driver's seat, had collected a fire extinguisher and was hosing down a grease fire that had erupted above the grill. The oily smoke curled from the shattered entrance.

Though the rubberneckers arrived under the guise of good intentions and a helpful spirit, Kleingarten knew the truth in their sorry hearts: they were hoping for a little peek of blood, something they could tell their spouses about over dinner while waxing philosophical about God's random hand.

Fuck God. Religion was just another calculated risk, a sucker's bet. For Kleingarten, all the religion he needed was a Glock semi and a pile of unmarked bills. The kind of stack his employers had mailed to a Burlington post office box, the address of a fictitious consulting business Kleingarten had launched a decade ago after leaving the security industry and becoming an entrepreneur.

He'd be picking up his next stack that afternoon, in person from Briggs, the down payment on a little job involving one Dr. Alexis Morgan of the UNC medical faculty.

The lone siren amplified and now was joined by others. The wailing chorus pulsed off the surrounding buildings and meshed in the urban valley around him. From behind the tinted window of his Nissan Pathfinder, where he'd slipped after launching the unmanned auto, Kleingarten could track the approach of emergency vehicles.

He should leave the scene, but where was the joy in creating a masterpiece if the end result couldn't be savored? Sure, the crash would make the newspapers, and already a Channel 3 TV van was zooming into the parking lot, nearly outpacing the first ambulance.

But this was reality TV at its finest, with all the color and drama of life even when viewed through a tinted windshield.

He let the binoculars rest against the steering wheel. These days everybody had a cell phone that took pictures and, since the documented beating of Rodney King had created a self-made homeless millionaire, all those budding Jerry Springers and Geraldo Riveras out there were itching for their turns. So a low profile was the next best thing to invisible.

The Looker in the fringed leather jacket had regained her composure, and she leaned against one of the cars parked in front of the restaurant.

His employers were aware of the parking setup, almost as if the entire lot was some kind of oversized game board, the cars and people nothing more than set pieces. They'd assured him the Slant and the Looker would have their regular Thursday breakfast at the Over E-Z Waffle House, they'd take a booth near the back, and the late-model Ford Escort would be parked and pointed in a direct path to the window. Little had been left to chance, which had taken some fun out of the job, although the whole game was just weird enough to keep him playing along.

He thought of them as "employers" in plural form because, even though all his communication had been with the same prick on the phone—through cryptic text messages or directly from the mouth of that eggheaded asshole Briggs—he believed some type of group or organization was behind the orders. Maybe more than one. It wouldn't be the first time.

He couldn't imagine one person rigging such an elaborate prank. A jilted lover, somebody still stewing because the Slant had clamped her legs shut and cut off the Bamboo Express? Or maybe the Looker was doing another dude on the side?

No, jealousy led you to act quickly and irrationally. Hell, women in general made you do that. But these folks—

Kleingarten checked his wristwatch. Seven minutes had passed. Soon emergency response would give way to an investigation. Even the cops, as stupid as they were, would figure out the unoccupied car hadn't started itself and shifted into "Drive."

But he still had a few minutes, plus he was sporting a stolen license plate that some harebrained mall shopper probably hadn't even noticed was missing. He wielded the glasses again.

The ambulance crew debarked and sprinted to the front of the crumpled Escort, rolling latex gloves up to their wrists. The TV van screamed to a stop and a camera operator got out, one of those shaggy-assed, bearded hippies who always seemed to get the easy gigs. A chick with the same hairstyle as the Looker exited the passenger door, checking her reflection in the side mirror.

Seeing the video camera, the Slant covered her face and lurched away, apparently peering between the cracks of her fingers. Shy, paranoid, or something else?

His employers must have had a reason for targeting the pair. It wasn't his job to know, only to follow instructions, however bizarre. But he had to admit, this situation was far more interesting than shattering a kneecap or arranging a drop for a heroin import.

The Looker seemed none too eager to make the six o'clock news, either, and the pair slipped away from the other victims, who appeared prepped for prime time. The gathered throng, including those who had gotten out of their cars when the ambulance blocked the lot exit, also wanted a piece of the action, the latest crazy move on God's pecker-headed checkerboard.

He grinned at the notion. Games of chance, games of risk. He had a feeling his employers weren't ready to cash in their chips just yet, that they wanted another few spins of the roulette wheel. He focused the twin lenses as the Slant and the Looker got behind the wheel of a faggoty new Volkswagen Beetle that was as silver as an alien's anal probe—and parked outside the lot, where they weren't hemmed in by the ambulance.

He noted the tag number. His memory wasn't eidetic, but when he put his mind to it, a brief series of symbols was no challenge.

Martin Kleingarten started his SUV, pulled out slowly so as not to arouse any notice in the chaos, and took the rear exit, wondering how long he'd have to wait before his employers called again.

If they wanted the two women scared shitless but still breathing, Kleingarten was the man for the job.

And if they wanted to drop that "breathing" part, why, he could oblige them on that as well.

He whistled as he drove away, a man who loved his work.

CHAPTER SEVEN

Call 911. Don't call 911?

The body in the bathroom was cold, and even the world's fastest ambulance would prove useless. But if Roland didn't call right away, the suspicion would build, because the desk clerk would be able to confirm the time of the wake-up call.

Roland knew he was innocent (wasn't he?), but the fact remained that he was behind a locked door with a dead woman in his motel room. Worst of all, he couldn't account for a period of time that could range from hours to days. Maybe even weeks.

Roland glanced at the wallet lying on the bed. He couldn't even prove his identity, at least not immediately.

How do you tell the cops you're not David Underwood?

Wrestling his trembling legs into his pants, he collected the rental-car keys, painfully aware of all the surfaces he had touched. It was only when he found himself thinking about wiping down the doorknobs, the phone handset, and the light switches that he realized he was planning to flee.

A glance at the clock showed it was nearly ten. The maid would be by any minute, knocking on the door and reminding him to check out. Roland considered calling the front desk and putting another night on David Underwood's credit card.

That would buy him some time to think. But he couldn't stay in the room while a stranger's body went through the early stages of decomposition a mere ten feet away. A soft gurgle echoed off the tiles in the bathroom, gastric acid settling inside livid flesh.

Had he touched her? Had sex with her? Not likely, since he'd awoken wearing his briefs. Then again, he had no idea how long she had been dead. He might have killed her two days—

No, he hadn't killed anyone.

Right, David?

"I'm not David." His own voice sounded alien to his ears. The name sounded vaguely familiar, like a character from a cancelled television show.

Or college. Most of college had been one long blackout. But that wouldn't explain why he was here now with a corpse.

Possibilities ran through his head, and he pictured himself in a night club, buying her a drink, flashing that salesman's smile. He might have asked her back to his place ("Short on charm but long where it counts, babe"), but even the friendliest woman was reluctant to go solo with a man she'd only just met. Serial-killer movies and Facebook perverts had all but snuffed out the chance for random hookups.

If she were a professional, then Roland had definitely fallen off the wagon and probably bumped his head in the bargain. She might even be someone he knew, maybe an old friend or previous encounter, or someone he'd met through one of the online dating sites.

Roland lifted the water glass from the nightstand and sniffed for lingering signs of liquor. Only the crisp smell of chlorine from municipal water treatment.

Some drugs are odorless and tasteless...

He tossed the inch of clear liquid into his dry mouth, working it down his throat, and replaced the glass, studying it for fingerprints. He wiped it with one of his socks, which was silly because his prints were all over the room. But this was one little detail he could control.

It was now two minutes after ten. He eased toward the bathroom door. Leaving more fingerprints, he reached inside and probed for the light switch. When he touched it, the phone rang, causing his heart to skip a couple of beats.

Four rings later, the sound abruptly died, and the ensuing silence, marred only by the muted whisper of traffic outside, was almost as jarring.

Roland peeked around the doorjamb as if respecting her privacy. Her left foot was nearest to him, toenails painted dark burgundy. Her legs were shaven, the skin smooth and unmarked. The robe had ridden up to just under the tuck of her buttocks, and her thigh was shapely, though the portion against the floor was heavy and blotched by lividity.

Farther up, near her waist, the robe was soaked with blood. In the greasy yellow light above the bathroom sink, the blood appeared crusty and brown. It was difficult to tell how long she had been dead without a closer examination.

He sniffed. No taint of decay filled the air, although the bathroom smelled faintly of mildew and cheap shampoo. The shower head leaked, creating an arrhythmic tick that measured its own time.

Roland glanced at the sink countertop. No sign of toothbrushes, razors, floss, aftershave, or the other usual detritus of the traveler. No clues.

Her face was turned away from the door, toward the tub. The hand nearest Roland was curled as if gripping an invisible ball. The fingers bore no rings. Her hair trailed in unkempt, luxuriant locks over her shoulders, though the blackness had lost a little of its natural luster and resembled a wig.

Eyeing the toilet, wondering if he'd be able to step over her if he needed to vomit, he edged toward the tub. Careful not to touch her, he knelt and peered under the folds of hair at her face. Her eyelids were sunken and grayish purple, mouth parted, lips gone pale.

Good. Never seen her before.

She appeared to be a few years younger than he was, but the bottle had aged him fast and he hadn't spent a lot of time looking in mirrors lately. She was made up, the fake eyelashes a little exaggerated.

Her right hand, dangling on the rim of the bathtub, appeared to be pointing. It was most likely an act of rigor, tendons shrinking and tightening in decay. But Roland found himself looking at the back wall of the shower stall, in the direction of the finger.

Faint soap letters were scrawled in the shower residue: "C-R-O."

Cro. Crow. Cro-Magnon. Crocodile Fucking Dundee.

The letters might have been there for weeks. In a low-budget motel, the shower might only get a good scrubbing twice a year. Some guest could have been playing a joke, goofing around, leaving a message for a spouse.

Sure, and some guest might have left a dead body in the bathroom for Roland to find upon awakening. Roland was grasping for bizarre explanations because he didn't like the simplest one. Then again, he always looked for someone else to blame, no matter what the problem.

Unwilling to explore the body, both because of revulsion and a fear of leaving trace evidence, he glanced around the bathroom to see if he'd left any sign of his stay. For all he knew, she might be lying on top of one of his razor blades, a brand advertised to bring the girls up close and personal.

In any case, she certainly wasn't carrying identification, since she appeared to be naked beneath the robe. Another theory that Roland didn't have the stomach to confirm.

Instead, he left the ceramic-tiled tomb and retreated to the relative sanity of the sleeping area. He checked the closet but saw no purse, underwear, or clothing. No lipstick, no condom wrappers, no high heels.

Ten minutes had passed since the ringing of the telephone, and though his mind still ran frantic loops, his hands no longer trembled.

He was slipping into his shirt when the knock came. The interior of the bathroom was hidden from view of the front door. Roland glanced once behind him to reassure himself of the bathroom's angle and cracked the door, making sure his foot was planted firmly behind it.

A Hispanic woman, wearing blue jeans and a white uniform shirt with a towel draped over one shoulder, gave him an uneasy smile. She stood before a cart that held the tools of a maid's trade: stacks of folded linen, spray bottles, mop, toilet brush, and a bucket of gray water that smelled of pine cleanser and bleach. She'd obviously expected to find an empty room and had given a perfunctory knock out of habit.

The woman pointed at her wrist, though she wore no watch, and said, "Time for checkout?" in a thick accent. A question, with the tone of one who had learned the hard way the customer was always right.

Roland managed a return smile, though his lips felt numb and paralyzed with shock. "Slept late," he said, faking a yawn. "Give me ten minutes. I need a quick shower."

The woman nodded and looked at a piece of notebook paper taped to her cart, then at the room number. "Okay, Mr. Underwood. But you tell the desk."

She said "desk" as if the destination was some sort of principal's office for wayward adults.

"No desk," Roland said, the smile frozen on his face. He was hiding a corpse, but he could lie with his eyes and his face and his hands and his heart. Some habits never died.

"*Por favor*," he said in bad Spanish, and he actually winked. He lifted a hand and realized it was still covered by the sock. He worked it like a puppet, grinned like an idiot, and then removed it. Digging into his wallet—*David's* wallet, he chided himself—he pulled out a ten-dollar bill and held it toward the maid.

She shrank back as if it were the badge of a U.S. Immigration Service agent. She glanced from the office below back to the money. "I want no trouble."

"Neither do I, but I don't want to meet my wife at the airport smelling like a pig."

"The desk finds out, I have trouble."

"My wife can be trouble, too. *Mucho* bad."

The maid hesitated, as if calculating the risk and mentally converting the dollars to pesos. "You hurry?"

"Five minutes, I promise."

Roland was sickened by the look in the woman's eyes and was ashamed how cheaply she could be led into conspiracy. But he was quite possibly a murderer, and bribery was several notches down the moral scale.

She took the bill and secured it in her pocket. Roland wondered if, when the police interrogated her, she would tell them about the money. He figured its DNA and fingerprint evidence would never enter a courtroom. He only hoped she had a green card, for her sake.

"Five minutes?" she asked, glancing at the office again and the omnipotent front desk that was hidden behind its tinted glass.

"Cross my heart," he said, declining to complete the last half of the promise. He closed the door, found that sweat had stained the underarms of his shirt, and wondered if five minutes would be enough.

Even if he mustered the will to touch the body, the maid would find it whether it was tucked in the closet or hidden under the bed. He considered turning on the taps in the bathtub and locking the door, letting the maid assume he was showering. That might buy him an extra half an hour.

But minutes meant nothing in the face of eternity. In recovery from alcoholism, Roland had practiced principles of rigorous honesty and self-examination, including a core commitment to purposely harm no one.

Somewhere in the space of maybe three days, he had not only traveled five hundred miles but had lost his identity. Or maybe he hadn't lost his identity at all, but found it.

If I'm David Underwood, who the fuck was Roland Doyle?

As he gathered his belongings and wiped down the telephone with the sock, he realized the police would be looking for David Underwood, not Roland Doyle. The world believed David had rented this room, and the police would put out an All Points Bulletin not for Roland, but for his spontaneous alter ego.

Despite the roiling of his gut and his hop-scotching pulse, he found comfort in the idea that David would be the fall guy. The latest contestant to suit up and show up for the Blame Game.

The car keys jingled in Roland's jacket pocket. He pulled out the orange plastic vial and gave it a shake as he held it up for inspection. It contained maybe eight pills. A plain white label bore bold print that read simply, “D. Underwood. Take one every 4 hrs. or else.”

Or else what?

LSD? A kick-ass barbiturate? Diazepam?

And, the bigger question, how many of them had he taken? Enough to blot out a murder?

He shoved the vial back in his pocket. Two minutes until the maid returned.

Run now, sort it out later.

That’s what drunks and cowards did.

That’s what Roland Doyle had always done.

Familiarity gave him comfort.

A drink would offer even more comfort.

He slipped his bare feet into his Oxfords, gathered his laptop and satchel, and took a final look at the bathroom. Hand in sock, he twisted the door handle, exited the room, and hurried along the balcony, hoping that bastard David had left him the right car key.

The outside surroundings were urban, but rounded hills and a river bordered the low buildings, a series of steel bridges glistening in the morning sun. The air smelled of coal smoke and chemicals. He recognized the city now as definitely Cincinnati, its Revolutionary War roots giving way to redevelopment, the arts, and young corporate professionals.

And the occasional surprise corpse.

He picked out the car and slid behind the seat.

Sitting on the dash in front of the speedometer was a handwritten note. It said, “Or else you’ll remember.”

CHAPTER EIGHT

"The chair recognizes Dr. Morgan. Alexis?"

The chairman of the President's Council on Bioethics, Dr. Michael Mulroney, had an irritating habit of referring to all committee members, and those providing testimony, by their formal titles. Except for the women.

No doubt he assumed it was part of his Texas charm and he probably wasn't even aware of it. But Alexis had noted, even in a cutting-edge field where women had credentials equal to men's, a sly sexism still existed. And the Good Ol' Boy network drew even tighter the closer she got to the Capitol Building.

She gave no sign of her feelings, though. "Thank you, Dr. Mulroney. This seems to be more of a moral issue than a scientific issue. From what I've heard here, we tend to view social anxiety as a welcome trait. Indeed, as an essential survival mechanism. When the monkeys came down from the trees, we couldn't instantly trust all the other monkeys—some wanted to steal our food or our mates, and maybe even kill us to protect their territory or eliminate competition. Fear was not necessarily a bad thing."

She could always count on Wallace Forsyth, a wispy-haired former U.S. representative from Kentucky, to stir himself any time she used a monkey metaphor, and she had taken to using at least one per session just to keep the old codger awake. As the token Christian Coalition appointee to the President's Council, Forsyth made it his mission to frame every issue as a war on religion.

Specifically, *his* religion, which to him was the only one.

Alexis was privately a Taoist of no fixed beliefs and was willing to throw anything at the wall and see what stuck. But she took an agnostic approach in professional matters. Her work was complicated enough as it was.

Crossing thin ice is even more dangerous if you believe you can walk on water.

"Mrs. Morgan"—Forsyth refused to call her "Doctor," as if he resented the fact that she had neglected to wear an apron and serve up coffee for the committee—"we all respect your behavioral research, and I'm sure we've all bought your book. I'm still on page eight but I'm enjoying it so far."

The chamber erupted in uneasy laughter. *All's Well That Ends Well* had been released four years ago, and though it had received brief attention in pop psychology circles, it had gone out of print within a year.

Since most of the committee members had published books, Forsyth's veiled jab went directly to their own egos—scholarly tomes had notoriously low print runs, and unless you were featured on *Oprah*, *Dr. Phil*, or one of the network morning shows, the fruits of your loving labor ended up buried in the eBay graveyard.

Alexis managed her most winning smile, having learned that in the political world, the best response was often the exact opposite of your true feelings.

"Then I envy you the pleasure of discovery," she said. "But many of the points in my book have already been covered in this session. The core question is not whether we *can* make people feel better about themselves, but whether we *should*."

"If this was just a question of physical illness, there wouldn't be no debate," Forsyth drawled. "If a brain tumor was causing somebody to misbehave, we'd cull it out like a rotten apple in a bushel basket. But if somebody's misbehaving all on their own, because God made them that way, would we really want to be messing in that?"

To his credit, Forsyth refrained from referring to the brain as "God's domain," as he'd done during his first few months on the committee.

"Mr. Forsyth, the deeper question is just who we are," Alexis continued, noticing Mulroney had opened his mouth to interject. "If our thoughts are nothing more than a series of electrical impulses, and our actions are nothing more than responses to those impulses, then you could argue we have no self-control at all. And whether you couch it in physical or spiritual terms, it comes down to chemistry versus individual will."

Mulroney leaned toward his microphone in an overt gesture of control, perhaps sensing Forsyth was about to shift the discussion toward God's will trumping the will of man. And especially the will of woman.

"You've given us much food for thought, Alexis, and now it's time for some food for the belly," Mulroney said, tapping his gavel. "We'll reconvene at one thirty."

Alexis busied herself sliding documents in her briefcase. Dr. Rita Wynn of Harvard patted her on the shoulder in passing, as if to congratulate her for fighting off the lions. Forsyth wiped his bald spot and gave his American eagle glare. She smiled in response and hurriedly left the conference room.

Nine of the fourteen people in there are doctors, and I wouldn't trust so much as an aspirin from any of them.

The meeting was a two-day affair at the Crown Plaza Hotel, and while many of the council members gathered in the hotel cafeteria, where the brave would take a glass of wine with their Alfredo pasta, Alexis caught the elevator. Just as the doors were closing, company stepped inside.

"Hi, honey," Mark said, leaning forward and giving her a kiss on the cheek.

"You were out late last night."

"Damned Senator Burchfield," he said. "He's got a hammerlock on the health care committee. We did everything but juggle and dance for him."

Alexis reached past Mark and pressed the button for the fourth floor. In the first year of their marriage, she would have taken the opportunity not only to rub her breasts against him, but maybe even hit the "Stop" button for thirty seconds of frantic foreplay.

The honeymoon five years over, now she looked forward to sitting on the bed, removing her high heels, and maybe coaxing him into a foot rub.

"So what's Senator Botox up to these days, besides keeping widows from getting cheap Canadian prescription drugs?" Burchfield had earned his nickname during his transition from congressman to senator, when the wrinkles in his forehead miraculously vanished and the gray in his hair had been reduced to two distinguished patches near his temples.

"He's been fast-tracking a lot of experimental drugs, leaning on the Food and Drug Administration to discreetly lift a few bans. That could be good for us, but it could also be good for our competitors. When we're gambling with supply and demand, one jackass like Burchfield can cut us out of the game while the cards are being dealt."

"You'll have him eating out of your hand before the weekend's over."

"I'd rather be eating out of *your* hand," he said. "And other places."

Mark Morgan, junior vice president of CRO Pharmaceuticals, was a smooth talker who had come up through the marketing department, and his science background was limited to a few undergrad biology classes in which he'd eked out a C. Luckily, he'd met his future bride there, the straight-A grad student.

That was all fine with Alexis. She battled wits with enough eggheads as a researcher and professor at the University of North Carolina, so after hours she preferred the company of a guy whose interests included sex, swimming, and televised sports, though not necessarily always in that order.

And he looked dynamite both in and out of a suit.

"Maybe you'll get your chance," she said. "I have a whole hour for lunch."

"Quickie?" He kissed beneath her earlobe and blew against the moistness, causing her to shiver. "How's the meeting going?"

Adopting a Southern accent, she mocked, "Dr. Forsyth thinks I'm the darlin' little flag-bearer for the Antichrist."

"He's a close friend of the president. Even though he got smeared in the election, he's still got clout. I told you, that's just the way this town works."

"I can't wait to get back to Chapel Hill myself."

The elevator dinged open, and Mark took her briefcase, leading her down the hall. "I'm afraid I'll have to stay over."

Alexis gave a fake pout. "I thought we were flying back tonight."

"*You* are. The council should wrap up by dinner. I'm going to be tied up lobbying the health committee. They're working on some make-or-break bills for the next session, and we've got to whisper in their ears the whole time or the idiots will forget who put them in office."

"You make it sound so noble."

Alexis swiped the room key in the slot, and Mark brushed past her and went into the bathroom. As his urine drilled into the toilet bowl, he raised his voice and said, "There are two bottom lines, honey. One is helping people, and the other is helping the company. If we can't get our drugs out there, then people will suffer."

"Please. I've heard enough of that from the council."

Mark sat beside her on the bed. He'd left his fly unzipped. "Poor baby. Want me to get you a tranquilizer?"

"Hell, no. With CRO's markup, it would probably run me ten bucks."

"I know a guy with the company," he said, kicking off his shoes and crawling behind her to rub her shoulders. She relaxed and let her head hang forward, wishing she could let down her hair and undress.

Mark's strong hands kneaded the back of her neck, eliciting a sigh. They hadn't made love since the previous weekend, and though statistically it was considered normal for ardor to decline during the early thirties, Alexis considered sex a foundation of good mental health.

The Centers for Disease Control should set a recommended minimum daily adult requirement of at least one orgasm.

"Hmm, if you gave Senator Botox this kind of treatment, he'd hand you the pen and let you write your own legislation," Alexis said with a purr.

He scooted against her until the hard heat between his legs pressed against her back through her blouse. "Yeah, but think of the rumors. People already believe Congress is in bed with the pharmaceutical companies."

"If they only knew," she said, yielding as his hands slipped from her shoulders and around to her breasts. Her nipples hardened even before his fingers reached them. A classic case of conditioning.

"That feels good, honey," she said, and now his breath played along the nape of her neck and his lips sought the vulnerable flesh where her scalp met her spine.

He slid his hand inside her bra, stroking the underside of one breast while his thumb teased her nipple. His other hand skillfully released the buttons of her blouse, his fingertips trailing along her belly as he did so.

She reached behind him and fished inside his pants, heat radiating as his erection filled her hand. "You're fast."

She raised her hips from the bed so he could hike up her skirt. He stroked the outside of her cotton panties. She was already moist, a little embarrassed at her own sluttishness.

"Forsyth would demand an exorcism if he knew you were wearing garter hose," Mark said, easing aside an elastic leg band and stroking the soft hairs beneath the fabric.

She licked her fingers and felt along Mark's length until she reached the soft, sensitive skin beneath the head. "Don't screw up my fantasy."

"I'm only screwing one thing," he said, slipping a gentle finger inside her and smearing her juices up to her clitoris. He rubbed in steady, teasing circles until it swelled, and then he caressed the underside in counterpoint to her manipulation of his penis.

She writhed, pressing back against him, debating whether to turn but reluctant to break the electric flow from his fingers to her vagina. Maybe if she lifted up slightly, he could slide into her from behind and—

The page buzzer was like the shriek of a bomb siren.

Mark stopped the movement of his hands. "Damn," he whispered.

"Damn? Everything's still in the right place, isn't it?"

"I shouldn't have started this," Mark said, slipping his hand from her panties and reaching toward his jacket on the bed. "I've got cocktails with some FDA suits in half an hour, and with traffic like it is—"

Alexis groaned, still holding him in her hand. "'Work before play' is for responsible grown-ups, not us."

"We wouldn't have time for the full monty, anyway. You've got the council meeting this afternoon."

"And I'm going to have to sit through it with moist panties."

"Well, leave them at home." Mark adopted a light tone, trying to minimize her disappointment. "Maybe give Forsyth a peep show like Sharon Stone in *Basic Instinct*. Torture him with all the delights of heaven and hell."

Alexis squeezed his fading erection as a farewell and reminder. "Or maybe give him the first one of these he's had since the Eisenhower administration."

"You packed the vibrator, didn't you?"

"No. With airport security like it is, I didn't want TSA to charge me with smuggling torpedoes. Besides, that's a placebo effect. I need a dose of the real thing."

He rolled off the bed, tucked himself back into his fly as best he could, and adjusted his necktie. She pointed at the jutting tent of his pants. "You going to catch a cab like that?"

"I'll picture the president's wife. That ought to stifle it." He gave her a spousal peck on the cheek. "Tomorrow night, I promise. We'll go for a double."

"Big promise."

As Mark brushed his teeth, Alexis rummaged in her luggage and found a granola bar, choking it down with one of the hotel's eight-dollar bottles of spring water. Good thing the federal government offered a generous per diem, or she couldn't afford to serve on the bioethics council.

Mark's salary was in the low six figures, but she still insisted on keeping their expenses separate when possible. Even though she understood the male's traditional role as provider, she was enough of a feminist to keep gender issues neutral in her own marriage.

Man smart, woman smarter. Acting like the weaker sex.

And my sex is feeling pretty damned wobbly right about now.

She got one more kiss out of Mark before she returned to the bioethics committee and more debate about the use of psychopharmacology to make people happier, more productive, and better socially adjusted.

In short, whether drugs should be used to make everyone feel the same. To feel "normal."

God, what she wouldn't give for a normal life.

CHAPTER NINE

Wendy was only ten minutes late for her noon class.

The eight students in Studio Drawing II were working in their sketch pads, some with charcoal, some with Conte crayons, and two with fat pencils. A tape of eighties synth-pop band The Cars thumped and squished from a cheap boom box in the back of the room, and Wendy was grateful for perhaps the hundredth time that she didn't have a demanding career with a fire-breathing boss.

This class was self-selecting, juniors or seniors with a serious yen for art, and they didn't really need motivation. In fact, they seemed as joyful not to have a "real class" as Wendy was not to have a "real job."

After the odd incident at the restaurant, the reprieve was doubly welcome, and the aroma of paint thinner cut the memory of bacon grease and chaos and Anita's recollections of the past.

"Hey, folks," she said, and most of them nodded or gave quick waves before returning to their work. "I'll just be chilling at my desk in case you need me."

Wendy had a tiny office, with a long counter and slots underneath for students to store their portfolios, but in typical bureaucratic shortsightedness, a battleship-sized metal desk took up much of the floor space. She parked herself behind it to collect herself before launching into instructional mode.

She picked a piece of glass out of her pocket. The E-Z's front window had been comprised of safety glass, although the square shards were still capable of cutting flesh, as evidenced by the wound on Anita's forehead. Wendy tilted the piece of glass like a prism, looking for a rainbow in its oblique surface.

Although she was still shaken by the incident, and the fact that officials had offered no explanation, she'd shrugged it off as just another bit of crazy in a world built of the stuff.

Once settled into the scarred wooden chair that looked to be a holdover from the days of segregation, she fiddled her cell phone from the folds of her jacket.

Anita answered on the second ring. "I think it was Halcyon," Anita said.

"Calm down, hon. I knew I shouldn't have left you."

"Briggs did it."

"Nobody did anything." Although she couldn't understand why an unoccupied car could navigate itself into a building, she failed to see a looming conspiracy theory that would make Oliver Stone cream his jeans.

She was annoyed that Anita brought up the name of a drug they swore they'd never mention again. "It was just an accident."

"But he knew I was there." Anita paused and then added with an anxious rush, "First my psychiatrist and now this."

"Your psychiatrist died of a heart attack."

"I don't know that for a fact. Besides, there's only one way to die, and that's when your heart stops beating."

"Anita, you're worrying me." Anita had been so distressed at the scene that Wendy, despite a vague sense that she probably should have offered some sort of eyewitness testimony to the police, had yielded to her friend's frantic desire to leave. Not that Wendy had really seen anything. It wasn't like she could have identified the driver.

"Did you see the way they looked at me?"

"Who?" Wendy was used to people staring at Anita. Besides being beautiful, her friend often evoked a feeling of vague recognition, as if the viewer had seen her somewhere before but couldn't place the face. Some did but couldn't admit it in polite company.

"The cops," Anita said. "They know."

"You told me you quit drugs when you left LA. You've never been paranoid before."

"Just like the trials. Freak out, and then forget."

"You didn't take more of that stuff your dead psychiatrist gave you, did you?"

"Right after you left. I couldn't wait till noon."

"Damn. I told you to consult your doctor before you took more."

"I needed it. Those monsters in their holes—"

"Listen—"

"I have to go now. They're coming. Like they came for Susan."

"Nita?" Her query fell into the white noise of a dead connection.

Susan. Who is Susan? And why is that name scaring me?

She wondered if she should call the police or 911. Given Anita's persecuted state of mind, the sudden arrival of uniforms might drive her to—what? Wendy didn't know.

Her friend, though flamboyant and prone to deep depression, had never suffered from irrational complexes. Anita lived only two miles from campus, but with college-town traffic, it might take half an hour to reach her apartment.

I shouldn't have left her, but she seemed fine.

Wendy tried the phone line again but gave up after seven rings. She was about to try again when she sensed movement in the office doorway behind her.

Her chair squeaked as she turned, the grating noise causing her to grimace. The door seemed far away, the office walls appearing to stretch from her and tilt at steep angles.

The sudden onset of vertigo disturbed her. She wondered if she was catching the flu, or if the Long-Haul Breakfast was making a contaminated run. Her head had been aching and mildly stuffy all morning, but she had no fever.

The morning's events had been stressful, but she considered herself adaptable and able to handle the unexpected. She was bracing for an attempt to stand when a shadow fell over the door.

"Wendy?" It was Chase Hanson, a student who wore his hair in a 1950s duck and favored checkered shirts. Mediocre talent, but like many aspiring artists, he thought attitude and style far outweighed the need for craft. "Got a sec?"

She swallowed and closed her eyes, hoping he wouldn't notice her unease. She motioned to a chair in the corner. "Sure."

Chase closed the door behind him, and the room felt impossibly cramped, like a mausoleum vault.

Like the factory.

He turned and gave her a smile, but his teeth descended in vulpine proportions. The look on her face must have startled him, because the boyish grin froze.

"I thought..." He looked past her to *Madonna of Egypt*, one of Wendy's surrealist creations, an oval-faced, hollow-eyed female swathed in filthy bandages like a mummy. "About yesterday."

"Yesterday?" Wendy gripped the arms of the chair, hoping the solidity of the oak would reaffirm her corporeality. Her pulse beat a steady path across her temples and her ears rang with a high-pitched whine.

Chase waved his hand at the desk. "What happened."

Not trusting herself to stand and face him, she sagged into the chair, which was now as unaccountably soft as a stack of pillows. She nodded, barely hearing him, focused on the three spots of cadmium-yellow paint that adorned his left boot.

"I know you could get in big trouble for something like that," he continued. "Probably even lose your job."

The implications of his words finally broke through the sensory gauze. She attempted to sit upright but failed. "What are you talking about?" she said thickly.

He grinned again, but this time the expression was lewd instead of gregarious. "Ah, I get it. It never happened, right?"

"Chase—"

He fell into a mockery of an old advertisement for laundry detergent. "Ancient Chinese secret, huh?"

"That was lame in seventh grade. What's wrong with you?"

The real question was what was wrong with *her*, but she wasn't willing to ask that one. The potential answers were too disturbing.

"Hey, don't go getting all upset," he said. "Although you're sexy when you're all scrunched up."

Chase's tone had changed from cautious to cocky, an "Aw shucks" charm he donned as if it were a thrift-shop beret. If only the walls weren't leaning in opposite directions, she would stand and usher him out the door. As it was, she scarcely trusted her lips, because she wasn't sure they would move at her command. She tried anyway.

"You're making me uncomfortable," she said, though in truth she had been uncomfortable before he had even entered the office. Now the floor was a jiggly magic carpet of Jell-O.

"I know, sweetie," he said. "I've been getting hot and bothered myself. You know what they say about guys my age."

Chase must have picked up a crossed signal somewhere, and she searched her memory for some suggestive classroom joke or double entendre she might have dispensed. She was cautious around her students for the very reasons Chase had suggested: she could get in big trouble and maybe even lose her job.

"Whatever you think is going on, you're the only one," she managed.

A print of Munch's *The Scream*, taped to the wall behind the student's head, seemed to ripple, and she could swear she heard the desperate ululation arising from that rounded O of a mouth. Or maybe the sound was coming from *her* mouth.

Chase put a finger to his lips. "Shh," he said. "Wouldn't want anyone getting the wrong idea."

"What's the right idea?" she said, feeling angry and foolish over her own helplessness.

"That you want this," he said. "Just like last time."

He reached his painting hand toward her, black flecks under his fingernails, the skin smelling faintly of linseed oil and turpentine. Instead of drawing away, she found herself leaning closer to let the rough fingers graze her cheek. He stroked the soft skin beneath her cheek. It tickled but she was unable to laugh.

"See there, babe?" he said. "You haven't forgotten after all."

He stooped so their faces were at the same level and she stared into his glacial blue eyes. His puckered lips glided toward hers, and something about the movement was familiar and disturbing.

To her horror, she felt her own mouth part in welcome and the wet cement of her arms set with a weighty permanence against her chair.

Then their lips met and her body broke free of its trance. As she jerked her head away, the unwelcome kiss cut a slick trail across her cheek.

She exploded from the chair, throwing her shoulder into his chest and knocking him off balance, the anger clearing her head.

The icy eyes grew narrow and colder, and Chase's swollen lover's lips shifted into a sneer. He hovered over her as she retreated into the corner. "Hey, what's your problem?"

"If you leave right now, I won't file a complaint."

"Didn't bother you any yesterday," he said. "You practically jumped my bones, remember?"

The trouble was, she *didn't* remember, and he spoke with such conviction that the student judicial affairs committee would be as likely to take his side as hers.

"You're mistaken," she said, hating herself for going on the defensive.

"Hell with it," he said. "You're just a yellow cock-tease. So you want a one-off, that's fine. Slam, bam, fuck you, ma'am."

Her lungs were marbled sculpture, but she managed to force air past her vocal cords. "I don't know what you're talking about."

"Man, I'm lucky you didn't yell 'Rape.' Glad I used a rubber. You're probably boning every guy in the department."

"You'll drop the class," she said, with a surprising modicum of calm. "I'll approve the paperwork."

"Damn right," he said. "I'll take it under Wingate. Her tits are so withered she doesn't go around shaking them in her students' faces."

He retreated and fumbled with the door handle, and it was only then she realized he had locked it upon entering. What exactly had happened the last time he had locked her office door?

Alone, heart pounding, she held her head for a full minute, eyeing the telephone. It looked fat and liquid, the handset like a swollen grub. Should she call an ambulance? Would she be able to punch the numbers?

Some of the disorientation left her, the geometry of the room falling more or less into right angles. Her respiration and pulse rate were only slightly above normal.

Anxiety attack.

That would explain a lot, except for Chase's behavior. He had moved with a practiced confidence. Like he'd done it before. Here.

Could she have done the things he'd suggested?

No. Don't give it an inch.

She didn't want to think about it. She would call Anita instead of the hospital.

First, she would fill out the form that would drop Chase Hanson from the class. His painted canvases would soon be gone from the studio, the garish Rothko imitations consigned to a dusty dorm closet until the artist needed them to impress some eager coed. Somebody else to slam bam.

The rage helped clear her head as she opened the drawer. Lying on top of the shuffled stacks of memos were paper clips, pastel crayons, a solar-powered calculator, and a dull linoleum knife.

And a ripped square of foil that had once housed a condom.

Unconsciously, her thighs squeezed together. She lifted the empty wrapper and rubbed a thumb along the serrated edge.

Not ours. Please let it not be ours.

Behind it, in the shadows of the drawer, was a plastic pill bottle.

Burnt orange, for prescription medicine.

The label bore script as if from a pharmacy but contained no drug store or medical logo. The bold text in the center of the label wasn't the sort prescribed by a physician: "W. Leng. Take one every 4 hrs. or else."

Glancing at the open door, she twisted the cap free. The pills resembled tiny green breath mints. She poured them on the desk. One rolled past the telephone and arced to the floor, where it bounced off the dirty tiles. Wendy retrieved it and then counted them.

Eight. The bottle was large enough to contain at least fifty of the green pills.

And they looked disturbingly familiar.

Oh my God. How many of these have I taken?

She nudged the pills onto a sheet of paper, funneled them back into the vial, and tucked the container in her pocket. Chase Hanson's paperwork could wait. Right now, she wanted a look at Anita's Halcyon prescription, because she had a feeling those pills were also green.

Every four hours.

Wendy wondered when she'd last taken her prescribed dose, and what would happen when she failed to take the next.

CHAPTER TEN

Roland reached the West Virginia mountains in early afternoon.

Whatever the pill was, it hadn't impaired his driving. In fact, it had helped clear his head, and Cincinnati seemed years away. Sure, it had been crazy taking the pill, but the orange bottle seemed like the only reliable and honest thing in his life.

The radio offered no reports of a murderer on the loose, but he had no way to tell whether the body had been discovered or simply that murder was no longer major news.

Despite the rental-car receipts being made out to "David Underwood," Roland veered off the interstate in Kentucky and stuck to the back roads, crossing the Big Coal River and entering the mountains. His brother, Steve, a dentist in Fort Lauderdale, kept a log cabin there as a summer getaway and had shared a key with Roland.

"We all need to hide out now and then," Steve had said, flashing a six-figure smile. Roland figured Steve was talking about entertaining mistresses and fishing for trout, not evading capture for murder.

But it wasn't murder, he reasoned, as he eased past a goat farm on the outskirts of Logan, heading up the gravel road that led into a dark hollow of the type praised in old Appalachian folk ballads.

Or, it may have been murder, but it wasn't mine.

He thought of all the cop shows he'd seen. Most of them were built on the simple words "It wasn't me." If you believed the fairy tales, nobody ever did it, especially the good guy.

And despite a blackout, despite blood on his hands, despite a pile of evidence that would make any prosecuting attorney salivate, Roland still believed he was one of the good guys. At least until proven guilty.

And I'm not David Underwood. Only Roland can feel this shitty and scared.

The gravel road gave way to twin muddy ruts, and Roland wondered how Steve navigated the driveway in his BMW. The neighboring goat farmer, whom Steve said took pride in monitoring the row of mailboxes for signs of vandalism and theft, had no doubt observed the unfamiliar vehicle passing by.

The Ford Escort was not exactly the wheels of choice for a deer hunter or fisherman, and there was a slim chance the farmer would jot down the license-plate numbers just in case. Nosy neighbors could be just as much a blessing as a curse, but Roland figured he'd be safe as long as he didn't poach any goats.

The key fit the lock, which was comforting. Further proof that he indeed was Roland who had a brother named Steve who owned a cabin near Logan. It may as well have been a jail cell, however, because Roland was imposing his own sentence.

Although his plan was to think the problem through, inaction would be seen as the resignation of a guilty man. The DA would have a field day retracing his movements in court.

Stale, musty air, with a wet-fur accent, wafted from the cabin's interior as the door opened. Steve rarely visited it, and Roland hadn't been there since a business stopover two years before.

The cabin was stocked with the usual rodent-proof fare: canned beans, a rusted tin of coffee, and powdered milk on the shelves; sherbet, ice cubes, and a graying, cellophane-wrapped hunk of mystery meat in the freezer; and a half-bottle of flat ginger ale and a crusted mustard jar in the refrigerator.

The cabin had no telephone, even though cellular reception was spotty in the mountains. "Part of getting away from it all," Steve had said.

Roland was afraid to even switch his phone on, much less make a call, fearing the signal would somehow be traceable. He didn't know if the police had ways of tracking phone locations using global-positioning satellite data, or whether the rental car contained such technology.

All he knew was that someone had planted links to the pills, the murder, and the car, and if one person could connect the dots, then so could the cops.

A distant dog brayed, a lonely sound that reminded Roland that he had no one to trust. Steve, the younger, overachieving brother, was almost his polar opposite, too slick to take on serious problems. Their father was dead, hammered by a coronary thrombosis, and Mom was living in that fragile state of denial that afforded no room for adversity.

The close friendships of his early twenties had given way to the forced camaraderie of coworkers and business clients, all his old buddies poured down the drain with the contents of that last half-bottle of whiskey. Only one person would have shared this dark burden, even at risk of being charged as an accomplice to murder.

No, he couldn't think of Wendy. That was over, a marriage killed by his selfishness. One of the sayings in his twelve-step program was that drunks didn't have relationships, they took hostages. And Wendy had paid her ransom with dignity and two years of counseling.

Roland checked the bedroom, wondering if he should air out the blankets. Even in March, the mountain air was humid. As he sat on the bed, he realized how exhausted he was. The adrenaline that had fueled him during that morning's discovery and subsequent flight had receded, though his thoughts still raced down the same avenues of the past few hours.

Had he killed someone? What had happened during the missing chunk of memory? And who was David Underwood?

He pulled the pill bottle from his pocket, a solid link to what had happened in Cincinnati. It had been over four hours, but damned if he was taking any more pills.

It was only after he'd stretched out on the bed that he realized he had no course of action. Too wired to doze, he stared at the ceiling. Harry Grimes would be expecting a sales report this afternoon.

He was supposed to be in Kentucky tomorrow, visiting a few tire dealerships to present a new style of rubberized signage, complete with tread marks. Now the wheels were bare, the road reaching a dead end, no exits.

Actually, that wasn't true.

One detour remained.

Steve, like many weekend hosts, stocked an array of cocktail staples. Though alcoholism stemmed from a genetic predisposition in many cases, Steve managed fine as an occasional imbiber. The very existence of a liquor cabinet was proof enough that his brother had dodged the affliction. Roland had never owned more than one bottle at a time, and he never slept until that bottle was empty.

Sweat arose in his armpits, his palms, and along the line of his scalp. He was convinced that the murderous blackout had not been caused by drinking, but now that the insidious whisper filled his head, it would not stop its siren song until he crashed on the rocks. Two years of sobriety, and what had he gained?

And it wasn't like this was *his* fault. After all, he didn't kill the woman. David Underwood did, and Roland wasn't David, was he?

She was just in the wrong place at the wrong time.

And because of her, Roland's world had been tipped off its axis.

Clearly, she was the one to blame.

He sat up. One of the ground rules of recovery was to maintain daily contact with your sponsor. Especially when the monkey climbed on your back and dug in its dirty claws.

No cell phone signal. Roland couldn't call.

He sighed, relieved, though his gut clenched in craving.

No Harry. So Harry shared in the failure as much as the dead woman did.

Fuck it.

Fists tight, Roland stood. He was almost to the closet when Wendy's voice came to him.

"What did you ever do to deserve this?" he'd once asked when they were exploring the damage of people who loved alcoholics.

"What did *you* do to deserve it?" she asked.

And he'd had no answer, then or now.

She'd been as supportive as any spouse should be. She even attended Al-Anon, the support group for family members of alcoholics. She'd sat with him in open meetings, listened as he made his required amends and worked through the steps; she memorized the little homilies, including the one that reminded drunks to remember the futility of control, resentment, and selfishness.

But where was Wendy now?

Out of his life, living across town from him, both of them financially damaged by the separation and legal battle.

Of course, when you got right down to it, God had set up the bowling pins for this particular split. Why cast about for blame when there was One who had all the power?

In the Blame Game, you didn't need to point the finger at yourself. The real target was in the sky, everywhere, pervading the fabric of reality.

Or, alternately, God was nowhere.

The grin was a grim rictus on his face. Justification, that savior of drunks the world over. He licked his lips. His hand was actually trembling in a way it hadn't since he'd beaten *delirium tremens* during a thirty-day stay in a treatment facility.

If God didn't want him to drink, God would cause him to trip over the living room rug and break a leg. And God wouldn't have stuck Steve's liquor in the cabin, just waiting for him like manna.

God's fault. God's desire. God's will.

He was heading for the liquor cabinet when someone knocked on the door.

He glanced at the ceiling, wondering if God was up there laughing, the hoary old bastard.

He thought about hiding, or maybe going for the back door and running into the woods, but that would be stupid.

No, the best thing was to answer it and act like he belonged there.

Roland opened the door, smiling but with a little hint of annoyance at being disturbed. A man stood there, beefy, dressed in a flannel shirt and overalls. He wore a new straw hat on his head that looked uncomfortably stiff. One side of his mouth was slack, as if he'd worn out his muscles from chewing tobacco in that cheek.

"Can I help you?"

"Howdy," the man said, waving vaguely off to the left. "I own the farm down there and keep an eye on the place for Steve. Thought I might check in and see if you need anything. Place has stood empty a while."

Yeah, right. And not a bit curious, I'll bet.

"I'm just stopping over on a road trip," Roland said. "I'm Steve's brother."

The man squinted. "I see a little resemblance, now that you mention it."

"Yeah, he got the brains, but I got all the looks."

The man nodded, no sense of humor. "Well, if you need anything, just holler."

Roland glanced at the man's feet, expecting to see scuffed boots flecked with goat shit. Instead, the man wore shiny leather dress shoes.

"I'll do that, sir," he said, though the man was only ten years older than him.

The man turned, and Roland noticed there were no other vehicles in the driveway. The farmer must have walked at least half a mile. Without scuffing his new shoes. "All right, David, enjoy your stay."

"My name's not David," Roland said. "It's—"

He caught himself as the man turned. "Steve said he had a brother named David," the man said.

Roland thought about lying, but he planned to be long gone soon. "It's Roland."

The man's lips pursed, and then they broke into a grin. "That's right. I was just testing you. We get all kinds of weirdos out in these parts. It pays to be a little suspicious."

"Sounds like good advice."

"You'll be heading back to North Carolina soon?"

How the hell did he know? "Depends on how much I enjoy my stay."

"I wouldn't enjoy it too much. You might never want to leave."

The man laughed, but the humor was off, like an inside joke he didn't want to share. Roland watched him walk down the road, those new shoes slapping in the dirt and gravel.

He slammed the door. Soon it wouldn't matter if he was Roland or David or the fucking ghost of Kentucky Colonel Jack Daniels.

He reached the cabinet and swallowed hard, throat stinging with the anticipated heat of the liquor. Steve's drink was Crown Royal, out of Roland's price range, but there would be rum, vodka, gin, and probably some brandy as well. Enough.

The cabinet was oaken, the door slightly warped by dampness. But now it was the gate to paradise.

As he opened the door, he closed his eyes, half-hoping for a final reprieve, some cosmic gesture that would gird his spirit.

The cabinet door creaked open. A warm, putrid odor wafted out with the force of floodwater.

A goat hung in the cabinet, a hemp rope tangled in its horns. Its body cavity was peeled open, red ribs exposed, offal spilling in trails of gray-green and pink.

As Roland dry-heaved for the second time that day, he realized the kill must have been recent. A strange jubilation surged through him; here was proof that he was not the killer.

On its heels came a deeper relief. He had stayed sober. Maybe through a little luck, maybe through the divine hand of that Big Bastard in the Sky.

But sobriety didn't change reality. The sacrificial slaughter had occurred while he was in the car, on his way here. Someone must have left the mutilated carcass for him, someone who knew his destination, someone who had anticipated his moves after leaving the Cincinnati motel.

Someone who knew he'd open the liquor cabinet sooner rather than later, because the killer had left a message.

Scrawled in congealed blood were the same cryptic letters he'd observed in the motel shower stall: "CRO." And beneath it, "Every 4 hrs. You're late." The symbols were smeared as if by a callous finger.

As blood continued to drain from the goat, it pooled around the message, and Roland realized the letters would soon be obscured.

The crime techs would be able to decode it. They'd be able to match evidence with the crime scene in Cincinnati and he'd be off the hook. Of course, there was still the problem of the missing time and his new identity—

"It's not *my* identity, damn it," he said, the words scouring his ravaged throat.

Roland couldn't stay in the cabin now, not while that hideous face leered from the cabinet with its strange, milky eyes. He reached past it and grabbed the only bottle there, half a pint of vodka. He twisted the lid free.

Here's to you, you glassy-eyed fucker.

Roland turned up the bottle, craving the sweet relief, no matter what price he'd pay later.

He'd forced down three swallows before he realized the vodka didn't burn. He pulled it away and smelled it.

Water.

The laughter hit him hard, and he leaned against the wall, air leaping from his lungs in painful grunts. He was such a fuck-up that he even fucked up getting fucked up. His sides hurt, then he punched the wall, and the pain brought him around.

Roland pulled the orange bottle from his pocket and glanced at the bloody letters on the cabinet door: "You're late."

The rage came over him almost instantly, and he had retrieved a butcher knife from the kitchen and was about to hack into that goddamned goat, with its glassy, accusing eyes.

Who are you to fucking judge me?

Trembling, he dropped the knife and fled to the back bedroom, crawling onto the bare mattress and huddling into himself.

They were coming. They'd find out he'd drunk the vodka.

He thought of the farmer with the spiffy shoes and city hands.

The farmer's words came back to him. *"You'll be heading back to North Carolina soon?"*

And another question, maybe one from David Underwood up in the peanut gallery:

Why did you kill Susan?

He hadn't thought of the girl in years, and he didn't even know he'd forgotten her, but her rounded face slid into his mind, eyes wide and mouth screaming and chubby cheeks bleeding.

Roland felt the world sliding away and the black walls of the room closing in. Then Susan blended with the dead woman in Cincinnati.

Every 4 hrs.

Or else.

Or else more of this. More memories, more corpses.

He pulled out the bottle and shoved one of the pills into his mouth, wishing he had the bogus vodka to wash it down.

The fear vanished in minutes, and he found he was exhausted from the tension.

Sleep.

Then Wendy.

CHAPTER ELEVEN

“Let me see your pills,” Wendy said.

Anita turned from the window of Dr. Hannah Todd’s fifth-floor office. After hanging up on Wendy, she’d made an appointment and caught a cab to the NC Neurosciences Hospital, where she waited in an outpatient room. Anita had finally answered one of Wendy’s repeated calls, and Wendy had hurried down to make sure her friend was okay.

And part of her wanted to make sure Halcyon wasn’t back in Anita’s life, because Halcyon should have died along with Susan Sharpe.

“Do you believe me now?” Anita asked. She was dressed in street clothes, the bandage still on her head, though she’d changed for her appointment and wore a loose white blouse and pleated slacks.

“I don’t know what to believe.”

“I thought I was freaking out, having little fantasies. I know we’ve been friends for a long time, but I couldn’t remember when I met Roland.” After a pause, Anita lowered her voice and added, “Or Susan.”

“Don’t say that name.”

“You don’t remember, do you?”

“Show me your pills.”

Anita rummaged in her handbag and came out with the orange bottle. She read from the label. "A. Molkesky. Take one every four hours or else."

She tossed the pill bottle to Wendy, who nearly dropped it, though they were only three feet apart. "These are just like mine," Wendy said.

"These are just like the ones from ten years ago."

Something tugged at Wendy's memory, but she pushed it down. She recalled what Anita had said about "monsters in their holes." Oh, she'd had holes, all right.

"Are you taking them on time?" Wendy asked.

"Now I am. After I figured out the 'Or else' part."

"I thought you were going to turn these in."

"I don't think I better do that."

"Are you crazy?"

"Yeah. And the pills help. Because when I don't take them, it all comes sneaking back."

"What does?" Wendy wasn't sure she wanted to know.

"Dr. Briggs. Us. The Monkey House."

"Us?"

"You, me, and Roland. You talked us into it, said it was a chance to make some extra cash. Plus we thought it was real anti-establishment stuff, brain research without a net."

Wendy felt jittery, because she caught a vivid image of a smirking Dr. Briggs. Sebastian. He'd been a doctor here, hadn't he?

Something else. She could see his face, smiling, leaning forward with his lips puckered. And from his voice came the words, "*Wendy, my sweet little Igor.*"

"No," Wendy said, willing the image from her head.

"Yeah," Anita said. "I don't know where the others came in. David and Susan. They probably just wanted money, too. And Alexis, but she was tied in with Briggs."

Wendy had kept in touch with Alexis over the years, though the casual meetings for coffee had become less frequent and more awkward, as if the only things they had to talk about were things they couldn't talk about.

"Alexis," Wendy said. "Is she still on staff?"

"She has a lab here in the basement, but her office is in the nursing school. I see her in the hall once in a while when I come for therapy."

"Does she…say anything?"

Anita shook her head. "Not about Susan Sharpe. She's got professional standing to worry about now."

Wendy wanted to change the subject fast. "What's the longest you've gone without the pills?"

Anita looked at the clock on the wall, which was pushing six o'clock. "Five hours is about as long as I can stand. Then it all starts crashing in and I remember what happened out there at the factory."

"I don't know what you're talking about."

Anita sat on the sofa, unconsciously perching in a pose that might have passed for seductive. Wendy had drawn Anita many times, and even the most innocuous figure studies had turned out erotically charged. Wendy wasn't sure whether it was something in Anita's nature, the connection of the friendship, or some secret carnal impulse in Wendy that was always trying to escape.

She suspected her impulse might have broken loose a few times, and that frightened her more than Anita's recollections.

"We did these drug trials," Anita said, with the patience of an adult lecturing a child. "The drugs were supposed to help people dealing with trauma, so we pretended to attack one another to stimulate violence and trigger our fear responses so Briggs could monitor the results."

Wendy had a vague memory of a high ceiling, dark clutter all around, stalking through corridors to find someone.

And not just the image but the *feeling* returned, the hunger of the predator, the rage that Susan was after Dr. Briggs, but Susan could never have him because Briggs belonged to Wendy.

The nerve of that fucking bitch.

"You haven't told this to anyone?" Wendy asked. Now it was her turn to look out the window. A long way down.

"No."

"I wouldn't. It sounds totally crazy, and they'll lock you away in a nice rubber room on the seventh floor."

"I'm not telling anybody anything. They might take away my Halcyon."

"Why do you call it Halcyon, anyway? There's nothing on the label."

Anita smiled. "You're playing me, aren't you?"

"Huh?"

"Pretending like you don't remember. Halcyon was the drug Briggs was testing."

Because the room was for voluntary outpatients, the window wasn't barred like those on the top floor. She could open it and lure Anita over. Then no more talk of Susan and Briggs.

"I'm tired of remembering," Anita said. "I'm taking my next dose. Give me my bottle back."

Wendy realized she was still gripping the orange bottle. She crossed the room and gave it to her, then watched as Anita poured the remaining seven pills into her palm.

"That's barely enough to get you to morning," Wendy said. "Do you want some of mine?"

"Bad things might happen when we take each other's pills."

"Bad things happen anyway."

Anita took a bottle of water from her purse and washed down a pill. "In a couple of minutes, it'll dumb me down pretty good. But I want you to remember something very important for me."

"Sure, Anita."

Anita gripped her hands and gave her an imploring look. Then she pulled Wendy close, their breasts pressing together.

"I want you to need me," Anita said.

"Nita? What are you doing?"

Anita moaned and she clutched the back of Wendy's neck, whispering harshly in her ear: "This is what happens if I don't take my pills."

Wendy wrestled to break free, but Anita's strength was almost demonic. She fell back onto the sofa and yanked Wendy on top of her. She brought her face to Wendy's. "Love me, Wendy," Anita said, and it was desperation, not lust, in her tone. "I need to matter."

They'd never kissed, despite the occasional teasing. Wendy wasn't horrified by her friend's bisexual leanings, her pornographic past, or even her depraved and sudden assault, as if a sexual switch had been flipped and she'd lost all her control.

No, what really scared Wendy was the image of Briggs and his slightly parted lips that had superimposed over Anita's face.

Do you want to play "doctor," Doctor?

Their lips touched and the contact shocked Wendy to her senses. It was Briggs she'd been surrendering to, not Anita. She broke free and headed for the door, wiping her mouth. "Good luck with your appointment."

Just before she closed the door, Anita called her name. Not angry, just frustrated.

"Yeah?" Wendy asked.

"Take your pills. Don't become like me."

By the time she got to her car, Wendy was starting to remember things. Chase Hanson. Dr. Briggs. Susan.

Those things never happened if you keep forgetting them.

She took a pill by the light of the dashboard before driving home. She would take as many as she needed to keep the past away.

And to keep her from her true self.

CHAPTER TWELVE

The black limousine turned off the street in front of the hotel and glided through the narrow underground tunnel to the service entrance Mark waited in front of.

Mark Morgan peered at the tinted, bulletproof glass, wondering what they thought as they sized him up. As the limousine came to a stop, Mark caught his own reflection in the window, a pale smudge painted by the unhealthy yellow of the security lights.

The car stopped, its engine so quiet that Mark thought the ignition was off, though the exhaust quickly made him lightheaded. The driver's door opened and a man in a dark suit emerged, nodding and bending to take Mark's suitcase. His face was cold, lean, and wolfish.

"I can do that," Mark said.

The glass on the rear window slid down. "Now, Mark, let Winston feel useful. He hates to be stereotyped."

"Good morning, Senator."

"I hope we're not running too far behind."

"No, my plane doesn't leave for another hour."

"Fine. Get in."

The door opened as the driver carried Mark's bag to the trunk and loaded it. Mark settled into the spacious rear compartment.

Senator Daniel Burchfield, the Republican from North Carolina, moved into the middle of the brown leather seat.

"You know Wallace Forsyth, don't you?" the senator said.

"Yes," Mark said, reaching across the senator's abdomen to shake Forsyth's hand. "It's been a while."

"That wife of yours is some kind of hell-raiser, Morgan," Forsyth said. "And I mean that with all due respect."

"She keeps my hands full," Mark said.

Forsyth's skin was cadaverous and cool, as if he'd been dipped in a thin layer of wax, and his cologne was overpowering. "Well, you need to rein her in a little," Forsyth drawled in his rough, Kentucky-inflected voice. "She's got the bioethics council chasing its tail. You ever seen what happens when a dog chases its tail?"

"Afraid not, sir."

"Well, it either catches it, or it drops over dead. I don't know which one will come first with this bunch. The president put too many liberals on the council, for one thing."

"Now, now," Burchfield said. "You really mean he put too many atheists on it."

Forsyth *harrumphed* as if he saw no difference in the two. "A good scientist can work God into anything. Especially if it makes better people."

"Save it for the council, Wallace," Burchfield said. "We're all on the same page here. Right, Mark?"

"Right."

A pane of soundproof glass separated the driver's compartment from the rear. Winston settled behind the wheel and negotiated a turn between the hotel shuttle vans.

Mark had planned to take a taxi. Alexis had left the previous evening, and Mark had an extra stop on his itinerary. He didn't feel he could trouble a U.S. senator to make a pit stop, however. He decided to get to business.

"We can give the FDA—"

Forsyth held up a chapped palm. "Is the car clean?" he asked Burchfield.

Mark didn't comprehend the remark. The interior still had that acrid chemical scent of new upholstery.

Burchfield nodded. "Secret Service swept it."

"You trust the Service?"

"You know me better than that. I had my own people go over it after that, in case the NSA wants a piece. Defense has been sniffing around, too."

Mark finally understood they were talking about bugs. He'd never considered that a senator's car might be bugged, especially by the very federal agencies whose budgets passed through one of Burchfield's other committees.

"Okay," Forsyth said with a crooked grin. "Now that Mr. Morgan knows we're not playing matchstick poker here."

"The subcommittee on health care is meeting Thursday," Burchfield said.

"They moved it up a week?" Mark asked. Congress usually moved at glacial speed on legislative matters.

"I had to call in some favors. There's a certain blowhard Democrat who is scheduled to be in Afghanistan this week, and I wouldn't mind if he misses a few votes. One thing you can count on in the current political environment—no politician dares cancel a photo op in Afghanistan."

The limousine merged into afternoon traffic, took an exit, and was soon on the freeway headed for Dulles International. Mark looked out at passengers in nearby cars, who stared back at the dark glass and no doubt tried to guess what type of important person was shielded from their view.

He'd noticed the same phenomenon in Los Angeles, where stargazers imagined Tom Cruise or Sandra Bullock behind every tinted windshield.

Only in New York did people not give a damn one way or another, as long as you weren't cutting them off in traffic. In that case, it wouldn't matter whether you were a pope or a polar bear, you'd be in for a horn blast and a middle finger.

"Where are we on Halcyon?" Burchfield asked.

"We've got our best people on it," Mark said.

"How long have the trials been going on? FDA doesn't like to fast-track. It's been bitten on the ass too many times. Look at the Vioxx mess."

"Well, there's a minor problem with that, sir." Mark resorted to the salutation because it might soften the bad news. Burchfield didn't buy it.

"Problem? Hell, Morgan, I thought the problem was getting this through the red tape and putting Halcyon on those blocks of sticky pads in your friendly neighborhood doctor's office. Don't tell me we're shaky on the approach?"

"We've had some trials and rigorous testing. We're doing a double-blind study right now."

"Then what's the problem?"

"Ain't it obvious?" Forsyth said. "The boy's walking on mule eggs. He has no idea what Halcyon can do."

"I have a real good idea, Mr. Forsyth." Mark looked past Burchfield to the wispy-haired fundamentalist. "Trouble is, I'm not sure we want the whole story out there."

"Now, now," Burchfield said. "Either you can deliver the damn drug or you can't."

"We've had the trials. Years of trials. Our lead researcher has been on it for a decade. But not all of it's documented."

"What do you mean, 'not documented'?"

"There are gaps in the record. The FDA likes a timeline, the introduction, the animal testing, the check for cross-reactions, all that. But we kind of skipped a step."

"It's a little late for surprises." Burchfield had the politician's knack of changing moods quickly, at least when not in front of the camera or on the Senate floor. His cheeks blotched with anger. "Fill me in."

"Well, it's an offshoot of a drug we had in trials a decade ago, before I joined CRO. The original testing was a little..." Mark shopped around for the right word.

"Squirrel-eyed," Forsyth finished. "You got some bad results and you chucked them off the back porch."

"The results were mostly positive," Mark said. "But the testing started with human trials."

"Goddamn it," Burchfield said, unapologetic for cussing in front of his Christian ally. "Can the FDA trace that to Halcyon?"

"Not likely. The only link is Sebastian Briggs, the doctor who—"

"I know Briggs. He gave a briefing to the subcommittee years ago on the ethics of mood-enhancing drugs. Before he went in the shitter."

"That was before the creation of the bioethics council," Forsyth said. "The Senate would let any nutcase present evidence."

"You were in the House at the time," Burchfield said. "And I didn't hear you raise any objections."

"Briggs is a heathen," Forsyth said. "Can't keep his fingers out of God's pie."

"Save it for the pulpit," Burchfield said. "Or your next campaign, if you ever have one." To Mark, he said, "So, is that the worst of it? Clinical trials without FDA approval?"

"As if that ain't bad enough," Forsyth said.

The limousine weaved in traffic and Mark glanced at the driver, who appeared to be checking his rearview and side mirrors. They were on the Beltway, making decent time for late afternoon, maybe half an hour from the airport. Mark was eager to get out of the car. The air seemed stifling, and Forsyth's cologne was giving him a headache.

"Well, Briggs had a few offshoots in the works," Mark said. "As you know, researchers often don't look for just one single thing. A lot of times, it's a case of seeing what pops up."

"I don't care about that end of it," Burchfield said. "I just want to know if any of this can come back on me."

"Briggs was studying serum levels in Gulf War veterans with PTSD. He found elevated levels of certain neuroactive steroids correlating with a high rate of suicides and—"

"Get to the point. Don't play Michael Crichton with me."

"Basically, Briggs wasn't satisfied with his test pool. After all, you can't very well wait around for the next war for a decent supply of near-death accident survivors. So he found ways to elevate normal serum levels. In effect, he created a drug that caused fear."

"You're telling me he had to create the disease so he could find a cure?"

"Fear is not exactly a disease," Mark said. "It's simply a condition, a state of awareness, a feeling. Some would argue it's a valuable survival mechanism."

"If you're scared, you run like hell," Forsyth said. "We had this debate on the council. The consensus was that human emotions were natural, a gift of God."

Because of his wife's membership, Mark was well aware the bioethics council wasn't designed to reach a consensus, merely to serve as an advisory board that addressed potential concerns.

And although God had a rightful place in the council's deliberations, the government God was a theoretical, all-encompassing, and even generic deity, not the punitive, white-bearded denizen of the Old Testament. Not that Forsyth appreciated the subtle distinctions.

"So Briggs was messing with some fear stimulants," Burchfield said. "Nothing much new there. The DOD has been working on that since the LSD and mescaline experiments. The trouble is they've never found a drug that has the same effect on every person. If you dose your enemy, you're just as likely to create a savage, bloodthirsty war machine as you are a man-mouse. Same with your own people."

"Well, maybe Briggs succeeded," Mark said. "I'm still not clear on that."

"Don't tell me you don't have a handle on him." Burchfield, the son of a tobacco farmer, had been studying for his chosen career since being elected class president in grammar school, and he was used to moving human chess pieces.

But in Mark's world, control was limited to laboratory tests and board rooms and didn't extend as readily to the scientists who concocted the substances. Science required rigid discipline, but a revolutionary creativity was essential for breakthroughs. Briggs was revolutionary in more ways than Mark cared to admit.

"I'll have it all by the time we go to the trials," Mark said. "I have to dig through some records at UNC, where the original testing took place. Don't worry, we'll put on a good show for the FDA. He's running two test groups, apparently. And we can always retroactively adjust the data."

“I can push on this, but the FDA is still going to want at least six months of solid numbers,” Burchfield said. “A flawless six months.”

“Some of the elements are patented, so we’ll have to do some shuffling,” Mark said. “CRO doesn’t want anyone coming in claiming intellectual theft right before Halcyon hits the shelves.”

“Sounds like Halcyon’s got more holes than a rusty milk bucket,” Forsyth said. To Burchfield, he added, “I’d tread mighty careful, Daniel. One slip and no Oval Office in two years.”

“I’ll want a full report on what Briggs is up to,” Burchfield said to Mark. “This ‘fear drug’ might even wind up being more valuable than Halcyon. I don’t like question marks, and I don’t like our security agencies getting to it before I know what’s what. Understood?”

Mark frowned. CRO had invested heavily in Burchfield, even more than it had invested in Briggs. “I’ll handle it personally, sir.”

Burchfield pressed the button to summon the driver. “Next exit.”

Winston nodded, and the limo glided up a ramp. The senator said, “You’d better take another route to the airport. It’s probably best if we’re not all seen together.”

“I’ll miss my flight,” Mark protested, still shaken but eager to get out of that mad city.

“We’ve taken care of everything.”

The limo pulled into a gas station. A taxi waited by the kerosene pump, a dark-skinned man in a turban at the wheel. Winston stopped beside the taxi, hopped out, opened Mark’s door, and unlocked the trunk. By the time Mark stood blinking on the crumbled tarmac, Winston was putting the suitcase handle in his hand.

“Is it safe?” Mark asked, meaning the cab, but he figured the question applied equally to the entire situation.

"Just don't go steppin' in nothing unless you got your hip waders on," Forsyth said.

"Get your data in line," Burchfield said. "Just make damned sure it all looks good on paper. And keep a tight rein on Briggs."

"And your wife," Forsyth added.

Winston got in and drove away, and Mark looked around before slowly approaching the cab.

"Airport?" the driver said.

CHAPTER THIRTEEN

Alexis wound through the clusters of students milling on the commons. It was Friday morning, and most upperclassmen were wise enough to manipulate their schedules for a three-day weekend, so the college was less crowded than usual. Even so, the changing of classes launched a human tidal wave across the well-kept grounds.

Not everyone was worried about the next class, however. Students sat under the ancient oak trees with fat books, iPhones, and laptops, while others enjoyed leisurely games of Frisbee or hacky sack. The aroma of coffee and rancid fryer oil wafted from the student canteen. A golden retriever chased a squirrel across the grass, nearly upending a girl on a bicycle.

Alexis loved the older part of the University of North Carolina. The country's first public university still had some of the landmarks from its 1700s origin, and care had been taken to preserve the traditional heart of the campus.

She'd been an undergrad here, receiving twin degrees in psychology and chemistry. She still had many fond memories of basketball games, frat parties, late nights in the library, strolling through the arboretum in the fall, smoking pot at the Bell Tower with Mark during the traditional Friday "High Noon," and barhopping on Franklin Street.

She'd lost her virginity her freshman year in the woods behind the outdoor amphitheater, then wished she had it back when the guy turned out to be a self-absorbed asshole. *Never date a concert violinist, no matter how skilled his fingers.*

Despite tradition, expansion had pushed the campus toward the south, where the buildings rose in gleaming towers of glass and steel surrounding the hospital. Most of Alexis's classes were in the Morton Building, named for a prominent disciple of Carl Jung, with her lab in the Neurosciences Department.

It was the same lab where she had served as a graduate assistant to Dr. Sebastian Briggs, although she only had a few papers of notes from that era. So much of it was lost, but she had a feeling the loss was for the best.

Today, though, she had to pay a visit to the Chancellor's Office to sort out some matters related to her upcoming leave of absence. She planned to take a year off to write another book.

"Dr. Morgan?"

Alexis turned. Celia Smith fell into step beside her, a freckle-faced young lady in pigtails and a Decemberists sweatshirt. Although Alexis had about fifty students each semester, she made it a point to memorize their names. Celia was one of those unspectacular students who turned in assignments on time but rarely made the leap from rote recitation to genuine insight.

"Hello, Celia. How are you?"

"Great. I didn't know they let the scientists over on this part of campus. This is liberal-arts turf."

"Some people would argue that neurobiology isn't really a science."

"Well, you've got a lab and stuff."

Alexis smiled at the "stuff." "As we come to understand more about the brain, the closer psychology edges toward science. Mood, disorder, and emotion are nothing more than various combinations of electrical impulses and chemical compounds."

"You sound like Dr. Briggs."

Alexis drew to a halt, spinning to face Celia and grab her forearm. "Briggs?"

Celia looked down at her flesh, where Alexis's fingers pressed hard enough to create red rings. "Ow."

"Sorry." Alexis drew back, appalled. "I didn't mean…are you talking about Sebastian Briggs?"

Celia nodded, eyes wide with a look Alexis realized was fear. "Yeah. I'm a volunteer in one of his research projects."

"Briggs is here?" Alexis couldn't believe it. She would have seen his name on the faculty roster, and he almost certainly would have been assigned to her department. Besides, Briggs had left UNC with a black mark on his record, and in academia, no administrator was willing to risk repeating a mistake. Especially one of the magnitude made by Briggs.

She had shared in that mistake, but her resume was spotless. However, the ledger in her memory bore a few smudges and eraser marks.

"He's working under contract," Celia said. "I drive over to RTP once a week. They pay us fifty dollars a session."

So Briggs is working in private industry. "What's the project?"

Celia shook her head, eyes narrowing in suspicion. "We're not supposed to say. We signed a whatchamacallit, where we have to keep it a secret."

"A nondisclosure agreement?"

"Yeah. I could get in trouble just saying this much. Plus I could lose the bonus at the end of the trial."

The crowd around them grew denser, people picking up the pace as the next class loomed minutes away. Alexis felt the urgency in her own bloodstream.

She didn't know how to fish information from Celia without further frightening the girl. "I won't tell anybody, Celia. I used to work with him and—well, I didn't know he was around. I wouldn't mind saying hello."

Celia backed away, looking over Alexis's shoulder. "Sorry, Dr. Morgan. I'm late for chemistry lab."

Celia turned and hurried into the crowd, which seemed to have thickened in the space of seconds. Alexis was about to shout at Celia, but someone bumped into her, causing her to drop the books she was carrying. As she was flung forward, she bounced against a tall man with the muscular physique of an athlete.

"Hey," the man yelled in a deep, gruff voice. In the commotion, Alexis felt a sting in the small of her back.

Her first thought was *bee*, even though it was March and bees were still a little sluggish in the cool air. A spider was more likely, since the spindly arachnids were so ubiquitous and would bite if trapped in clothing. She reached to rub the wound as the jock turned and sneered.

"Why don't you watch where you're going?" he said, obviously used to inciting fear through a display of force.

Classic case of insecurity and overcompensation. He probably had performance issues in bed. But, despite Freud's own suspect logic in linking every problem to sex, maybe this case was simpler. Maybe the guy was just a flaming asshole.

"Sorry," Alexis said, looking past the gathering crowd in hope of sighting Celia. The student was gone.

The jock kicked at one of the books that had fallen near his foot. "You could have broke my toe," he said. "Knocked me down a few rounds in the draft."

Alexis gave her most winning smile, though the spreading pain of the sting tightened her lips. "I advise you to get your degree, then, so you'll have a fallback position."

"Fallback? I'm a fullback."

"I'm sure you are," she said. Another student, a geeky guy in a ragged knit cap, bent and collected her books as the crowd, now bored and running late, lapsed back into its chaotic stream. The football player trudged forward as if it were second down and goal to go from the three.

Knit Cap Boy handed her the stack of books. "You okay, miss? You don't look so hot."

The stung area had begun to swell, and heat radiated across her back and down her buttocks. She looked around, her throat dry, wondering if she might be suffering anaphylactic shock. A campus policeman stood watching from the steps of a nearby student-services building.

"I'm fine," she said thickly, taking the books. "Thanks."

Alexis wiped a sudden sweat from her temples, wondering if she'd be able to finish the quarter-mile walk to her office. The student infirmary was across the compound, behind the library. Anaphylaxis could kill in minutes by constricting her throat and cutting off her air supply. The campus cop, evidently noticing her distress, hurried down the steps.

She swayed, dizzy, and Knit Cap Boy reached to steady her.

"Here, let me," the cop said, taking Alexis by the shoulder. "Are you okay, ma'am?"

The cop's eyes were hidden behind sunglasses, and the dwindling trickle of pedestrians reflected in the twin black lenses. He slid his arm around her shoulder and guided her toward a concrete bench that was half-surrounded by low shrubbery.

She sat, gazing at the oak canopy above, the new leaves bright green in the sun. The clouds drifted by in a cotton-candy kaleidoscope.

As an undergrad, Alexis had eaten hallucinogenic mushrooms once, and this experience mimicked that trip. Her body felt simultaneously weightless and thick with fluid, as if she were a warm, water-filled balloon.

"Can you talk?" the cop said. His face was pocked with large dark pores, one side of his mouth drooping. The roundness of his shoulders suggested a former weightlifter whose muscles were now making their slow surrender to gravity and age.

Something about his demeanor tugged at her, but her sensory distortion prevented her from focusing. She noticed the books were gone from her hands. The grass of the courtyard buckled like the waves of a turbulent sea, the people crossing it bending and swaying as if made of soft rubber.

Oxygen deprivation. It's making me hallucinate.

Yet she could feel air circulating in her lungs. Indeed, she could imagine the oxygen entering her bloodstream, flowing through her limbs, racing back through her system to be exhaled out her nostrils, laden with carbon dioxide. Her skin itched with cellular regeneration, and she was acutely aware of her saliva glands. This was no ordinary spider bite.

Clarity descended, and with it a deep unease, as if something had gone horribly wrong and couldn't be fixed.

"Listen to me," the cop said. He bent forward until she could smell his mint toothpaste.

I'm all ears, she wanted to say, and the image of her naked flesh, covered with aural cavities, made her giggle. If she could make her fingers work, she would get rid of these clothes. The sun was a glorious patch of golden pleasure, melting against her skin. The bright-green odor of spring was as thick as the curling clouds.

"Do you remember talking with Celia Smith?" the cop said, though his tone was not like that of a demanding interrogator working a victim behind a two-way mirror. This was no detective-show copycat, a type she'd found most university cops to be. Though trained and certified, they often had inferiority complexes that sometimes caused them to overstep their authority.

Not that a cop implied menace in her new, vivid world. She licked her lips and found they tasted of mangoes. A phrase, a name, niggled at the back of her mind like a thin wire trying to fish a wedding ring from a drain. *Celia?*

"Dr. Briggs wanted me to give you a message," he said, maintaining his low, melodic voice. She gazed into his sunglasses, saw her own face doubled, both reflections smirking with swollen, leering lips.

Briggs.

The name stirred something inside her. Briggs had taken something from her, long ago. Was he some frat boy she'd dated? Someone who had treated her badly?

The cop's head tilted toward the sky. The Bell Tower clock clanged in the distance, the vibrations tickling Alexis's cochlea, digging into her skull like the fast, silvery bit of an electric drill.

The sudden pain caused her to clamp her teeth down on her tongue and the sensation was that of biting tinfoil. Her hands and feet, which had been so bloated and warm moments ago, now burned with static. The pain allowed her to focus, finally recognizing she was on a campus bench.

"Briggs wanted me to tell you this," the cop said, leaning close enough that she thought he was going to kiss her cheek. Instead, he whispered, "The Monkey House is open for business."

The man drew away, the dampness of his breath lingering a moment on her earlobe before evaporating. He stood, looked around, adjusted his sunglasses, and headed for the nearest building, his simian movement a reminder that evolution was an ongoing process.

Monkey House.

Alexis rocked back and forth, fever sluicing up her spine, the limbs of the nearby oaks swaying as if driven by a frantic, fierce wind. No, the limbs weren't swaying. They were reaching, scooping down with spindly, cracked hands to claw at her, tangle in her hair, scratch her face and bare skin.

The roots lifted, shaking away dirt and the stiffness of long sleep. The nearest one stepped toward her, quivering with eagerness.

Nothing in her index of diagnostic manuals, textbooks, and clinical observations could explain away these hallucinations. And though her trained mind insisted trees could not walk, the massive oaks couldn't care less about symptoms of delusion.

Crazy people always believed in the peculiar reality that imprisoned them, and Alexis understood for the first time that a delusion wasn't just a distorted perception.

For the sufferer, it became reality. And even a delusion could make you bleed.

She wiped her face with the back of her hand. Students sat around the compound, oblivious to the monstrous miracle in their midst. A blackbird lifted from one of the tree branches, fought a waft of wind, and rose into the sky.

Alexis leaned back, shielding her eyes from the grasping limbs, the tannic aroma of green oak burning her nostrils. Her legs were damp sand, her throat a cold pipe, her lungs buckets of dead ash scooped from an ancient burial pyre.

The gathering oaks breathed, their whispered words taunting her in the voices of wood. Lumber creaked, sap spat, leaves rattled.

The Monkey House was real.

"You okay, miss?"

These trees, which had been young when the first English speakers had landed on the Eastern shore with their muskets and axes, had their own language. How could she reply in any way but a scream? She clamped her hands over her ears and wriggled against the unyielding concrete bench.

Nothing like the "brink of madness" existed. She understood now. No soft gray fog created a foreboding borderland between sanity and the land beyond.

The two states existed simultaneously, commingling in the same ether, built of common atoms. The stuff of stars was all the same, only some burned while some bled.

"Miss, you don't look so hot."

She blinked. Students crowded the sidewalk around her, moving in twin but opposing streams. The young man in the knit cap held her books, brows scrunched above the plastic frames of his glasses. Across the stretch of lawn, the trees stood majestic and gray, and a whiff of cigarette smoke trailed past as a student grabbed a nicotine fix before class. The sun reflected off the neat rows of windows, the bricks of the buildings as solid as the hands that had stacked them.

Reality.

It wasn't a state of mind or an illusion of perception. It was nothing more than a shared and mutually accepted madness. An agreed-upon delusion kept the Earth fixed in the heavens and the trees knitted deeply into the soil.

And Briggs was no longer a fantasy. He had happened. The Monkey House had happened.

The Monkey House was real.

And she couldn't let it show. No matter what, she had to maintain appearances. She was Dr. Alexis Morgan, respected neurochemist, not some trippy-dippy English professor.

"I'm fine," she said, taking the books as she spied the knotted shoulders of the fullback bobbing above the crowd, hurrying away. From the concrete steps, the campus cop observed her behind frigid shades.

A fugue experience. Mind slip. Déjà vu of an event that couldn't have happened.

Yet the warm glow of a pinprick emanated across her back, and she was afraid the dizziness would return. Before the cop could climb down the steps, before the trees could walk, before the injected venom could taint her bloodstream, she smiled in gratitude at Knit Cap Boy and hurried across the compound, toward the center of campus and the safe, familiar walls of her office.

CHAPTER FOURTEEN

Kleingarten smirked.

The university cop uniform had been easy to fake, and nobody looked at patches or badges. In fact, by changing from the blue shirt to a brown shirt, he could just as easily have passed for a member of the landscaping crew. He'd paid a little visit to Dr. Morgan's office and the crowd in the hall had parted like a creek around a boulder. These college brats were so damned cool they couldn't even acknowledge authority, much less respect it.

The day was warm and he enjoyed ogling the sweet young coeds, and probably a few were into men in uniforms. He might find out if he held his post long enough to draw them in. But despite all the budget cuts, a real university cop might show up and cause trouble.

Kleingarten could handle trouble, but part of the fun was in working outside the system. Any idiot could go out guns blazing, playing *Die Hard* and hoping for a sequel. It took real skill and genius to go completely undetected.

And he liked this little game Briggs was playing. Hell, he might have taken the job for half price.

Still, he had overhead, like the jock sidling his way, trying to blend in despite his letter jacket, spiked hair, and a steroid-bloated neck that made his head look like a ferret-covered bucket of rocks.

Kleingarten rolled his eyes to a secluded alcove that led to a basement entrance, indicating the jock should follow him.

The guy mouthed, "What?"

Fucking amateurs. Kleingarten gave an impatient jerk of his thumb and turned away. After a moment, the jock followed.

"Did I do good?" he said.

"Sure, kid," Kleingarten said, pulling the roll of unmarked bills from his pocket. They were bound by a rubber band. He should have tucked the money in the envelope, but this was part of the game, too.

"It won't hurt her none, will it?" The jock was making an effort to be concerned, but compassion was a few too many rungs up the IQ ladder.

"Would your government do anything to harm one of its citizens?"

The jock shook his head, visibly stiffening as if looking for a flag to salute. He struggled to stuff the bills into the pocket of his too-tight jeans.

"What about…you know, the other stuff?"

"Of course."

Kleingarten handed over the vial of anabolic steroids. "This should be good for six extra touchdowns and moving up a couple of rounds in the draft."

"Sweet. You know how hard it is to get this stuff these days?"

"Hey, there's always the Canadian Football League."

The guy didn't catch the humor. "Yeah, sure. So, are we done here?"

"That's it. Easy as pie, just like I promised."

A couple of students passed, and Kleingarten gave an exaggerated slap to the jock's arm and guffawed for their benefit. "You kick State's ass for us, okay?"

The jock nodded. "If Coach gives me the ball more."

Kleingarten winked as the students moved on past to join the human stream. "Take enough of that, and he will. Now, how about that needle?"

"Right," the guy said, as if he'd forgotten. He reached into the pocket of his letter jacket. "Ouch. Fuck."

He pulled the needle out and looked at the little pinprick on the side of his thumb. "You *sure* this stuff is okay?"

"Safe as mother's milk, my friend. And, remember, it's a secret."

"A matter of national security," the jock recited, those magical words that allowed people the world over to get away with murder.

"Now get out of here and forget you ever saw me."

The jock hunkered away and Kleingarten pretended to check the locks on the doors. Someone might be watching. These eggheads lived in their own oblivious little fantasy land, though, and considered their island immune from the ills of the real world.

They were worried about people taking the word "nigger" out of books and how many goddamned butterflies were dying in the rain forest. That stuff was too important for anyone to notice an anonymous rent-a-cop.

A cute coed walked by and gave him the once-over, and Kleingarten resisted the temptation to open the door for her. Instead, he just touched the bill of his cap in greeting. He didn't smile too broadly or she might remember him.

As she entered, he followed, using his foot to hold the door open. He retrieved the backpack he'd tucked behind an air unit, and then went to the private faculty restroom that was little more than a closet. Those with extra college degrees couldn't just shit in a stall like the rest of the crowd.

Kleingarten removed the uniform shirt and now wore only a "Go Heels" T-shirt featuring the horned head of a ram, the school mascot. He never could figure out why a school nicknamed "Tar Heels" used a ram, but he supposed you couldn't just walk around at halftime holding up a black, splotchy Styrofoam foot.

He crammed the cop hat and blue shirt into the backpack and changed into scuffed loafers. He was mussing his hair when someone tried the handle and then knocked.

"Just a sec," Kleingarten said, and then cut a fart so the room would smell authentic.

He flushed and exited, and a preppy dude in a sweater vest stood there tapping his foot like he had diarrhea. "All yours," Kleingarten offered.

He went down the secluded hall with the backpack slung over his shoulder, just another middle-aged, nontraditional student working hard to improve his lot in life.

There was a chance the jock would talk, but it would have to be before he took his first injection. A 90 percent solution of calcium gluconate in the steroids would stress his heart to the bursting point.

And there was a chance a brilliant, astute medical examiner would detect the elevated calcium levels, assuming he or she had any reason to suspect anything but a case of steroid toxicity.

Kleingarten had already filed an anonymous tip that the star fullback was using illegal performance-enhancing substances. While the letter mailed to the UNC athletics department would likely be buried fast, and the one mailed to the NCAA would sit idle for months while policymakers figured out how to spin it,

UNC's conference rivals would probably wave their copies of the letter from the tops of their ivory towers and scream their self-righteous bullshit about fairness, as if anyone expected the world to be fair.

The jock might get his touchdowns first, and the autopsy might even raise suspicion.

But it was all part of the game.

And this game wasn't fair.

Kleingarten exited the building and headed across the sidewalk, so nonchalant that he almost forgot to fake it.

CHAPTER FIFTEEN

Mark Morgan's flight landed ten minutes behind schedule at Raleigh-Durham International. As the jet taxied to the terminal, the man in the seat beside Mark powered up his laptop computer and, despite the pilot's admonition against using wireless devices, connected to the Internet.

As the man punched up his Yahoo home page, Mark found himself straining to browse the news headlines. Senator Burchfield's national profile had been heating up, both on the rumors of a presidential run and his hard-line stance on defense spending. Of course, those two could be intimately entwined.

"Stock market's down thirty points," his seatmate said. "I thought the damned Democrats were supposed to turn things around."

"Money's bigger than politics," Mark replied, though in his own experience the wealthy and the powerful fed side by side like hogs sucking at a bottomless trough.

Mark hadn't been fully forthcoming with the senator and Wallace Forsyth. Though Briggs had indeed been engaged in unsupervised research without federal approval, he hadn't confined his diabolic dabbling to memory suppression. Briggs's fear drug had rolled through CRO's internal rumor mill, but because such a drug wasn't deemed commercially useful, no resources had been directed toward it. That didn't mean Briggs didn't have an intention for it. Mark didn't trust Briggs any more than he trusted Burchfield. But for the time being, they all needed each other.

The cabin began emptying, and Mark waited a few minutes before retrieving his carry-on luggage. He was inside the terminal, heading for the front entrance and his ride, when two airport security guards flanked him.

In the era of shoe bombers and hijackers and TSA Nazis, Mark had given up his reasonable expectation of privacy, but most surprise searches occurred while passengers were boarding planes, not while debarking.

Both guards wore blue uniforms, stripped to short sleeves despite the air-conditioning. The taller one was armed, and Mark, who had traveled to many countries as a CRO executive, had seen his share of airport militia.

The shorter guard increased his pace and moved alongside Mark. The terminal was filled with the food-court odors of fried onion rings, hot dogs, and hazelnut coffee. The public-address system boomed a change of gate numbers, and a baby was crying in a waiting area.

Mark took a detour toward the restroom, though his bladder was tight and dry. Hopefully it would be crowded and he could blend in and escape scrutiny, or at least have witnesses for any shakedown. The guards continued toward the front exits, the taller one still trailing.

Mark stood at a urinal and unzipped, the suitcase propped behind him. Even with Burchfield on his side, other federal agents might have an interest both in Halcyon and Mark's involvement in the health subcommittee's deliberations. He didn't think a public kidnapping was likely, but Burchfield's political opponents might apply a little extra surveillance and pressure to flush out any subterfuge.

After standing at the urinal for two minutes, Mark washed his hands, taking his time. When he left the restroom, the two guards were nowhere in sight. An Asian man raced by, arms loaded with baggage. A mother with two small children in her lap read *USA Today* by a ticket counter. A teenage couple swayed to the rhythm of separate headphones, and Mark couldn't tell which set was emitting a bass beat loud enough to be heard from twenty feet away.

He gripped the handle of his luggage and was joining the crowd again when the guards suddenly appeared, one at each elbow.

The tall guard took the suitcase while the other gripped Mark's upper arm. "Has this bag been in your possession the entire time?" the tall guard asked.

"It's never left my sight," Mark said.

"Are you sure it's yours?" the short guard said. His head resembled a thumb.

"Yes. It has my name on it, as well as stickers with numbers from other flights."

"This way please," the tall man said, nodding down the corridor toward a less-traveled area of the terminal.

"Can you tell me what this is about?"

"Routine baggage check."

"It was cleared at Dulles when I boarded."

"Please, sir. You wouldn't want to make a scene, would you?"

Mark wondered if a scene might be required. The DEA, CID, FBI, CIA, and National Security Agency could all have an interest in Halcyon, or, more likely, the rage drug Briggs had discovered through the back door. Any of the agencies might want to hang a bull's-eye on Burchfield, particularly if the president viewed him as a rival.

"Look, I can open this right here if you want," Mark said. "Someone's picking me up in a couple of minutes and you know how traffic is."

Thumb finally spoke. He even sounded like a thumb. "National security."

Mark sighed. No one could fight against those words. Best to go through the dog-and-pony show and let the puppet masters flex their strings.

They led Mark to a door as innocuous as that of a janitor's closet. Mark entered to a brightly lit room containing nothing but a wooden table and a chair. Thumb planted the briefcase on the table. "Open it."

Mark turned the serrated metal wheel of the lock until he'd dialed the proper combination and stepped back. "Please keep my papers in order," he said.

Thumb grunted and opened the lid. The contents looked just as Mark had left them. He tried not to smile. He suspected Thumb wouldn't trust a smile.

The tall guard removed his sunglasses and flashed gray eyes. "Mark Morgan."

"I didn't tell you my name."

Thumb emitted a guttural noise that might have been satisfaction. He pulled an orange pill bottle from some hidden crevice. "Prescription?"

"Never seen it before," Mark replied.

Thumb gave the bottle a shake. No rattle. Grimacing, he twisted the lid free and a piece of paper fluttered to the tabletop.

The tall guard picked it up and unfolded it. "'This could have been ten years in jail,'" he read in a monotone.

"I don't know where that came from," Mark said.

"A joker, huh?"

"No joke."

Thumb rummaged around a little more, checking every pocket and flap until he was satisfied.

"Ten years," the tall guard said, handing the vial back to his partner, who dumped it in the briefcase and snapped the lid shut.

"I don't know who you're working for, but I didn't put that there," Mark said. He knew it wouldn't have mattered, because the note was right. The bottle could just as easily have contained twenty grams of cocaine, TNT, or stolen jewelry.

"You might want to be a little more careful, then, and quit lying about letting a bag out of your sight." The tall guard held out the briefcase, his eyes like winter clouds. "You might get yourself in trouble."

Mark nodded and headed for the door. Even if there had been no bottle, the guards could have easily planted one. He wasn't sure if the encounter had been a friendly reminder from Burchfield or a wry warning from his CRO superiors or even Briggs. With the stakes mounting, the players would be pushing their bets. He would be glad when Halcyon was out of his hands.

He straightened his tie and exited the room, joining the stream of travelers. He glanced at his watch and didn't wipe the sweat from his brow until he had reached the far end of the terminal. He punched numbers on his cell phone. "Meet me out front," he said.

The green sedan with the tinted windows was so modest that it drew attention. Mark glanced around, wondering which of the exhausted, sullen-faced travelers might be an agent of some sort. Then he slid into the passenger's seat.

"You're late," Briggs said.

"The flight attendant insisted on a second bag of peanuts."

Briggs navigated away from the curb, gaze fixed straight ahead. His eyes were onyx, large pupils ringed by deep brown. The hooked nose gave him the aspect of a bird of prey, and touches of gray hair at his temples suggested a professorial, distinguished demeanor.

"How's the senator?" Briggs asked.

"Is the car clean?"

"You've been watching too many spy movies. I picked this up at Hertz. Cash, no reservation. Therefore, no bugs."

"You can't be too careful," Mark said.

"Do I have the go-ahead for the experiments?"

"*Carte blanche*. Just don't harm any innocent bystanders. A little collateral damage is okay, as long as it stays inside the building."

Briggs twisted one corner of his mouth in a smirk. "Selective ethics, Mr. Morgan. Maybe there's a career for you in politics after all this is over."

"I work for CRO," Mark said. "If there are fringe benefits like helping the human race, then fine. But don't forget who's boss."

"A lesson we should all keep in mind." Briggs merged off a ramp onto I-40, headed for Chapel Hill. "How's your wife?"

Mark froze. "She's out of this. That was the deal."

"Relax. Just inquiring about a colleague, that's all."

"She told me about the original trials. What little she remembers. She thinks you're a charlatan, or worse."

Briggs cackled. "Alexis believed in the goal. You can't treat people's trauma until you know where the border lies. We all have different breaking points."

"But you enjoyed breaking people, not putting them back together. That's the difference. And that's where Halcyon comes in."

"What's that saying? 'You have to crack a few eggs to make a good omelet.'"

"Alexis said the trials were a failure."

"The real failure was that she didn't get any credit. She always wanted a breakthrough, and that could have been hers. Don't you find she's just a little bit bitter?"

Mark was annoyed, because he sensed some truth in the words. "She came out of it just fine. She's resilient. But she thinks the other subjects might have suffered permanent damage."

Briggs took his eyes from the teeming traffic to study Mark. "Anita Molkesky, David Underwood, Roland Doyle, and—"

"Wendy Leng?" Mark clutched the briefcase. "Handy that three of them are still in the Research Triangle."

"We have to finish those trials."

"They're off the books. You know we can't present any of those old results to the FDA. Stick with the new group, the above-board project."

"But at least we know Halcyon works. All the subjects dealt with their fear and trauma and have gone on to productive lives."

"'Subjects'? They're *people*, Doctor. Alexis had years of therapy to deal with those issues. They nearly ruined our marriage."

"Halcyon would have eased those problems."

"By erasing whatever happened in those trials. You seem to be the only one that remembers everything."

"You make it sound so wrong."

"We learn from our mistakes. Flight or fight. If you snip those wires, all you have is a puppet."

Briggs turned up one corner of his mouth in what might have been a grin. "Ah, the military application. One of them, anyway."

"Above my pay grade," Mark said. "But this is the kind of stuff I don't want to monkey around with."

"Good choice of metaphor. The amygdala is the foundation of our evolutionary brain, the mysterious center over which all that complex gray matter blossoms. But give it the slightest bit of stimulation and you might as well be a caveman, whimpering in the dark as the beasties roar."

Briggs veered off the interstate onto NC 15-501 and began winding along the wooded, gently bending road toward the university. "You know, Mark," Briggs continued, "there's a chance for Alexis to make her name in this after all. There's enough credit to go around for everyone, and it could really advance her career. Grants, peer reviews, all those honorary degrees."

"Forget it," Mark said.

"Ah, the protective male. Why don't you let her decide for herself?"

"I told you the deal," Mark said. "We've already given you the others. That should be plenty."

"I'm a mad scientist, remember? I won't be happy until I accidentally destroy the world."

"I'm not so sure it would be an accident. But there's bigger stuff at stake than just the future of the world."

"CRO's stock value, I know. I hear shares are slipping while all this is cooking, but they're poised to make a miraculous run after Halcyon is announced and the government invests. And I'm sure they give stock options in your pay grade, right?"

"I have my own motives. Just like everyone."

They had passed the golf course and the turnoff to the Dean Dome, the cavernous gymnasium named for the venerable basketball coach Dean Smith. More university structures began appearing on the wooded lots, identifiable by their brick facades and large windows. They would reach the main campus within minutes.

He wasn't sure he wanted to ask the next question, but he needed to know. It would reassure him that he still had some vestiges of a conscience and hadn't become a complete sociopath. "How many more will you need for trials?"

"I've administered mild doses to half a dozen subjects," Briggs said. "They think they're in clinicals for a new anxiety treatment. That's not on CRO's dime, it's through a CDC grant with a real professor heading it up. But that's a cover. We need the original subjects because they've already been exposed to Halcyon. The pump is primed, so to speak."

Mark didn't want to think about the neurochemical time bomb ticking in his wife's brain. Maybe sociopaths couldn't truly love, but he was deeply passionate about her. He was slightly comforted by the notion that sociopaths wouldn't have such a thought.

"So we stop at four? Leng, Underwood, Doyle, and Molkesky."

"I love the old part of campus and all those brick sidewalks," Briggs said. "Too bad they kicked me out. Once I restore my good name, maybe I'll see about an adjunct position."

"Four."

Briggs pulled to the side of the narrow road, near an old stone amphitheater girded by oaks and maples. "Is four your limit, or is that a direct order from the senator?"

Mark slammed his fist against the dashboard hard enough to hurt. "That name stays out of this."

"Ah, so you're the satchel man, or whatever they call it in the movies."

Mark opened the door. His wife's office was half a mile away, and he would be a little late. But he had another stop to make first, one that was long overdue, and one he didn't want Briggs to know about. "You'll get your satchel soon enough."

Mark collected his suitcase and hurried away without looking back. Briggs called from the open window. “Tell your wife I said hello.”

Mark turned, his fist unconsciously clenched again. *If you weren’t so critical to CRO’s future, I’d give you a dose of medicine you wouldn’t forget for a long, long time.*

“Just kidding,” Briggs said, then rolled up the window and eased away from the curb.

Traffic was picking up, and the wind sent leaves scuttling over the sidewalk. Mark crunched them underfoot as he jogged up a short rise of stairs. The brittle noise was like the breaking of many tiny bones.

If Burchfield had ordered Alexis into the Monkey House trials as well, he wondered if he would have nodded in acquiescence.

He wasn’t sure which master he served anymore. It seemed there were far too many.

CHAPTER SIXTEEN

"That was a little risky, don't you think?" Briggs asked, glancing around his office as if expecting to see cops in the shadows. "An open attack on Dr. Morgan in broad daylight?"

"You said try to embarrass her," Kleingarten said, tossing a handful of unshelled sunflower seeds into his mouth. "Besides," he said amid crunches, "only sneaky people come under suspicion. The important thing is I got it done."

Kleingarten looked around the bizarre office as he chewed. Briggs had rigged up a temporary lab on one side of the old factory, and he'd stuck most of his gear in what looked to be a zoo cage. It had a hinged grid of steel for a door, with a thick lock, as if Briggs anticipated the need to keep people out. On a low catwalk above, sophisticated equipment of some kind was at work, but Briggs had little more than a computer, some rows of test tubes, an autoclave, and moldering reams of research journals.

Somebody had sunk a fortune in state-of-the-art video monitors and what looked like a security and light system operated by remote control. The main gate was set on a rolling track, and it appeared Briggs could run the whole show from right here.

It seemed like a lot of trouble for a building filled with old tractor parts and farm equipment. He'd had a hard time even finding the place, and the closest buildings were about half a mile away. The huge factory was made of light-red brick, the concrete joints gray with age and spotted with moss.

It seemed like a weird place for a super-secret project, but everything about Briggs and this job was weird.

A large charcoal drawing of a nude woman was taped to the bars on one side of the cage. It wasn't one of those boring pictures they usually did in art classes. This was like porn, with her tits stuck out and a smile on her lips as the fingers of one hand trailed between the dark patch between her legs. She looked Oriental, and Kleingarten wondered if it was a self-portrait of the Slant, because it was framed like a mirror.

But that wasn't as strange as what hung above it. A Curious George clock, with George's skinny arms pointing out the hour and minute, was tied to one of the cell bars with baling wire.

Maybe that's why he calls this the Monkey House.

Briggs didn't fit the criminal type, but he had the glittering, intense eyes down pat. The guy was wired, and Kleingarten had found over the years that obsessed people tended to make mistakes because all they saw was the finish line, not the track. With his soft hands and pale skin, he looked like he'd melt if stuck under a heat lamp for too long.

Kleingarten smiled and spat some salty shells onto the stained concrete floor. He'd have to try that sometime.

"I dosed her close to her office, and I trashed it just like you wanted," Kleingarten said. "She had time to get there before she freaked out. Plus, I got to admit, I was curious to see what would happen. I've been juicing up all these people and I still don't see the point."

"Lucky for you, I've worked two time-release mechanisms into the compound," Briggs said, heading into the cage of his office. "One is the diminishing effect of the chemicals, which occurs naturally as the substance is broken down by the body's processes. The other is a narrow window of disintegration. The time between breakdown and complete eradication is so short that no trace remains even if the symptoms linger."

"Symptoms? I thought you were trying to fix these people." Kleingarten was bored with the man's babble. It reminded him of his high school chemistry class and the time he'd had to set the asshole teacher's lab on fire.

"Sorry. I meant 'effects.' My terminology is a little rusty."

"Yeah, a long vacation will do that."

Kleingarten always checked on the background of the people he worked with, for, or against. Research was just as important in his line of work as in this headshrinker shit.

Sebastian Briggs had been bounced from the UNC faculty after that stupid incident with the trials, but the university had tied it up in a nice little bow so that it looked like Briggs had resigned "to pursue other opportunities in private industry." The Sharpe family had threatened a lawsuit but they got their hush money and everybody lived happily ever after. Except the Sharpe kid, of course.

"My reputation isn't your concern," Briggs said. "Your concern is following instructions to the letter."

"There wasn't no letter. You said stick the lady and I stuck the lady. You said run the car into the coffee shop and I put the pedal to the metal. You said kill the hooker and plant her with Doyle after I dosed him. You said mess with them and I messed with them plenty."

Kleingarten omitted mentioning the murder of the football star. But it wasn't really murder, to his way of thinking. It was suicide. Whether the guy died fast or died slow, what difference did it make?

And the Looker's shrink. But that was a mercy kill, too. Saved her from a life of having to hear other people's bullshit problems.

A metallic banging emanated from the bowels of the basement, as if someone were tapping on a large pipe with a cloth-covered baseball bat.

"Sounds like a toilet's backed up," Kleingarten said.

"A building this old, I wouldn't be surprised," Briggs said, now fidgeting in his top desk drawer.

Kleingarten heard a faint drumming on the high, flat roof and wondered if it had started raining. The day had been overcast but not really threatening. He didn't want to get his new shoes wet.

He glanced at the monitors, anxious to get his money and his next assignment. Pictures from a dozen security cameras filled the video screens. It was a nice system, a Sentinel brand with a mix of wireless cameras and motion sensors so nobody could knock it out by snipping a couple of wires, with a main monitor that was currently blank.

But few of the cameras monitored the outside of the building or its entryways. Most were pointing down the long canyons of abandoned lockers, stainless-steel tables, machine presses, and conveyor belts, as well as tangles of old plows, balers, cattle trailers, mower machines, and fat-threaded tires.

If the factory were in business today, Kleingarten could see where you'd need all those secret eyes on the floor to keep the workers from slacking off or nabbing the merchandise. But now the cameras just pointed at lots of stained concrete and rust.

"So, do you want to me to follow up on that Molkesky woman?" Kleingarten asked.

"No, that situation will resolve itself."

"You don't seem none too happy about it."

"People are predictable, Mr. Drummond. That's why I knew Roland Doyle would stop over in West Virginia at his brother's cabin and would need that extra booster to keep him moving. That's why I knew the two ladies would be in the waffle house. Our subjects will all be gathering soon, because they're going to remember what happened ten years ago."

"Christ, Doc, you got me driving to Cincinnati and then West Virginia when you knew they'd all end up here anyway? I had to buy a straw hat and overalls. I got expenses."

Briggs held out a plain brown envelope. "Fifty thousand. The next installment."

"Well, tell your people I might be billing for overtime," Kleingarten said.

"Not necessarily. Roland Doyle will be in town this afternoon."

"What did you do? Hotwire these people's brains?"

"It's a drug I call Seethe, and I was poised to introduce it to the world ten years ago. But I had to go underground and refine it a little after…well, after we had a little setback. Now it's time our subjects came together again, so I can observe the long-term effects. A decade is a long incubation period, don't you agree?"

The doc said it like he didn't expect Kleingarten to know what "incubation" meant, but his family had raised chickens. He'd dosed Roland twice, assuming Roland hit the vodka bottle like Briggs had predicted, and the Slant and the Looker also took liquid doses, but he'd had to inject the Morgan woman this morning because she was behind schedule.

"Yeah, I can see where you'd be getting impatient," Kleingarten said. "I understand giving them the juice. But I don't get why you want to play games with them."

Briggs gave him a smug look, like every schoolteacher whose face he'd ever wanted to bust, and launched into egghead talk. "My drug chemically alters pathways in the brain until the subject reverts to the dominant core impulse, filtering out reasoning and mitigating stimuli until the subject is obsessed and consumed by that basic impulse. You might say they become more like themselves, the people they would be without all the socialization, inhibitions, and morals that our so-called 'evolved' intelligence has imprisoned us with. Each of the subjects has a specific trigger that amplifies the effects of Seethe. That's why your contribution is so important. You're the trigger man."

Kleingarten squeezed a little common sense out of the mumbo jumbo. "Like that guy in the comic book who gets mad and turns into the Incredible Hulk, right? And then starts smashing shit."

"Yes, but anger is just one of the possible impulses. Each subject will have a reaction unique to their personality, which is why I need to observe their behavior and verify my thesis. The doctor, she's proud and ambitious and aggressive. Roland is an alcoholic, so he's his own evil twin just waiting for permission to mess up, but he's also our problem child who needs additional exposure. Anita Molkesky is insecure and craves attention. Wendy..."

Briggs glanced at the framed nude drawing on the wall, confirming Kleingarten's suspicions.

So you got the hots for the Slant, huh, Doc? And you don't want to say what her weakness is. But I got a pretty good guess. Yes, sir, indeed.

The drumming was louder now and Kleingarten squinted up at the high sheets of gray windows that girded the uppermost five feet of each side of the cavernous facility. The glass was so smoky and dirty that he couldn't tell how much of the gray came from rain clouds.

Then the drumming increased and Kleingarten saw movement in one of the cameras. It was gone before he could focus, but his impression had been of a hunched, pale form, as if maybe the monkey cages held one of those albino chimps they showed on Animal Planet. "There he is!" Briggs said, rushing from his office.

Kleingarten looked at the monitors and saw Briggs appear in one of the screens, gracelessly jogging between two rows of corrugated metal storage containers, leaning and peering anytime he came to a crevice. Briggs was near the end of the aisle, beneath a baler chute that had metal packing straps dangling from its opening.

The pale blur exploded from the darkness, slamming into Briggs.

"Easy!" Briggs's shout echoed through the cavernous structure as Kleingarten ran toward the commotion. He wasn't on the clock at the moment, but he was curious.

Curious Fucking George, that's me.

The pale form scuttled over the machinery and Kleingarten wondered if he should draw his firearm. Maybe the doc had been testing monkeys on the side. He seemed like the kind of guy who could never get enough data.

Briggs was shouting and cursing, searching through the maze of abandoned equipment. Kleingarten followed, glad the old building was relatively isolated, especially for the Research Triangle Park. If Briggs had let loose a crazy monkey, it might need a round or two from Kleingarten's Glock, and he hadn't packed a silencer.

One bullet, maybe charge them five thousand bucks. Sounded like a fair deal, especially if the monkey attacked Briggs again.

Kleingarten was out of breath by the time he caught up with Briggs, who was also panting. The doc stood with his hands on his knees, peering under a metal work table whose top was pitted and scarred. The form was huddled beneath it, mostly in shadows, and emitting a low murmur that bordered on a growl.

"Need help grabbing your monkey?" Kleingarten asked, trying to hide his exerted breath.

"Shh," Briggs said. "Keep your voice calm."

"You're the one who was yelling," Kleingarten observed.

Briggs took a hypodermic needle from his pocket, removed the cap, and squinted at the tip as he pushed the plunger. A dewdrop of fluid oozed from the tip. It looked like the same kind of rig Kleingarten had passed to the jock to stick in Alexis Morgan.

"This is a special part of the experiment," Briggs said. "Can I trust you?"

"Sure." Kleingarten didn't deal with people who expected trust. People like that deserved being lied to. "Don't the bosses know about this?"

"Of course," Briggs said, leaning low and approaching the huddled form. "But they don't know that they know."

Kleingarten braced for the monkey to come bursting out of the cranny and slam into the doc again. He didn't think much of a man who couldn't control his monkeys, no matter how well he paid.

The doc knelt, talking in soothing tones. "Come on, David, it's going to be all right."

David. That wasn't a good name for a monkey. You named your monkey George, or Roscoe, something silly like that. You didn't give it a regular name because monkeys were too much like people and both of you might get the wrong idea.

But Briggs seemed to have some practice with this game. Maybe David the Monkey had escaped before and the doc knew just how to get the job done. When Briggs reached in with the syringe, the creature scuttled away to the far end of the table. Kleingarten went around it, figuring to scare the monkey back toward Briggs.

With a screech, the animal burst from the shadows, all claws and waving arms, a liquid hiss coming from those too-wide lips. The monkey was on Kleingarten before he could react, and though he'd trained in boxing and self-defense, he found himself falling backward onto the cold concrete.

Kleingarten managed to twist and avoid cracking his skull as moist, rancid breath spritzed his neck, and he wondered if Briggs's monkey had rabies. Despite the small, wiry frame, the monkey was strong, and Kleingarten didn't want those claws digging into his skin. He'd seen monkeys in the zoo throwing shit, which meant those nails were nasty.

He spun and flexed, jabbing his thumbs toward the creature's eyes, but stopped when he realized they weren't primate eyes.

A man. Sweet Mary in a manger, it's a man.

The naked man clambered away, passing up the chance to rip at Kleingarten's skin.

"Get him," Briggs yelled, rushing around the table.

Kleingarten blinked alert and grabbed at the man's leg, encircling one thin ankle. He tugged and the man fell flat, his bony chest slapping against the floor. The man immediately curled into a fetal position, quivering beneath Kleingarten's grip.

"Easy, David," Briggs said, moving in and sliding the needle into the man's arm. "You're safe now. Nobody's going to hurt you."

Nobody besides whoever did this to him.

CHAPTER SEVENTEEN

Wallace Forsyth took a sip of Glenlivet single-malt scotch. He liked to think of it as his solitary moral weakness. But a forgivable one. After all, Jesus drank wine and gave it to others.

It was a ritual in which he often indulged while visiting Senator Burchfield. However, the senator was a teetotaler and had none of the common failings of the flesh. No, Burchfield's addiction was power and influence, and even though he'd achieved success in the business world, he cared little for money. All money did was help him control those who didn't share his views, a means to an end.

But as a rising star on the Foreign Relations Committee, the Health, Education, Labor & Pensions Committee, and the Armed Services Committee, Burchfield was uniquely situated to change people's minds.

Many of them.

Burchfield's library was elegant, with polished maple shelves, marble busts of Aristotle and Thomas Jefferson, and a dark leather sofa that sucked Forsyth into its depths. A fire crackled cheerily in the fireplace, though the room's air was carefully controlled to protect the vast collection of books.

Burchfield was proudly pointing out some of his prized editions, such as an early printing of Hitler's *Mein Kampf* and a copy of Lyndon B. Johnson's biography signed by the late president.

"Top of your head, Wallace, who was the most intellectual of our nineteenth-century presidents?" Burchfield said.

Wallace went for the easy pick, mostly because he could only name half of those presidents. "Lincoln."

Burchfield pulled a hard plastic sleeve from the shelves and held it aloft. The clear sleeve contained a ragged, salmon-colored paper. "Wrong. Millard Fillmore. He had a personal collection of more than five thousand volumes, and he established the White House library. He presided over the slavery compromise of 1850, which was the last time a senator drew a pistol on the Senate floor."

"Now you threaten one another with so much greater subtlety and charm," Wallace said, letting his Kentucky accent stretch the words a little.

Burchfield waved the document in the air. "He's generally regarded as a footnote, the kind of trivia question that stumps a history major on finals. But Fillmore was the first president who didn't come from a background of wealth and privilege."

"Is that the reason you summoned me to the castle? A little history lesson? I'm too old and forgetful to squirrel away any more useless information."

Burchfield laughed. "We're more alike than you imagine. Play a little bit dumb so that people underestimate you. You get your best work done when attention is diverted to louder, shinier people."

"You're hardly a shrinking violet, sir. Or are those presidential ambitions just more smoke to veil a different agenda?"

"You know my agenda. That's why you're on the team."

As Burchfield replaced the Fillmore manuscript, Wallace took another sip of the scotch. It was sweet and cold as it flowed through the ice cubes. Worth tempting the eternal flames of hell.

"I don't always agree with Dr. Morgan, but I'd hate to see her crucified for this."

"That's one of the risks," Burchfield said. "You knew going in that there would be collateral damage."

"I knew going in that the atheists, Communists, and radical liberals were winning the war against God."

Burchfield gave his confident bellow of a laugh. "Don't confuse the Democratic Party with the Illuminati. It's all about timing. You just happened to come up for reelection when people were in a mood to dump a few incumbents. But, like all of us at the trough, once you know the way there, it's not so hard to get back."

"I'm serving a higher power here." Forsyth drank more liquor. Scotch tasted better and better with each sip.

Burchfield nodded, suddenly somber. "And sacrifice is the hallmark of all good Christians. So we sacrifice a little now in order to save more people later. Christ took the nails so others might live eternally, right?"

"I reckon so, Senator."

"So Dr. Morgan is serving a greater good. And there might be other casualties as well."

"This here Halcyon…if you change people's minds, are we making them better? Or are we making them less than human?"

Burchfield opened the glass doors on the hearth and grabbed a metal poker. "You're always so concerned with free will and the state of the soul. That's an old-fashioned sentiment."

"That's the Christian's burden. To carry the message and save people from the flames of hell."

Burchfield rolled one of the logs, and the sudden rush of oxygen caused the fire to roar. "Hell is right here, Wallace."

Forsyth rubbed the cold glass against his lips, relishing the numbness. How fortunate to be numbed. If Halcyon was half as good as liquor, then maybe there was hope for the world after all, especially as evil ideas crept toward the United States from every corner of the globe.

"One in every eight American adults is on some kind of happy pill, Wallace," Burchfield said. "Prozac, Xanax, Zoloft, so many drugs with the letters X and Z in them, all creating billions in drug profits."

"So Halcyon is a golden goose."

"It's presented as a drug to treat post-traumatic stress disorder. I can already see the television ads, a grinning, all-American soldier returning home, sweeping up his kid in a slow-motion reunion. What doctor would have the balls to let even one vet walk out of a check-up without a prescription?"

"You know how I feel about messing with people's minds."

"Don't play 'holier than thou' with me, Wallace. You'd like nothing more than to change people's minds so they believe the right way. Hell, you'd practically consider it your sacred duty if you had the means."

Forsyth hadn't considered the potential of influencing people's emotional conditions so that they were more susceptible to God's grace. He wasn't sure if such manipulation would be sinful, but God surely wanted his servants battling for the greater good with whatever weapon was at hand. The Old Testament was a litany of war, genocide, and enslavement, violence and conquest made ethical and right. "You think Halcyon has that sort of widespread potential?"

"This is a bait and switch," Burchfield said. "Halcyon is a winner, to be sure, but it's this rumored 'fear drug' I'm most interested in. But I can't let anyone inside the Beltway know it. On the commercial front, imagine a low-level exposure to such a drug, one that left a certain population uneasy. Maybe something in the public water supply, or toward a targeted group like at a college or hospital. One would expect prescriptions of a drug like Halcyon to increase dramatically."

"And profits along with it." The thought evoked the need for another sip of scotch.

"But that's only the beginning." Burchfield spoke faster now, in that dynamic rhythm that kept members of both parties in line. "Think of the military applications. Can you imagine widespread exposure to a fear drug in a place already ripe for violence?"

"What, you turn crazy-eyed terrorists another notch crazier? That doesn't seem so smart."

"Fear and anger are the same thing when you get right down to it. If you can dose a sensitive area—say, the border between Afghanistan and Pakistan—then the situation's bound to escalate."

"So, while they're busy killing each other, we send in the troops and play hero?" Forsyth said. "Another win for America?"

"You're too old-school, Wallace. You worry me sometimes. The real effect would be protracted war, because American troops would be among the victims exposed to the drug. Protracted war means conservative policies, a chance to consolidate power, and a good time for a hawk to run for the Oval Office."

"Damn, Daniel," Forsyth said. "You're more ambitious than I thought. And as ruthless as a rattlesnake in an Easter egg basket."

"This is good news for your people, too. Hit Muslim areas first, then we can start on Africa. It's about time America discovered a moral imperative in all those countries where tribalism is leading to the slaughter of millions. Of course, Africa's home to the next gold rush for natural resources. And after that, who knows? China's booming but still vulnerable."

"And with so much war, trauma, and violence, Halcyon will become nearly universal," Forsyth said. "I can see Halcyon doled out even before the trauma occurs. Just in case something bad happens. You owe it to your family to protect them from all the horrors of the world, right?"

"It's a world of possibilities, old friend. Christian relief agencies—government funded, of course—move in and help clean up the rubble, with a Bible in every box of rice, socks, and soap. Missionaries have been using that carrot-and-stick for centuries."

It wasn't the way the Book of Revelations mapped out the final battle, but maybe it was metaphorically close enough. While Forsyth's power in the capitol had declined, he was still a figurehead among fundamentalists and his support meant votes. But Forsyth needed a little more convincing, despite their long-time friendship. "But first you need to win the White House, or none of it matters."

"Right. And you know there's a place for you in my administration. That's why I want you as an ally in this."

Forsyth beamed. "I can side with Dr. Morgan and swing the bioethics council toward wider acceptance of mood-changing drugs."

"That would help lay some groundwork. The NSA and CIA are already snooping, but Halcyon will sail through the FDA hearings and go aboveboard. Protecting our vets is the right thing to do."

"More legislative tomfoolery's been committed under the banner of 'the right thing to do' than every other reason put together."

"Because the right thing is never questioned or explained."

Forsyth was simultaneously intrigued and appalled. "And would you say inciting war is the right thing, Daniel? Using drugs to spread American ideals and influence?"

“I’m a freedom fighter, Wallace. And I’ll use any weapon at hand.”

Forsyth looked at his glass, wondering if Burchfield might have secured a liquid sample of the drug. He might right now be artificially subjected to deep forgetfulness. Or that other drug, which seemed to interest Burchfield even more.

And what if I’m afraid? What if the Lord has called on me, and this is my test of faith? Do I take up the sword?

All Forsyth could think was what he had thought before, that the devil was loose in the world and the forces of God were mightily outnumbered and had their backs against the wall.

Burchfield waved the poker in the air like a conductor’s baton. “One other little detail about Millard Fillmore.”

“Yes?”

“He was raised a Presbyterian and married the daughter of a Baptist preacher. Yet later in life he became a Unitarian.”

The Universalist Unitarian Church. The liberal mask of the anarchists, the ones who taught that every spiritual belief was valid and that individuality should be worshipped above all. A church that was actively eroding the country’s foundations and freedom.

“I see what you mean,” Forsyth said. “Knowledge leads you away from God.”

Burchfield leveled the poker, not in a threatening manner, but like an instructor drilling a point into a student. “And people with knowledge must be controlled or destroyed.”

Forsyth smiled. Of course he’d join the battle. It was the right thing to do.

He glanced at the crystal scotch decanter on the sideboard, wondering if he might have another before he left.

CHAPTER EIGHTEEN

I'm not like that. Not anymore.

Wendy's hand shook. The pills rattled in the bottle.

"It didn't happen that way," Alexis said. "Tell me it didn't."

"That's the trouble," Wendy said. "We all remember it differently."

"Or not at all."

"Thank God you called me."

"Once I remembered, I had no choice."

Wendy looked around the confines of her off-campus apartment, still feeling vulnerable even with the doors locked. She'd learned that even inside—maybe especially inside—you still couldn't escape yourself, your fears, your deepest impulses.

Alexis was just as nervous. She leaned against Wendy's drawing table and stared down at the drawing spread across it. Wendy had been working on charcoal sketch, a huddled human form suffocating in shadows. She'd been driven, knowing a deeper message lurked beneath, but as always, art proved inadequate when it came to expressing the full breadth of human truth and lies.

"Is it happening again?" Wendy asked.

Alexis looked up with those ice-blue eyes that always projected a bright but cold intellect, but they both knew that blue was also the color of the hottest stars, the raging storm of a body consuming itself. They could hide their duplicity from the rest of the world, but the Monkey House survivors *knew.*

"When did it kick in?" Wendy asked.

"About an hour ago. I got dosed on the commons. It was in a crowd, when classes were changing, so I couldn't tell who stuck me."

"And you found the pills waiting in your office?"

"Whoever did it must have known my routine," Alexis said.

"You know who did it."

Wendy crossed the cluttered living room to check the locks again. After the separation, she'd taken a one-bedroom apartment within walking distance of campus. Neither she nor Roland had been able to afford the mortgage on their Chatham County farmhouse, and Wendy had always hated the half-hour commute to work. Now she longed for that remoteness and isolation.

"I don't think we have to worry about him getting in," Alexis said. "He couldn't be any more 'in.' He's already got a back door to our brains."

"I'm at least a day ahead of you. So grant me a little extra paranoia."

"I know. I'm feeling it, too. I walked here because I didn't trust myself to drive. It's Briggs, all right."

Wendy paced, irritated by the stacks of framed canvases and the art screaming from the walls. She fought an urge to rip down the fruits of her dreams and talents, to stamp them on the floor.

The works of colleagues also adorned her walls, ranging in style from surrealism and cubism to such postmodernist frenzy that it hadn't yet acquired a label. Alexis's arrival had originally comforted her, but now her friend was just another object fueling her claustrophobia and anxiety.

"How long before we completely lose it?" Wendy asked.

"How soon is now? How crazy is crazy?"

"Jesus, Lex, you're starting to freak me out, and I'm freaked out enough. You're supposed to be the brains here. You know, that academic voice of reason?"

Alexis sipped at the chamomile tea Wendy had made, a pitiful attempt at a calming antidote. "Sorry. In the trials, the window was eight hours, but it looks like Briggs has altered the formula."

"It's time we called the cops. Or the attorney general. Somebody."

"Right. They take us in for observation and seize the Halcyon." Alexis held up her own orange bottle, and Wendy realized they'd both been clutching their pills as if they were sacred talismans.

"And we go all the way to the end of the cycle."

"An uninterrupted ride. And I don't think we want to go there."

"Because you don't come back."

"Just like Susan."

The name invoked a silence on the room that penetrated beyond the walls, as if the whole world were hushed and eavesdropping.

"Besides," Alexis continued, more quietly, though she, too, appeared to be trembling a little. "That might open the door to questions about what happened ten years ago, and none of us wants that."

"I'm not so sure," Wendy said. "I'm an artist. I can do my thing just as well in prison or in an asylum."

"They take away your sharp things," Alexis said, studying the drawing again. "You'll be stuck finger painting with your own feces."

"Maybe Anita has the right idea. Take yourself out of the game before you lose."

Alexis crossed the room with such speed and ferocity that Wendy squealed in shock. Alexis gripped her wrists, right where the scars were, and squeezed hard enough to hurt. Alexis's eyes were as mad and glittering as a lost, stormy sea.

"Don't you dare say that," Alexis said. "Don't you dare even *think* it."

Wendy nodded, unable to speak. Alexis had been the first to come up with the idea of dealing with Susan. In many ways, Alexis was a born leader, an Aries, with a forceful sense of justice and a practical approach that could border on pathological.

But they all were sociopaths, each of the group members, and they would never know if they'd been born that way or made that way by Sebastian Briggs.

It's all her fault. She's still jealous over Sebastian. Just like Roland.

"Okay," Wendy whispered, her pulse rate still elevated. "I'm back."

"How many pills do you have left?"

"Three."

"Damn. I only have two left. Briggs started us all on different cycles. Do you recall getting bitten or stung, maybe a little pinch in a crowd?"

"No, there was just the accident this morning I told you about."

"Maybe during the chaos somebody injected you."

Wendy shook her head. "I don't think so. I think that was to get the adrenalin going and kick-start the fear response."

"He must have synthesized a liquid form." Alexis glanced out the window, where the solid brick buildings of academia in the distance suggested order and sanity. But the brick and ivy hid things that went on in the basements, where researchers sometimes took intellectual liberties in the interest of science.

And other liberties as well, Wendy thought.

"So we can't go to the cops or the doctors," Wendy said. "What about your Washington friends?"

"You don't have 'friends' in Washington. You have units of political capital."

"Your husband, then? Isn't he in that business?"

Alexis paused in her restless pacing. "I want to keep him out of it if I can. Something like this could ruin his career. Besides, he doesn't know who he married, and I want to keep it that way."

"I think you're a little more important to him than CRO."

"I wish I could believe that."

"Lex, that's the fear talking. It's already getting to you. Don't you see?"

Alexis hugged herself. "You're talking civilized logic, and this stuff is cooking away inside the lizard brain."

A buzzing sound erupted, and the noise was almost painful. Her anger flared. Taking a breath to focus, Wendy located her purse and pulled out her cell.

"Who is it?" Alexis asked her.

"I don't recognize the number. Should I answer it?"

Alexis shook her head. "We should limit outside stimuli as much as possible. If Briggs is playing with us, he'll infect us any way he can. Because his fear drug needs triggers. Anger, trauma, fear, excitement. He's learned our weaknesses and will hit us where it hurts."

Excitement. The way he touched me and inspired me...

Wendy found that she couldn't wait to see Briggs again. Maybe they'd finish what they had started.

All of them. Everything.

The phone quit buzzing after the seventh ring, and Wendy closed it. Alexis sat beside her on the couch, and they waited. For what, they didn't know.

CHAPTER NINETEEN

After Briggs withdrew the needle, the monkey man let out a final whimper and relaxed. Kleingarten also relaxed, although he was ready to pounce on the monkey man if he moved.

But Kleingarten's 210 pounds would smash the guy, who probably weighed 120 pounds soaking wet. His ribs showed and his hair was nearly solid white, which had helped fuel the illusion that he'd been an albino monkey.

"Lot of strength for an old guy," Kleingarten said, voice casual despite his hammering heart. He didn't want the egghead to know he'd been rattled.

"He's not so old," Briggs said. "He's only thirty."

Kleingarten released the limp, shivering man and studied the doctor with a newfound interest. Briggs's straight career had been derailed because he didn't play by the rules, and Kleingarten could respect that.

Hell, he himself had been a security guard making ten bucks an hour until he realized once they let you inside with the keys, the place was yours.

CRO was another story. Corporations like that were nothing but smoke and mirrors, and on paper they looked legit, with their executives hanging around the White House and running charities to help ghetto kids buy shoes endorsed by basketball stars.

But Kleingarten's digging suggested they were in deep with the military and national security organizations, people not necessarily allied with the White House. One thing for sure, CRO probably didn't want Briggs to make the front page for running some sort of Nazi funny farm.

Which meant Kleingarten might have to double dip and see if CRO would pay him to keep an eye on Briggs as well as follow orders from Briggs.

"Your bosses know about this?" he asked.

"This is the part the bosses wouldn't have the stomach for," Briggs said. "And they wouldn't understand it, anyway. Because they think they're the bosses."

Kleingarten surveyed the far end of the building, where closets and storage units had been added sometime after the factory had closed. "How many other monkeys do you have back there?"

"David is our only guest at the moment," Briggs said. "But we hope to have more visitors soon."

"The ones I've been sending invitations to?"

Briggs gave a distant smile. "We have plenty of room."

"You're not one of those Looney Tunes types, are you?"

"I work for a better tomorrow," Briggs said. "Now, help me get him up."

Kleingarten hesitated. He'd already gone outside the job description to chase the thing he'd thought was a monkey, and here was the doc expecting him to haul cargo. What next, a shoeshine?

Briggs must have read his mind. "Don't worry, Mr. Drummond, there's a bonus in it for you," Briggs said, still using the false name Kleingarten had given him.

Apparently the doc wasn't as shrewd about background checks as he was about his research. Another reason to worry about him.

“He’s not contagious, is he?” Kleingarten said.

“His disease is internal and self-inflicted, poor man.” There was no irony in Briggs’s tone. “Hopefully our research can one day help him return to society and lead a productive life.”

They stooped and lifted the naked man, who was half-conscious, eyelids fluttering. They walked him to the rear of the facility, and as they drew closer, Kleingarten saw the series of rooms were rigged with surveillance gear and outfitted like hospital rooms, with small observation windows in the heavy steel doors. The sterile, brightly lit environs were a stark contrast to the murky, dusty factory floor.

Somebody had spent more big money back here, which meant they expected big payback.

That was something Kleingarten could wrap his head around.

“Here we go, David,” Briggs said as they came to the last door on the right. The door was ajar and Briggs nudged it open. The walls were covered with images of eyes, hundreds, maybe thousands, every color, shape, and size. Some were artistic, others clipped from magazines, a few blown up to monstrous proportions.

Just entering the room made Kleingarten woozy. If this poor guy was staying here as a “guest,” it was no wonder he’d gone monkey-shit mad.

Kleingarten let Briggs finish the job of leading David to a small metal cot covered with clean linens. Aside from the wall art, the room was mostly bare, with the exception of some video monitors and speakers secured in the upper corners of the room, enclosed behind metal grates. A stainless-steel toilet and sink were bolted in place, like in a prison cell, except there was no mirror above the sink. The walls were covered in a thick white vinyl material, bradded into place, and it would take a sledgehammer to bust through.

Glints in small recesses revealed camera lenses, and the hundred-square-foot room stank of new carpet and chemicals. Kleingarten imagined the white background made a pretty good projection screen, and here and there were smears of blood, as if David had tried to beat and scratch the images away.

"Nothing to fear, David," Briggs said, sitting the man on the cot. "You're home."

David emerged from his catatonic state long enough to smile. "Home, home on the range," he spoke-sang, about as musically as a manhole cover grating across pavement. The tortured melody was made even more haunting by the echo in the building.

"That's right, David," Briggs said. "Home on the range."

The doc exited the room, closing the door behind him, and a wave of relief washed over Kleingarten. He'd killed a few people in his day, old-fashioned, honest, hands-on killing, but he'd never been this unnerved.

"Aren't you going to lock it?" Kleingarten asked.

"That would defeat the purpose of the experiment," Briggs said. "They have to *want* to be here."

"And it doesn't have anything to do with that joy juice we're sticking in people?"

Briggs sighed and stared off into the distance, as if envisioning a better future for everyone, where people danced in meadows and ate fruit and didn't worry about the beasties roaring in the night or inside their own heads. "Surrender is the first step to victory."

Kleingarten was going to have to conduct a little more research on this guy. He doubted if CRO knew what they'd turned loose.

The game had changed a lot in the fifteen years since Kleingarten had taken the field. In the old days, power was power. You got hit, you hit back harder.

In this crazy-assed twenty-first century, though, knowledge was power, and if Kleingarten learned more about what was going on than anyone else involved, he might make this his retirement project. He hadn't really enjoyed cutting up that whore in Cincinnati. The thrill was gone, and when the focus faded, a fatal mistake was sure to follow.

Yes, it was time to get out. A few more paydays and then maybe a rice plantation in Thailand, or a little cottage on the beach in Puerto Rico, or whatever the hell they did in Madagascar.

He followed Briggs back to the ape-cage office, and Curious George told him he'd wasted half an hour in the lab. Briggs slid open a desk drawer, and Kleingarten saw a recent color photograph of Wendy Leng.

So, you're hung up on her? Good. It's about time you showed me something I could use.

Briggs touched the photo tenderly for a moment, then nudged it aside and withdrew some documents and maps.

Smart egghead. If you sent out e-mails or phone calls, anybody could be listening.

CRO wouldn't get its hands dirty but wouldn't have any problem keeping an eye and ear on the doc from the safety of a computer somewhere.

That was one of the tricks of the Information Age. You didn't always have to outsmart people. Sometimes you could out-dumb them.

"Roland Doyle will be the most difficult," Briggs said. "He's always been my problem child."

"Is that why we did that 'David Underwood' thing with the fake IDs? To help him remember?"

"Roland has serious identity issues. He loves himself as a drunk, and when you take that away, he doesn't know how to deal with himself. He's a man of unreliable character. But one thing you can always count on with Roland—anytime there's trouble, he comes crawling back to the ex."

"The Chinese woman, right?" Kleingarten said it just to see the reaction in the doc's eyes. It was a mixture of anger, lust, and jealousy.

He'd seen idiots fall in love with hookers and heroin addicts and AIDS sluts, and he never failed to be amazed at the shit guys let their dicks do to them.

"She was actually born in Tibet, and we could engage in a political discussion about that, but we both have work to do."

"Okay. I bring the four people and then I get the bonus? All done?"

Briggs frowned. "Yes, but I'm afraid we'll lose one."

"Lose one?"

"Anita Molkesky will finally succeed in the one thing she was put on Earth for, which is to destroy herself. Her final cry for attention. But she'll need the others to help her with her mission. Bring her first."

"What do I use? You just want me to kidnap her?"

"She's already broken, Mr. Drummond. All you have to do is sweep up the pieces and bring them to me."

"She's been talking to shrinks. It might be trouble."

Briggs broke from his dark reverie. "Don't worry, you'll be paid for that one, as long as you bring in the others."

"Do I look worried?"

Briggs smiled, back to his usual self. "No. Not at all. You know the way out."

The doc turned to his bank of high-tech gear and flipped some switches and triggered the front-door lock. As Kleingarten wended his way through the skeletal machinery, he heard the strains of the old cowboy ballad, "Home on the Range," once sung by Willie Nelson, who wasn't a whole lot better than David Underwood at carrying a tune.

The music was concentrated in the area of the holding cells, and Kleingarten shuddered as he pictured David Underwood in that brightly lit room in front of all those eyeballs, with a dope-headed hippie droning on about where the buffalo roam. He told himself he was only hurrying because he was on the clock and headed for retirement, but he knew that was a lie.

The Monkey House was not a place anybody stayed too long if they wanted to keep their marbles.

It wasn't until he was in his Jeep and headed toward Chapel Hill that he realized he'd been humming.

Where seldom is heard a discouraging word, and the skies are not cloudy all day.

He punched up the radio and blasted the tune from his mind with ordinary, idiotic pop-rock, where there were plenty of discouraging words.

CHAPTER TWENTY

Damn, Wendy, never there when I need you. Some things never change.

Roland had been lucky enough to find the last working pay phone in the mountains of Virginia, at a run-down gas station where the pumps turned numbers on dials to tally the bill. Roland had made change inside, drawing a long look from the cigarette-huffing woman behind the counter.

He wondered if he looked suspicious as he staggered toward the phone. He was running from something, but that was nothing new. However, this one felt bigger than all those other forgotten failures.

And that damned David Underwood driver's license stared at him as he stood at the counter. He had to remind himself again that he was Roland Doyle, and in forcing the name into his brain, Cincinnati came back in a rush.

Hell of a week. Fall off the wagon, kill a woman, and turn into somebody else. That sounds exactly like the kind of thing that would happen to me.

"Can I help you, sir?" It was the woman from the counter, who'd taken a break from her cigarette break. She'd rolled the sleeves of her Jeff Gordon racing jacket to her elbows.

Roland realized he'd been leaning with his head against the phone, idly fingering the change slot. He might have been muttering to himself, because the words "Monkey House" spun around his skull like the metal ball of a roulette wheel. "I'm fine."

"You sure don't look so hot."

"A little touch of the flu," he said.

The woman jumped back as if the virus had wings. "You can keep it."

"I'm not contagious," he said. *Insanity is only catching in a crowd.*

"You ought to take something for that," she said, retreating to the safety of the store and its carcinogenic atmosphere.

Roland took the vial of pills from his pocket and held them aloft. "Got it right here. Just what the doctor ordered."

He looked at the vial's label and then checked his watch. Ten minutes to go. Until what? How many had he taken?

More importantly, how many did he have left?

Three.

The thing that would happen if he didn't take the pill was already building inside him. It was like a black tsunami, a force that would crush all thoughts and sweep away the foundations of all that made him Roland Doyle.

And as fucked up as Roland Doyle was, it was all he had.

He dropped coins in the slot. As he tried Wendy's number again, a dark Lexus with tinted windows pulled alongside the pumps. The car had that suspicious sheen of officialdom, though the plates were standard Virginia issue. Roland let the phone ring seven times, just for luck, before he gave up.

No one had moved from the car, though a large, hand-painted sign by the road said "Self Serve Only."

Could be anybody. Or it could be him.

Now why did I think that? And who is "him"?

Roland wondered if this was how schizophrenics thought just before they slid into an episode. Just clued in enough to know they weren't thinking quite right, but unable to escape their own buggy thoughts. He headed for his rental car, determined to be casual, though his legs wanted to break into a run.

He was sweating and lightheaded by the time he slid behind the wheel. He'd be in Chapel Hill at about the time he'd have to make a decision about the last pill. First he'd find Wendy, and maybe they could call their friend, the chemistry professor. He knew the professor's name but couldn't summon it. All he remembered was her glittering blue eyes, a beauty mark on one side of her chin, and sweeping auburn hair.

And someone else.

Susan? Was that her name?

He pulled onto the road, driving carefully, afraid of weaving and drawing police attention. He couldn't afford to get arrested, not like this. He'd only been driving a couple of minutes, five miles under the speed limit, when the dark Lexus gunned past him on the left.

Guess they had enough gas after all. Must not have been THEM, whoever they are.

But it could have been. He could run from a murder scene, but he couldn't run from whatever had happened ten years ago, and he couldn't hide from himself. Whoever he was.

He tried to concentrate on Wendy, because she reminded him he was Roland. As long as he had her, he couldn't turn into David Underwood.

He had met her as an undergrad in Wilson Library, literally bumping into her at the DVD archive, a popular destination of budget-minded students. She was looking for anything zany and breezy and he'd had a craving for a big-bug science-fiction movie.

They'd been one of those cases of "opposites attract," which they both should have taken as a warning, but the attraction hit hard and they never had a chance. The Tibetan artist and the Rocky Mount trailer-trash boy trying to make good.

It sounded like a quirky rom-com. Both struggling financially, they'd found ways to improvise, including showing up at artist's receptions to scarf down cheese and grapes, and they'd also sold their own plasma. Then they'd accepted that offer to serve in the experiment.

The experiment. Me, Wendy, that professor. Wasn't there some more people?

He had a headache so he went back to picturing Wendy, standing in the brilliance of a sun-splashed room, painting naked, breasts swaying sensually as she danced with the brush.

Then his vision shifted to what she was painting—Susan after what they'd done to her—and he nearly drove off the road.

He popped open the vial with one hand and swallowed the pill even though it went down like a bone.

God, please don't make me see that again.

CHAPTER TWENTY-ONE

The Eshelman School of Pharmacy was one of UNC's education and research wings, part of a complex that had grown over the years to connect the university with Memorial Hospital.

Mark had taken a few classes there to augment his business degree, because even as a teen he'd understood where the money of the future would be flowing. That was where he'd met Alexis, who was already working on her doctorate.

Now, entering the brick building, he saw how little the building had changed—the same uncomfortable benches, waxy potted plants, and somber portraits of past benefactors. That stood in stark contrast to how much he'd changed in the interim. He'd worked so hard to showcase his maturity to Alexis that he wondered if that was when he'd first become an actor and his life a role scripted by others.

He knocked on Dr. Ayanadi's lab door, even though he'd called ahead to make the appointment. The doctor opened the door, smiling and extending a brown hand. His jet-black hair was cut in a bowl shape, and his thick glasses were held in place by hairy ears. "Mark Morgan, my successful pupil."

"I only got a C, remember?"

"Yes, yes, but you've gone on to bigger things. Most of my C students are pushing lunch carts in the hospital."

"I married well," Mark said.

"That you did. And how is Dr. Morgan?"

I wish I knew. "She's busy with the bioethics council. You know how much she hates politics, but somebody's got to fight for what's right."

Ayanadi nodded. "But you didn't come here for a philosophical discussion. You sound worried."

Mark glanced around the small lab. Most major research was conducted off campus, in the RTP, but tenured faculty like Ayanadi were given personal-sized labs, mostly to support journal publication and justify grant requests. Ayanadi, though, had a modern electron microscope and gleaming gear that Mark didn't recognize, which clashed with the chipped counters and 1950s-era sink.

"What do you know about Sebastian Briggs?"

Ayanadi's dark eyes narrowed. "We don't like to speak of him around here. That could have been bad for all of us."

"It might be bad for all of us now."

"Mark, I appreciate CRO's contributions to our research, but we always must keep the business and the personal separate. We can be friends but a researcher avoids the appearance of favoritism."

"I'm not here for CRO. I'm here for my wife."

Ayanadi glanced wistfully at the papers and computer near his microscope, as if he'd rather be lost in routine. He sighed and said, "As you know, Briggs was something of a maverick. Early on, his flamboyance was…tolerated, because he brought in grants and published a few significant articles at a young age."

"I've read the records," Mark said. "I need to know what's under them, the stuff that got cut out."

"Even now, we must avoid that. Surely your wife told you more than I could."

"She doesn't remember. It seems like nobody remembers. It's either the biggest case of collective amnesia since the Holocaust or somebody's hiding something."

Ayanadi moved around Mark and closed the door. "Very well. I will tell you the rumors, but I must warn you, I have no evidence to support any of this, and you know how much that repels me as a scientist."

"I promise, Doctor, I won't dispute any of your conclusions. I have some of my own that nobody would believe."

"Briggs received doctorates in both psychology and neurobiology. We don't get many of the softer sciences in this building."

"Softer skulls" is what you mean. The touchy-feely doesn't go well with the numbers racket. "He was running experiments."

"You've seen the records. He used student volunteers, and while it's not unusual to use students in the early trials of drug testing, Briggs apparently conducted what one might call a 'bait and switch.'"

"Pretending he was testing one drug on paper while he was actually running something else?"

"Yes. Hardly uncommon, sadly, in the history of therapeutic drugs. Our branch has been just as complicit in some of the horrors of modern psychiatry, such as insulin shock therapy and the designer drugs of the fifties and sixties. And it's likely Briggs would have gotten away with it if not for Susan Sharpe. But I imagine your wife has told you about her?"

Mark was about to nod out of habit but realized he would get more information by acting ignorant. He'd never heard of Susan Sharpe. "She doesn't like to talk about that."

"We still aren't sure what happened, but we've pieced together a trial with six participants. Your wife, of course, was both a participant and Briggs's graduate assistant. Though who knows whether her participation was voluntary."

"Yeah," Mark said. "That was a traumatic experience, and I think she blocked it out."

Ayanadi nodded. "Briggs was testing fear response, one of the favorite subjects of psychologists. On paper, he was conducting a simple maze experiment, similar to the Stanford Prison Experiment in which volunteers divided into the roles of guards and prisoners. They soon socialized and adapted to those roles, so much so that guards turned violent and the prisoners had trouble adjusting back to their regular lives."

"In other words, the make-believe became real."

"Yes, and whatever happened out there with Briggs must have been terrible."

"Out there? The records said the trials were conducted here in the pharmacy school."

Ayanadi's face pinched in anguish. "Yes, that's what the papers say. There was a big hush-hush, so much at stake, lawsuits and funding. The dean and chancellor thought it best to have it appear as a tragic accident. Susan Sharpe's body was found at the foot of the stairs in the basement, suffering multiple contusions."

Mark wondered why his wife never mentioned the incident, but he also couldn't accept she had any part in it. "I don't understand."

"Whatever Briggs did to those volunteers, somehow Susan Sharpe was beaten to death as a result."

"No," Mark said, reluctant to believe the nation's oldest university had skeletons in its closet. But he of all people should know that the most polished veneer could hide the most alarming atrocities. CRO bent ethical rules as a standard operating procedure.

"No charges filed," Ayanadi said. "That would have been disastrous to all involved. The university police handled the investigation, the Board of Trustees negotiated in closed session, and a football booster funded the confidential settlement with the Sharpe family. The official report said she died here from a fall down the stairs. A tragic accident."

Mark had seen photographs of domestic-violence victims, people who had taken a pounding yet walked away. He couldn't picture the amount of blows it would take to kill someone.

He now remembered reading about the incident in the *Daily Tar Heel*. With a student population of 26,000 people, a death was unusual but quickly swept past in the bustle of rock bands, politics, frat parties, and sports.

"Susan Sharpe," Mark said. "She was a student?"

Ayanadi cocked a bushy eyebrow. "They were all students, except Briggs, who had recently earned his doctorate and was teaching part-time. Briggs couldn't stay on, of course. He didn't help himself with his refusal to cooperate. And his personality didn't lend itself to the support of allies."

"If these trials were going on in the building, how did he manage to keep it secret?"

"No. His research here was innocuous, camouflage for the real work he was conducting in the Research Triangle. He never divulged the real location."

"Surely the cops found the lab?" Despite CRO's involvement, Mark had never heard a mention of the tragedy within the corporation. No surprise there.

"As I said, this was hush-hush. No one looked because no one wanted to see."

Mark did a quick calculation in his head. That would have been nearly two years before he met Alexis. And, despite her generally positive demeanor, at times a shadow crossed her face as if doom had skirted past without her fully recognizing it. Like most young married couples, they'd been more interested in their future together than the mistakes and secrets of their individual pasts.

"These other…subjects. What happened to them?"

The professor shook his head. "I don't recall all the names, but I distinctly remember Wendy Leng, because she later joined our art faculty."

Wendy. Lex's friend. And they never mentioned the trials…

Wendy had married a man named Roland, who had been in school with the two of them. He and Alexis had attended the wedding, where Roland had gotten embarrassingly drunk and made a fool of himself. Mark wondered who else among his wife's friends had been involved, and how much that friendship was built around a shared secret.

"One last question, Doctor. Was CRO backing Briggs at the time?"

Dr. Ayanadi stared at the periodic chart on the wall, as if he could rearrange the elements and structure the world into something good, whole, and sane. "CRO has always been a generous benefactor of our program, Mark. A relationship we all hope to continue."

Mark tapped the counter on his way to the door. "No one looks because no one wants to see, right?"

CHAPTER TWENTY-TWO

Kleingarten held the little orange bottle of pills about six inches out of Anita Molkesky's reach. The hunger in her eyes was unmistakable. He'd handled his share of drugged-out hookers, and when the need sunk in its teeth, they would do anything for a fix.

Anything.

This Briggs guy was on to something.

"You know you need it, honey," he said.

"I need it," she murmured.

She was sitting on the bed like she knew her way around it. She looked a little rougher than she had in the waffle house, just before he'd crashed the car into it. Briggs had called the collision a "trigger" and said it would kick in the necessary adrenalin to juice her brain. Kleingarten had cut him off before Briggs launched into a lecture, but he understood the basic idea. He knew plenty about drugs and hookers.

The only thing he couldn't understand was why Briggs had gone for the Slant when this gooey candy on the hoof was available. Sure, she'd had some work done, and those melons were inflated by at least two letter sizes, but she looked like she was primed for partying.

He'd picked her up outside the hospital after her appointment with just a few well-chosen words. He'd use them again if he had to.

"Okay, Daddy will fix you up, but I just need you to do one thing for me, okay?"

She nodded. One thing was easy.

Kleingarten looked around the motel room. It was a lot like the one in Cincinnati where he'd killed that hooker while Roland Doyle was in sand land—cheap paneling, a chipped dresser, a single lamppost, and an EZ chair that, despite its obvious age, had no ass print in the seat. Nobody came to motel rooms to sit around in chairs.

He pulled the digital tape recorder from his pocket. He thought about playing with her a little, but the doc had said the recording was an important part of the job. In fact, it pretty much *was* the job. The rest was bonus.

"Are you going to hurt me?" she asked, her tone flat, like she couldn't care less one way or another.

"Maybe," he said, with equal ambivalence. She was taking the fun out of it.

He held the recorder out and hit the button so the red light came on. It was a basic Sony model, but solid, and it would record for a week if he needed it to. He didn't think he'd need it.

"Here's what you say, Anita. You say, 'Wendy, I'm in the Monkey House.'"

"But I'm not in the Monkey House. I'm in a motel room."

He wondered if she'd been hitting other stuff besides Briggs's happy pills. Maybe a barbiturate or oxy. He didn't know how the Halcyon would react with other drugs, but he figured it wasn't his problem.

"Take two. Say 'Wendy, I'm in the Monkey House,' only say it like you're scared. Like in a panic."

"I was an actress."

"Yeah, I bet. Weren't you with George Clooney in that, whatsit, the *Ocean's Fifteen*?"

"No, but I met him once."

One thing about human nature, you gave somebody a chance to brag and they forgot all about their problems for a second. Kleingarten shook the bottle to bring her back around.

"Wendy, I'm in the Monkey House."

She closed her eyes, maybe channeling Marilyn Monroe. "Wendy, I'm in the Monkey House."

"Not bad, but a little more energy. You sound like you're getting your nails done." Kleingarten cut the recording so he wouldn't have to edit too much later. "Picture the scene. This crazy guy has you locked away in a filthy, dark factory, and he's trying to put you in a cage. But" —Kleingarten acted out the next part, grunting as he spoke—"you kick him in the nuts and run. You get to his little office and there's a cell phone, right on the desk, like he wanted you to use it. You got no choice. You pick it up and call your only friend in the world—"

"I got lots of friends." Her nostrils flared a little.

"Yeah, I know, but nobody else who *understands*. You know you've got less than a minute, tops, and how could you explain it all to anyone else?"

She nodded. "Yeah, in that case, it would be Wendy."

Kleingarten hit the "Record" button. "So you pick up the phone, punch in her number and—"

"I don't know her number. Not off the top of my head. I'd have to dig around in my purse. Unless it was my cell phone, then her number would be stored in it."

"Okay, goddamn it, let's say it's *your* phone on the desk. You pick it up and get through and she answers and you go..." He pointed the recorder toward her face as the cue.

"Wendy, I'm in the Monkey House."

"Hey, not bad, a little passion, a little fear, a little drama. What movies did you say you were in?"

"Nothing you probably heard of. *Tommy Salami, Patti Cake Patti Cake*, and *Cherry Paradise*."

She'd named them with a perverse kind of pride. Kleingarten had heard of them, and had seen one, and now he knew why she looked familiar. "You did a lot of movies with food in them."

"Yeah." She gave him a glassy-eyed smile.

Kleingarten was angry now. He usually didn't get too worked up over a job, even an enjoyable one, but she'd just shot down one of his little fantasies of how this would play out.

After remembering the disgusting things she'd done with those guys in that video—guys of every color in the rainbow—he wouldn't touch her with a ten-foot pole. And that was a fucking shame.

"Can I have my pill now?" she asked.

He moved the hand with the vial behind his back. "Okay, now pretend he's got you again, and you go, 'Help me, hurry, we're in the old factory where we killed Susan.' Except rush the words all together."

She started and then forgot the line.

"Here, let me help you," he said, grabbing her wavy blonde hair and yanking.

"*Ow*."

"Help me, hurry, we're in the factory where we killed Susan." He was getting impatient, and that scared her a little.

"Help me, hurry, we're in the factory where we killed Susan."

He clicked the recorder off. That was an Oscar performance. Briggs would be pleased. "Okay, honey, it's a wrap."

Kleingarten slid the recorder in his pocket and shook out one of the green pills. He gave it to her and she tossed it in her mouth without looking at it. He figured she put a lot of things in there without looking.

The dose seemed to hit pretty quickly, because she looked around as if realizing she wasn't in the hospital or her apartment. "What were you making me say?" she asked.

He shook the vial. "These pills. They really help you forget, huh?"

"Forget what?"

"That movie we were talking about."

"Yeah," she said. "A movie. Did I get the part?"

"Sure. Didn't you get the script?"

"No. What happens next?"

"A little reunion. And then you commit suicide."

Mark was startled to find his wife's office door ajar and the lights off. During scheduled office hours, she kept it wide open. Otherwise, the small room was locked.

He glanced at his watch. He was only twenty minutes late, and she wouldn't have left knowing he didn't have a car. He tapped on the door as he opened it.

"Lex?"

He flipped on the light. Her normally neat office was in disarray, books pulled from the shelves, desk drawers open, papers and magazines scattered across the desktop. The computer was turned on its side, the mouse dangling by its cord halfway to the floor. A splintered pencil protruded from the forehead of the Styrofoam mannequin head he'd given her as a present, upon which she'd drawn a crude diagram of the brain's different lobes.

Scrawled across the foam forehead, in Alexis's handwriting, were the words "Every 4 hrs. or else."

Or else what? If you've harmed her, you bastard, I'll gut you like a frog in biology class.

He heard a purring electronic echo. Her phone was in the room. He found her purse upended behind the desk, the makeup compact, tampons, pens, coins, and car keys scattered across the floor, but it had quit ringing before he could answer.

Alexis was never without her phone. He checked the incoming number but it was blocked.

He jammed the phone in his pocket, swept up the keys, and grabbed the note. He locked the door behind him. A janitor's discovery of the mess might lead to questions.

On the way to the parking deck, he called Burchfield, who answered with a terse greeting. While Mark was part of the inner circle, the senator didn't like people calling without an appointment.

"Senator, we might have a problem with the trials," Mark said, making sure no one was in earshot. People seemed wrapped up in their own concerns and the evening rush hour that awaited them.

"No problems, Mark, everything is under control."

"But is Briggs under control? We knew he would be a big risk factor."

"It's only a risk when you have a choice." Laughter and music leaked from the background, suggesting the senator was at some vitally critical social function. Canapés and Chablis on the taxpayer dole in the name of national security. "Briggs is the only one who can pull it off."

"He's not exactly flying under the radar here. Not when he's dragging in a member of the bioethics council."

"Your wife?"

"Maybe. I don't know yet. But he's playing some kind of game. It's not just for money anymore."

"You're the boots on the ground there, Mark. Control Briggs and control your wife. Do whatever it takes."

Mark wanted to hurl the phone at the concrete pillars of the parking deck. Instead, he said, "Yes, sir."

"And Mark?"

"Yeah?"

"Watch your back."

The senator rang off and Mark took his advice, glancing behind him. After the incident at the airport, he felt exposed and vulnerable. The solid world of company profits, performance bonuses, Washington hobnobbing, and a big house in one of the brain centers of the South had given way to a landscape of ever-shifting horizons and illusory detours.

And a man in a dark jogging suit was now also in that picture.

Mark picked up his pace, wondering where Briggs had taken Alexis. Or if she'd been taken at all.

The man behind him began jogging in his direction. Mark gave one more glance back, and then began running. His hard-soled leather shoes slapped on the concrete, and a young couple eyed him suspiciously as he burst past the rows of cars. He made it to the stairwell before the jogger caught up with him. Mark waited, panting, on the concrete steps.

"Where is she?" Mark asked between gasps.

The jogger wore a stocking cap despite the relatively mild March weather, and it was pulled down to his eyebrows. He was trim, in his mid thirties, and clean-shaven, and had blue eyes that showed no hint of intention. "You're forgetting who you work for, Morgan."

"Christ. You're CRO?"

"Let's just say we're an 'allied interest.'"

"What's with the cloak-and-dagger shit? Why can't you just text me like everyone else?"

"Because they're watching. We have to put on a good show."

"They? There's another level above you guys?"

The eyes didn't harden, but the tone did. "There's a lot more riding on this than Senator Botox and his rumored run for the presidency. Word is that CRO is going to let a few crates of Halcyon slip through the cracks, up through Canada and over to our cave-dwelling friends in Afghanistan. It looks like the first extensive field trials are going to involve U.S. troops."

"No way. CRO is as red, white, and blue as Uncle Sam's Saturday beer."

"The only flag CRO waves is green."

A teenager wielding a backpack shuffled around the turn in the stairs above, either too stoned to find the elevator or else on a misguided bout of self-inflicted physical activity. Mark thought over this new information until the student passed.

"Why should I believe you?" Mark asked.

"Your wife told us."

Mark balled his fists and approached the man. "She's out of this. That's the word from the top."

The man didn't draw back or stiffen from the threat. "You're assuming there's only one top."

"Tell me where she is."

"You're not in a position to make demands, Morgan. In fact, there are some who think you'll have to be moved out of the way after this is over. Even though you don't know as much as you think you do, it's still too much."

"More cloak-and-dagger bullshit. Just tell me what you want and get out of my face."

"We hear Briggs is developing a spinoff. A rage drug."

"Never heard of it." Mark wondered how well he'd hidden the lie.

The man gave a snort of laughter. "I thought we were beyond all that. I thought you were in a hurry."

"What are you? CIA? FBI?"

"I'm with the good guys. We're checking out Briggs, but we need an inside source at CRO to tie this together."

"Do I *look* like the kind of guy who would know what's going on?"

The man looked him over as if deciding whether Mark would walk away breathing, or whether pain might elicit information. "Then maybe you better ask your wife about it."

"I will. As soon as you tell me where she is."

"We want to protect everyone."

"None of you people give a damn about my wife, or any of the people in this. All you want is a piece of Halcyon."

"Halcyon isn't the real issue here. It's the other stuff we want. The Seethe."

"Seethe? What's that?"

"Pray to God you never find out." The man jogged away in an easy, rolling gait, now just another fitness freak putting in miles.

Mark was pretty sure Alexis wasn't home, but he headed for the car anyway. He had something tucked away in the back of the closet shelf he might need.

Roland hit Chapel Hill at about four in the afternoon. The city had a population of 55,000, but its sprawling, wooded nature projected a small-town feel, which led many UNC graduates to stay in the area and often end up working at the university. Roland had wanted to leave after the marriage, but Wendy was reluctant to give up her career track in the art department.

It was just one of many conflicts that had led to their split, but Roland knew somewhere deep in his heart that the seeds of their ruin had been planted in the Monkey House.

Monkey House? Why the hell am I thinking of that?

He'd indulged in a Kurt Vonnegut binge in high school, just as he was discovering the mellow escapism of marijuana, and Vonnegut's story "Welcome to Monkey House" had been one of those mind-altering leaps of consciousness.

The story was based on the old joke of mathematical probability that if you gave a monkey a typewriter and he began pecking at random, eventually he would reproduce the entire works of Shakespeare. In Vonnegut's rendition, the monkeys immediately began cranking out flawless manuscripts.

But he'd read the story a few years before he met Wendy, and there was no reason to link them now. Except for the inescapable realization that the entire world was a crazy primate zoo, and humans were little more than hairless monkeys, only with more murderous habits.

Sure, I read the Vonnegut story, but I wonder if David Underwood did.

He could feel the vial in his pocket, deliberately jammed by the seatbelt so he was constantly aware of its presence. He glanced at the dashboard clock. He was determined to skip the next dose, no matter how distorted his mind became, but he was nearly due.

As he hit the business district, he passed an ABC package store, and the gleaming rows of bottles beckoned him. He licked his lips. The vodka in there would be real.

Wendy.

Roland didn't know why her name would be so clear when all else was fog, but he pictured her face and the craving fell away. He knew that was wrong, that he should seek a higher power instead, but it worked, so maybe that was the power he needed.

By the time he pulled into her apartment complex, his hands were shaking on the wheel and the car was weaving. He slowed and willed the sedan into an empty space, then pulled out the vial.

Should I take one now, or wait until I get inside? And what if she doesn't let me in?

What if I'm David Underwood?

No. Can't be. If I were David, I wouldn't be wondering about it.

He had trouble getting out of the car and the Earth tilted on its axis, threatening to spill him on the pavement. It was like being drunk except he didn't have any of the emotional numbness, the dumb rage, or the thirst for more pain.

A man riding a ten-speed swerved on the sidewalk to avoid him, shouting, "Hey, watch it!" before pedaling away. Roland had to fight an urge to chase the man, drag him from the bicycle, and beat him senseless.

Roland had only been to Wendy's apartment three times. Once, he'd helped her move. The second time, they'd had a serious replay of the breakup, ending up reminiscing and engaging in awkward lovemaking before a final argument. The third time, he'd personally delivered the signed separation agreement.

They'd bumped into one another occasionally because they still shared some of the same haunts, and the awkwardness lingered, as if something had gone unsaid.

And now here he was, turning to the one person who had the least reason to help him. And he wasn't even sure why he was there.

She answered on the third knock, but from behind the closed door and with suspicion. "Who is it?"

He hadn't meant to scare her. He tapped gently this time. "It's Roland."

"Roland who?"

He fought off a rush of anger. "Come on, Wendy."

"Who is this?"

He was about to punch the metal door in frustration, but he couldn't afford to draw any attention. Someone might report his erratic behavior and then he'd be explaining himself to the cops while his brain was peeling itself like an onion. "It's your husband, Wendy. It's important."

He was just about to knock again when the deadbolt clicked. The door parted a few inches, a thick security chain in place. One of Wendy's onyx eyes and half her face appeared in the gap.

"My husband?" she said.

Oh, fuck. They got to you, too, didn't they?

Instead of explaining, he simply held up the orange bottle and showed her the label. "We need to talk."

Kleingarten peeled off the latex gloves.

Hand rubbers. I hope she wasn't carrying anything.

He'd left her in the cell in the back of the Monkey House, a few doors down from David Underwood's hellhole. Anita's walls were tricked out with the same kind of freakish collages, except hers were more colorful—photographs of autopsies, gaping flesh wounds, and invasive surgeries.

Mixed in with the gore were lewd images of every conceivable kind of coupling, including one that looked like two women and a hairless dog, but Kleingarten hadn't checked closely enough to be certain.

Anita had felt damned good in his arms, despite her being a slut, but entering the room had sickened him enough that he'd dumped her on the cot and backed away. Briggs must have been watching from the monitors, because he immediately started a syncopated overhead light show of red and orange bulbs.

A soundtrack started, and it took a moment for Kleingarten to recognize it. He'd heard his share of porn voice-overs, where the actors pretended to groan and grunt in pleasure, and this sounded like a dozen of them stacked on top of one another and mixed together into one huge orgy.

Kleingarten hurried through the main alley toward Briggs's cage, anxious to get paid and get the hell out of there. As he reached the opening of the cage, he was struck by the impression that Briggs was just as much a monkey as the others, except Briggs was in his cage voluntarily.

"That thing about fear," Kleingarten said. "I'm starting to figure out your game."

Briggs looked away from the bank of video monitors, which were now divided between images of Anita and images of David Underwood. Briggs seemed annoyed at the intrusion, but like a true egghead, he never passed up a chance for a lecture.

"We each have a greatest fear," Briggs said. "And in some ways, your fear is also your greatest strength. When you overcome it, then you are ready for a higher purpose."

"You make people scared with your joy juice, and then you hook them on the pills so they forget they're afraid. Sort of like crack. The first hit is always free."

Briggs narrowed his eyes in a gesture of consideration that might have signaled respect. "If you can both induce fear and eliminate fear, you could help people control themselves. But fear is also our friend, a survival mechanism. Take Anita Molkesky here."

Briggs pointed to the screen that showed Anita sprawled on the cot, undulating in a faint but clearly sensual motion. Her eyes were closed and she seemed lights-out oblivious, and Kleingarten wondered how many brain cells Briggs's medicine chewed up and spat out in the process.

"Anita is afraid of abandonment," Briggs said. "It's so classically Freudian that it's too easy. Father left when she was seven, mother had a string of bad boyfriends. She wasn't molested, which was truly a miracle given the opportunities and cast of characters, but she formed an unhealthy need to seek attention and approval from this revolving cast of losers."

"So she started screwing for money?"

"You don't understand. This isn't about sex or pleasure or reward of any kind. In her pornography work, she doesn't display any enthusiasm."

Kleingarten recalled the disgusting scene in *Patti Cake Patti Cake* where two men and a woman had rubbed chocolate batter all over Anita's body and licked half of it off while plugging every hole in her body with different kitchen implements. Anita had uttered a few grunts and groans, although she might just as well have been complaining about a headache. But she went through the motions just fine and everybody got their money shots.

"No, Mr. Drummond, to Anita, it's all about acceptance. She is an exhibitionist because she expects to be rejected. She was a model who took her clothes off because her body was the one thing that no one rejected."

"She's sweet stuff, all right," Kleingarten said, then laid out his bait: "But the Sla—I mean, Wendy Leng—she's a lot hotter."

Briggs glared at him, and then glanced at the nude charcoal drawing. "Wendy's beauty radiates from the inside. She has the soul of an artist."

Kleingarten wondered why Briggs simply didn't have him just kidnap the Slant, drug her, and then tie her up in one of those cells where he could work his magic.

This game was getting way more complicated than the pay was worth. Still, it was tax-free, and if not for this gig, Kleingarten would probably be working as a bodyguard for some rich-kid drug dealer.

Movement on one of the corner monitors caught his eye. "What's that?"

Briggs huddled over the keyboard and clacked until the camera zoomed in. The monitor showed the outside perimeter of the lot, and a guy in a jogging suit was huffing and blowing, moving through the pine trees on a narrow trail that followed a creek.

"Penetration," Briggs said.

"Is that one of your people?"

"I don't have any 'people.' Except you."

Kleingarten wanted to lecture the egghead for a change, tell him that you didn't go engaging in double-crosses and setups unless you had a few layers of insulation. Instead, he touched the 9mm in his shoulder holster. "Guy must not be able to read. He just ran past a 'No Trespassing' sign."

"And the gate closed after you came through?"

"That's what you told me to check, right?"

"It's probably nothing."

Some egghead. The way Kleingarten did math, probability was measured on a scale between "Dead certainty" and "Don't take the chance."

"Want me to check it out for you?"

"Okay, but act like you're a security guard patrolling the property. Don't make him suspicious. I'll unlock the back door."

Briggs bent over his series of switches and buttons, hitting a couple.

Kleingarten wended through a series of wenches with hooked cables, once used for lifting motors, until he came to the emergency exit. The inside of the door had no handle, which probably worked great at keeping factory workers from playing hooky back in the old days.

He oriented himself to determine the location of the jogger and began strolling as if he were a bored plainclothes guard.

Most real security guards wore little uniforms to make them feel good and to intimidate those who equated a brass badge with authority. Kleingarten had a few like the campus-cop uniform hanging in his closet back home, but today he'd just have to fake it.

The spring air was crisp but not cold, and pine needles squeaked under his new leather shoes. He reached the creek, which was little more than a drainage ditch with a slimy green trickle of fluid ruining through it. A path meandered parallel to it, probably used by the wildlife that was fenced in on the twenty-acre compound, unaware they were imprisoned.

Kleingarten transferred the 9mm to his jacket pocket in case he needed a quick response. By his calculations, the jogger should be visible between the corrugated brown tree trunks any moment now.

After an enforced casual stroll of more than a minute, Kleingarten was antsy. *Ease up. The guy probably was winded and needed to catch his breath.*

Yeah, and he also accidentally climbed over a ten-foot fence topped with barbed wire.

Kleingarten gave it another minute, picking up his pace, before he decided to hustle back to the Monkey House. He reconstructed the image of the jogger in his mind, searching for possible clues. The man wore one of those hooded gray tops, a little baggy, so he could be packing. His jogging pants were the faggoty, snug sateen kind with no bulges in the wrong places, so no weapons were stuffed in there.

He was a little out of breath by the time he'd looped back through the trees, leaving the path so he could take cover. The jogger was standing outside the back door, running in place, the way those adrenaline junkies did when they were punishing themselves for taking a little break.

Kleingarten wasn't sure how to play it. If he let the guy run away, then Kleingarten would have to give chase, and his feet were already killing him. Best-case scenario, he'd get the guy's car tags, but if the jogger was a pro, the plate would be stolen or forged anyway.

Option Two was to see if the guy tried to break in, which meant he knew a little something, but probably not enough, or else he would have taken a different avenue into the factory. Like maybe getting a job like Kleingarten did, asking around, doing a little research.

No, this guy knew just enough to be dumb. And therefore he was dangerous.

On the other hand, the guy could be on the Home Team, paid by the same handlers as Kleingarten, except without Briggs's knowledge. That made the most sense, because somebody obviously had a lot invested in the Monkey House. And if that investment was riding on a wild card like Briggs, it was good business to see which other cards were in the hand or up the sleeve.

Okay, so we play it "pro to pro." That will cut the bullshit about me having to pretend to be a security guard and him having to pretend to be a lost jogger.

Kleingarten emerged from the woods. "Howdy," he said, trying to sound like a dumb-ass Southerner instead of a California ex-con.

The jogger quit with the leg-pumping-in-place and let out an exhausted pant. "Hey. I was running through the woods and saw this old building. What was it, a school?"

Yeah, right, a school that only has windows thirty feet above the ground.

"Nah." Kleingarten kept approaching, steadily, the nine in his palm but still tucked into the jacket pocket. "It's a secret research lab."

The jogger gave a "just guys" grin and wiped sweat from his forehead. "Ha, that's a good one. Like on that TV show, *Twenty-Four*, right? Kiefer Sutherland?"

"Yeah, just like that." Kleingarten had never seen the show, but it sounded stupid as shit.

A drop of sweat slid down the jogger's nose and dangled at the tip. "Nice day to be outside, huh?"

"Nice day to be on private property."

The jogger frowned. "CRO?"

"Hell, no," Kleingarten lied. "I'm with the Feds."

"Then you shouldn't know this is a secret research lab."

"And neither should you, I reckon."

The man made his move then—or maybe he was just reaching up to wipe that itchy drop of sweat from his nose—and Kleingarten reacted at the first twitch. If he was a Fed, he was poorly trained, and if he was a lone op like Kleingarten, he wasn't cut out for the job anyway.

Kleingarten had his nine out and smoking in less than a second, and the jogger gave a girlish squeal as blooms of red erupted on his chest.

Kleingarten knelt over the corpse, wondering what sort of gun the amateur was carrying in the pouch of his hoodie. *Probably a .357 Magnum. That's what guys pack when they watch too much TV.*

All he found was a water bottle.

"I'll be damned," Kleingarten said.

At least he'd discovered that the secret research lab was not so secret, so it wasn't like the murder had been a total waste.

CHAPTER TWENTY-SIX

"These are the same pills," Roland said, avoiding looking around Wendy's apartment because he was afraid of how much she'd changed without him.

"How the hell do you know?" Wendy said. "A green pill is a green pill. Unless you want to have the cops run a test."

"Be cool, Wendy," Alexis said. "If this is what we think it is—"

"No. If we go down that road, we don't come back."

Alexis, sitting on the sofa beside Wendy, took a tight grip on Wendy's forearms and pulled her hands from her face. "We can't hide anymore."

Wendy was nearly in tears, and Alexis was afraid if the dam burst, there would be no patching the pieces back together. The friends had drifted apart after Susan's death, but that had been an instinctive act of survival, not a conscious decision.

They had all stayed aware of one another, bound by the understanding that they held a collective fate in their hands. Any of them could break the code of silence at any time. But none of them seemed to remember it in exactly the same way.

Roland, standing by the locked door, shook his head at Alexis. His sudden appearance had served to unsettle Wendy even more. And, just like during the trials, Alexis now felt responsible, as if she'd let things go too far through her own fascination with untapped landscapes of the brain.

"All right, Wendy," Alexis said, hating herself for lapsing into the cold, academic bitch she knew slept inside her. "Let's look at the facts. We each got the same vial with the same pills and the same prescription. And you said Anita got them, too. That makes four of us."

"Where's David Underwood, then?" Wendy said.

"Right here," Roland said, and they both glared at him. He fumbled in his back pocket and pulled out his license and flipped it toward Alexis. It knocked over the three pill bottles they had placed on the coffee table.

Alexis retrieved it from the carpet and studied it. Roland's face and David Underwood's name.

"He's back," Alexis said.

"But why?" Wendy said. "He's got more to lose than any of us."

"You know why," Roland said.

Wendy burst from the couch and lunged at him, delivering a solid slap to his cheek. He reacted in time to catch her wrist as she began clawing at his eyes.

"Don't blame me because you fucked him," Roland said. "I forgave you, remember?"

"Oh, hell, no, you didn't," Wendy said, shrieking and kicking. "If you forgive, you're supposed to *forget*!"

Alexis hurried to help Roland restrain her, but Wendy seemed to have the strength of ten, just like the drug-war horror stories about arrests of criminals high on angel dust. But Wendy was fueled by an even deeper toxin: her own rage, fear, and shame.

Alexis took an elbow in the abdomen before trapping one of Wendy's arms, and by then Roland had wrapped her in a bear hug and was carrying her to the bedroom. "Grab something to tie her with, quick!"

Alexis opened the hall closet and found a couple of scarves dangling from a coat rack, along with an Ace bandage on the shelf. She carried them to the bedroom, where a wailing Wendy was now pinned to the bed by her ex, who straddled her and dodged her kicks. Heeding an unspoken command, she secured Wendy's feet at the ankles with the Ace bandage, then helped Roland bind her wrists.

Wendy let loose a stream of expletives loud enough to be heard outside the apartment.

"You fucking bastard," Wendy yelled at Roland. "I knew I should have got a restraining order."

"Like a piece of paper's going to undo the past?"

"Roland, please," Alexis said, pissed off at having to be the responsible one. "She's vulnerable right now and everything's raw. You know what the trials do."

"'Do'? You say that like they're still going on."

Alexis ignored him, leaning over Wendy to stroke her hair. "Hush, honey, or we'll have to use this scarf on your mouth, and we don't want to do that."

"Bitch," Wendy said, and spat.

Alexis wiped the gob of saliva from her forehead, triggering a flash of recollection: *Susan, nearly biting her face when Alexis had tried to calm her down.*

"Do it," Roland said. "She's no help in this condition, anyway."

Alexis wrapped the scarf around one palm and aimed toward Wendy's thrashing head. Roland was still perched atop her in an odd position that suggested sexual domination, but Alexis shook the image away and concentrated on her task. Wendy emitted one last scream before Alexis wriggled the impromptu, clumsy gag in place.

"Okay, now get me some duct tape," Roland said. "Look in her art stuff. She always has some around."

By the time Alexis had found the roll of gray tape and returned to the room, Wendy was a little more subdued. Roland took the tape from Alexis and held it close to Wendy's wide, dark eyes. "You know I'll use this if I have to," he said, a startling menace behind his words. "I've done it before."

Wendy closed her eyes and fell still, her chest rising and falling rapidly in her exertion.

"God, Roland, it's all happening again," Alexis said. "We're not like this, are we? Please, God, don't let us be like this."

"That never happened," he said, getting off the bed. "No matter what anybody says, we could never commit murder."

"She fell, didn't she?"

"Sure. That's what I heard. What about you?"

Alexis felt herself nodding, although it was the motion of a marionette directed by high, unseen strings. "It was an accident."

He glanced at his watch. "I'm fifteen minutes past due. Better take my medicine. Or else."

Wendy's phone rang in the living room. They both looked at her, restrained on the bed. The trials had barely begun and already she looked a manic wreck.

She might be the next Susan, Alexis thought, relishing a shiver of triumph. *Not me.*

"Should we answer it?" Roland asked her.

She was pleased at the deference. Despite his male strength and suppressed anger, she was the acknowledged leader. The graduate assistant all over again. The responsible one. She only hoped she could do a better job this time.

"Sure," she heard herself say. "We have nothing to fear but fear itself."

"And each other."

She let that one pass.

CHAPTER TWENTY-SEVEN

"We lost our man," Burchfield said, closing his cell phone. "So much for eyes on the ground."

"What happened?" Wallace Forsyth said, only half-listening. He'd been staring off at the tip of the Washington Monument in the distance, wondering why no terrorist had ever targeted it.

They were on their way along Pennsylvania Avenue to a caucus meeting, and since Forsyth was not yet a registered lobbyist, he was free to wield his influence as he wished.

He was a little old for a cabinet position, but if Burchfield took the White House, Forsyth wouldn't mind an advisory role. Somebody had to keep an eye on the Supreme Court, after all.

"He touched base after shaking down Mark Morgan, said he was heading for reconnaissance of the Monkey House posing as a jogger," Burchfield said. "It must have gone bad. Either that, or he got some goods and jumped ship."

Forsyth snapped alert. "You mean, he stole Halcyon?"

Burchfield nodded. "You never served on the health committee, but these companies run high-stakes con games on each other all the time. That's why there's so much pressure to beat everybody else to a patent, because usually everybody's neck and neck. There are more spies in the corporate world than in the world of political espionage."

"Your own staff member would double-cross you like that?"

"Sure, if the price was right. And he's not just on my payroll, he's officially on the books as a CIA consultant. We're not the only ones who work both sides of the fence. It's a pain in the ass, but we're all grazing the same pasture."

Wallace grunted. "That's what's wrong with Washington these days. You can't even buy loyalty anymore."

Burchfield thumbed his phone, clicking out a text message. "Riordan probably had some loyalty that ran deeper than a dollar. These agents sometimes forget which side of the fence they're on."

"What would he do with Halcyon if he had it?"

"The CIA would hustle it over to whichever company they're in bed with this time. CelQuest, Genesis Laboratories, BTDM, could be any one of the majors. They crack the compound and roll it into whatever they are already doing, so it looks like a new discovery. No proof that the formula was stolen, because it's a new formula."

"You don't sound too worried about it."

"Riordan will be easy to find. When a donkey breaks out of its pen, it usually stands around just beyond the fence, not understanding it's now free. The fence is what defines him, no matter which side he's on. Riordan will jump back through the same old hoops again and he'll turn up before you know it."

"And the other option?"

Burchfield concentrated on his text, hit "Send," and looked at Forsyth for the first time since they'd left his Georgetown condo. "That would be the one I'm worried about. It means Briggs is on the ball and won't be so easy to maneuver. He knows what his drugs can do...and that this is a legacy-maker."

"I thought this Briggs fellow was damaged goods. He doesn't have any career."

"That's why he's dangerous. He has nothing to lose. And Riordan is a desk jockey, a corporate snoop, not a muscle guy. His cover might have been blown, and he wouldn't have been prepared for violence. Maybe we're all underestimating Briggs and CRO."

"I thought Mark Morgan was in your pocket," Forsyth said. "That gives you CRO."

"Maybe, but it doesn't give me Briggs. If the CIA is in on the rage drug, the lid may blow off the volcano."

"Dear Sweet Lord Almighty," Forsyth said, instantly grasping the implications. A part of him had thought Burchfield's Afghanistan plan was a little pie-in-the-sky, but maybe other people were having similar ideas, only with different targets and agendas.

"We need this before any other agencies get their hands on it," Burchfield said. "I just don't think we can trust anybody to do the right thing anymore."

The gleaming dome of the Capitol Building loomed ahead, and despite the traffic, Winston was making good time. Dark limousines slid through the tide like sharks skimming through schools of lower members of the food chain.

"How many other people do you have on the job?" Forsyth asked. He didn't think Burchfield would trust a lone operative on something this important, though every additional person involved meant a doubling of the risk factor.

"One more, but he's working through CRO. He flushed Roland Doyle back to the Triangle, just to make sure he didn't take a detour."

"You said half a dozen were tied up in this. How come Briggs needs all of them?"

"Everybody reacts differently. Briggs needs to understand the range of reactions if we want any degree of predictability. And I don't want to let this stuff loose in Al-Qaeda country until I know what's in Pandora's box."

"Hardly seems American, dosing our own boys with this stuff."

"Think of the greater good, Wallace. Afghanistan will blame Pakistan, and India has to do something. China's sitting up there waiting. Of course, Israel will stick its bulldog face in the mess. If we're lucky, we've got Muslims killing Hindus and Buddhists killing atheists, and Uncle Sam rides in like the cavalry."

"It sounds like the revelations," Forsyth said. "Wars, pestilence, famine, and one horned beast on the seat of power."

"Damn, Wallace, I'm almost starting to believe you're sincere. But don't say that stuff in public. People will label you a wacko and I need you for the presidential run."

Forsyth gritted his dentures. He'd originally backed Burchfield because Burchfield had promised to allow churches to receive federal funds for charitable purposes, which Forsyth felt was the next step toward getting school prayer before the Supreme Court.

Burchfield hinted that a couple of the more liberal justices were due for some ill health that would force them to step down. Forsyth knew from his own political background that timing was everything when it came to paradigm shifts, and wise use of these potions could help shape the next administration. And in a world weakened by war, that administration could be very influential indeed.

And if Burchfield saw a more prominent role for Christianity in government, such a push was sorely needed. When the angels poured out the seven vials of God's wrath upon the world, the Lord would need foot soldiers, not just a white horse and a sword and the strong arm of righteousness.

Burchfield pressed the "Call" button on the back of the driver's seat. Winston's voice came through a tinny speaker. "Yes, sir?"

"Change of itinerary," Burchfield ordered. "We're heading south on I-95."

"Yes, sir."

"South?" Forsyth asked.

"North Carolina's a five-hour drive. We take a plane, everyone will know we're coming. This way, it's like a surprise party."

Forsyth wasn't sure he liked Burchfield's grin. But he found himself curious about these mysterious drugs that corrupted people's minds and eroded their will. When Burchfield had exhausted its military and corporate applications, perhaps it could have a place in Forsyth's arsenal for the bigger battleground.

After all, Armageddon was also a matter of timing.

Chapter Twenty-Eight

"Help me, hurry, we're in the factory where we killed Susan."

Roland stared at the dead cell phone, contemplating several reactions. He wanted to hurl the phone against the wall, but he no longer trusted his instinct. And a small part of him wanted to race into the bedroom and pummel Wendy with his fists. Not for any particular reason he could think of, but just because she was the latest contestant in the Blame Game.

"What was that all about?" Alexis said. She was visibly nervous, picking at her fingernails.

"They have Anita. They're waiting in the Monkey House."

Alexis sat down hard. "That place wasn't real!"

"Shut the fuck up," Roland said, and she looked at him, blue eyes wide. He realized his hands were clenched into trembling fists and he immediately opened them, cool air enveloping his sweating fingers.

"Sorry," he said. "It's happening."

Alexis pointed to the three pill bottles on the coffee table. "Take your Halcyon. This could get ugly fast."

"I'm afraid to take it," he said. "I don't even know what the hell it is."

"You're on Seethe, Roland."

"Seethe?" The word rang a distant alarm in Roland's head, but it was in a mental vault he didn't want to enter.

"The trigger. The drug that stimulates fear response. Seethe shocks the amygdala and floods the nervous system with neurochemicals."

He couldn't avoid sarcasm. "Thanks, Doctor. Maybe *you* were sleeping with Briggs, too."

She was angry, but Roland didn't care. If she had a hand in all this, maybe she should have been the one to die instead of Susan. But maybe it wasn't too late to set things right.

"Look, I was just a young researcher fascinated by the potential. I didn't know what was going on. It all appeared so…legitimate."

"Since you're the only one who remembers Seethe, what exactly does this shit do and how can I get it out of my head?"

Alexis rubbed her mouth, face twisted in concentration as she struggled to remember. "He had an injected form back then, but it needed an amplifier. That's why the trials were set up to shock us, to see how far over the edge we would go."

"And then he'd give us Halcyon to float us back from la-la land without remembering a thing?"

Alexis nodded. She bit her thumbnail, tearing off a ragged piece. She spat it out and said, "Halcyon is temporary, but Seethe is permanent."

Roland thought of all his drunken blackouts and wondered what acts he might have committed. He could have been Seething all along and never even known it. "You mean this shit's been sleeping in our brains for ten years?"

"Briggs has probably been planning this for a long time, and he finally found the backers to help him pull it off."

“Who are these ‘backers’?”

“I don’t know, but they must have deep resources if they can move us around like chess pieces.”

Roland picked up the closest vial and read: “D. Underwood.”

“What if I got the wrong pills?” Roland said.

What if I killed that woman in Cincinnati? I know I’m capable. Because I helped do it to Susan.

“You need to take it now, Roland,” Alexis said.

“Or else I’ll remember?” he asked.

“Yeah. It could get ugly. And we don’t know what we’ll turn into, what we might become…”

Or what we already are. Like maybe both of us are murderers and we don’t know it.

“We better tell Wendy,” he said.

“And then we find Anita.”

“No. Goddamn it, can’t you see that’s just what he wants? All his little monkeys back in their cages?”

“We have to stop him.”

“Yeah.” Roland glanced at the door as if expecting arrest just for thinking about it. “The cops are out of it, because we all have normal, happy lives now. Well, except me. And there’s no statute of limitations on murder.”

“I need to call Mark.”

“Mark?”

“My husband.”

“Damn. I forgot.”

“He’s with CRO Pharmaceuticals and they have connections. Maybe we can—”

“What did you say?” The red rage was simmering at the edges of his vision again, like sheets of rain building to a hurricane.

“Mark can help us.”

"CRO," he said, half to himself. "Those initials were in Cincinnati."

"Cincinnati? What's in Cincinnati?"

"The last person I killed."

She came at him then, her fingernails raised like the talons of a wildcat. "We're not killers, goddamn it. *Shut up.*"

Wendy's muffled voice grunted from the bedroom doorway, and she awkwardly ran toward them, hands bound behind her. Her shin hit the coffee table, knocking over the remaining two bottles, and she lowered her head and charged toward Roland like a missile. He fought an urge to drive his knee up into her face.

Instead, he stepped to the side and gave a small shove to her shoulder that sent her sprawling on the carpet. As she rolled over, Alexis jumped him, clinging to his back.

"Get off," he yelled, bucking and flinging her toward the couch. She fell a little short and slammed into the armrest. She spat out a *whoof* and rolled away, curling into a ball.

Roland backed into a corner and crouched. Now he knew how a caged tiger felt when those maniacs with their whips and chairs closed in.

But he wasn't going down without taking a piece of—

He looked down at the orange bottle, which he'd gripped so tightly that the plastic was cracked.

Take one every 4 hrs. or else.

"It's the Seethe," he whispered.

Then, aloud, so the two women could hear him. "It's the Seethe!"

A neighbor banged on the wall, the urban demand for "Quiet, goddamn it," and Roland focused on the throbbing spot where Alexis had banged the back of his head.

The pain helped him calm down. He was clammy, sweating, and hyperventilating, but he'd beaten the Seethe this time.

This time.

He gobbled down his pill and went to untie Wendy.

CHAPTER TWENTY-NINE

Sebastian Briggs was annoyed at the unwanted complication, and he was beginning to resent the hefty henchman CRO had hired for him. Kleingarten had been innovative in dosing and then inducing emotional trauma in the four subjects. But now Kleingarten had outlived his usefulness. The murder of the intruder had been the turning point.

Kleingarten stood outside over the intruder's body as if it were a bag of garbage waiting for disposal. "What do you want me to do with it?"

"The creek," Briggs said. "There's a concrete drain on the far end of the property. Stuff him in there and make some crows and raccoons happy."

"He might be a Fed. And somebody's going to notice when he doesn't check in."

"That's not your concern, Mr. Drummond," Briggs said, maintaining the pretense of the false identity.

"Sure, it is. Your bosses hired me to protect their interests, and that's what I'm doing."

"My guests will be arriving soon, and we can't afford any unwanted attention."

Kleingarten nudged the corpse with his foot. "That's why I'm taking care of business."

Briggs gave an absent nod. He might as well have been talking to the brick wall of the Monkey House. He surveyed the forest that surrounded the facility. The pines had grown taller and thicker since the original trials, and tangles of vines gave the property a wild, unkempt appearance.

And just as the vegetation had run its natural course, Seethe had slowly infiltrated his subjects, twisting and growing.

Of course, the human brain was a complicated organ, and he hadn't been as skilled and experienced ten years ago when he'd planted the chemical time bombs. Each subject could present a unique set of symptoms. But that was part of the fun, too.

Even experimental failure added to the canon of knowledge, so failure was a different type of success. Not that he expected either CRO or Senator Burchfield to be happy with that explanation, nor the increasing cast of characters that were sniffing around at the rumors.

"Okay," Briggs said. "Once you dispose of the body, we're done for a while."

"I don't know. You can manage the two women, probably, but this Roland guy seems a little unhinged."

"Don't worry. I'll have your final payment, and CRO will send your bonus once Halcyon is approved."

"You're forgetting something."

Briggs was growing impatient. "What's that?"

"I know where this place is," Kleingarten said, eyes narrowing. "I'm not sure what's going on in there, except you're fucking with some people's heads, and I don't really care. But I don't think the major players are just going to let me walk away."

"Ah, so you need some sort of insurance policy."

"Yeah."

Briggs pondered the possibility of keeping Kleingarten around. It was a little after four in the afternoon, and if he'd calculated correctly, then Roland, Wendy, and Alexis should be able to find the Monkey House by dusk, about the same time they would deplete their Halcyon.

He preferred to work alone, but David Underwood had already gone wild once, and the one reliable clinical outcome of Seethe was that it achieved unexpected results. Anything might happen.

"How about this, Mr. Drummond? I have a nice payoff coming from my employers. You stay on as my personal bodyguard and I will pay you double."

"On top of the CRO money?"

"You want insurance. I have the Halcyon formula. And as long as I have Halcyon, I'm safe. But I'm only safe as long as everyone involved knows that. So I need you to tell our bosses."

Kleingarten nodded, eyes shifting as if he were processing that information. "I get it, Doc. You want me to give a report on you, tell CRO you have the formula in your head, something like that? So word gets around?"

Briggs looked down at the dead man, who was beginning to exhibit some morbidity. "I'd hate to jog down the wrong path."

"Yeah. I can see that." Kleingarten grinned, his lips greasy and cracked. "Don't worry, I got your back."

That's what I'm worried about. But I have another bonus waiting for you, Martin Kleingarten, a.k.a. Mr. Drummond.

"Let's make the place presentable, because company is on the way," Briggs said, heading toward the steel door. By the time he entered the Monkey House, Kleingarten was dragging the body away with a scuffing of dead leaves.

Briggs navigated the corridors between the rusted, hulking rows of machinery. In the original trials, he'd let the subjects run free, because they had been willing subjects with no reason to run away. This time, they would be wary. At least for a while.

Once the Seethe set in, though, they'd be too busy turning on each other to worry about freedom.

He walked the eighty yards to the back of the building where he'd had the cells constructed, employing Mexicans without visas who were only too happy to work for cash and who were unlikely to talk to authorities about the place. The surveillance system had been a little trickier, but CRO had called in some favors with allied companies and built it to Briggs's specifications.

The electricity and water connections had even been moved to the perimeter of the property, just beyond the fence, so that meter readers would have no reason to explore the grounds.

From David Underwood's cell came the plaintive strains of his theme song, "Home on the Range." Every broken lunatic needed a theme song. But his condition wasn't really David's fault. He'd been Seething for two full years, and though Briggs had finally refined the Halcyon formula through persistent trial and error, David would go into the books as an experimental failure. Just like Susan Sharpe.

Briggs could have monitored the cells from his office, but soon the Monkey House would be crowded, and he wanted to enjoy one last peaceful moment with his veteran subject.

He tapped out the code on the electronic lock and eased the metal door open. The thousands of eyes glared at him from the walls.

David was huddled on his cot, but his head lifted at the noise. "Mom?"

"No," Briggs said. "It's Susan."

David pushed himself back hard enough to knock his skull against the wall. "You're dead," he said.

"No, David. That's the Seethe talking. That drug Dr. Briggs gave us. Remember?"

The way David violently shook his head suggested that he did not, in fact, remember. "We killed you. Go away."

"I'm sorry you feel that way, David. I thought you liked me."

David balled his fists and jammed them hard against his eye sockets. "*Go away, go away, go away*!"

"Okay, David. But our friends are coming. Roland and Alexis. And Wendy. Do you remember them?"

"*They're dead, too-ooo*," David wailed.

The poor man. If he'd had a stronger constitution, he might have resisted the Seethe. But the chemical worked on the primitive brain, and in that neurotoxic swamp of fear, there were few defenses. The world would find that out soon enough. It was time they all met the enemy within.

"I'm sorry you feel that way, David. Now get some rest, and if you're a good boy, I'll bring you some Halcyon soon and you can forget all about it."

David nodded and whimpered.

Briggs closed the door. It was time to visit Anita.

She wasn't Wendy, but she would have to do for now.

CHAPTER THIRTY

"Do you think you can drive?" Alexis asked, looking at the final pill in her bottle and the apartment walls that now seemed like a prison.

"Sure," Roland said. "I've had a lot of practice driving drunk. This can't be any harder."

He'd calmed down considerably, his jittery rage giving way to a placid, almost dull resignation in the wake of his final dose. Alexis studied the way he tended to Wendy, displaying a gentleness that masked the raging monster he'd been only ten minutes before.

Despite her horror and shock, Alexis was impressed by the efficacy Briggs had achieved with his Halcyon formula. If the drug went legit, it could ease the suffering of many people, not just the military veterans that were the intended patients. Rape, car crashes, and random violence often created long-term debilitating effects on the victims, and if science could alter or suppress the impact of those memories, it would be a welcome act of compassion.

But where was the boundary? How far into their heads could Halcyon reach, and how many memories, both good and bad, might be raked away with all the indifference of an orbitoclast jammed into an eye socket to peel away a frontal lobe?

Wendy rubbed the circulation back into her wrists after Roland released her bonds.

"He wants us to go back to the lab."

"What lab?" Roland said.

"The Monkey House," Alexis said.

Roland looked from one to the other, then back to Wendy. "What's she talking about?"

Wendy stood shakily and took Roland's hands. "Roland, you have to trust me."

He nodded without conviction. "I always trusted you, Wendy."

"He doesn't remember," Alexis said. "Not like we do."

"Are we going to forget, too?" Wendy asked.

"We're on staggered schedules," Alexis said. "Briggs must have counted on one of us freaking out at any given time."

She was thirty-five minutes from her final dose. She didn't want to think of the sprawling, open-ended nightmare that lay beyond that last pill.

Briggs must have been so close back then. If Susan hadn't fallen down those stairs, Briggs would have been hailed as a genius.

Of course, the success would have been a keystone to Alexis's own career, especially if she'd coauthored the research. The amygdala was the secret center where fear, sex, and food combined, a mysterious and complex stew of electrical connections and chemistry that offered endless opportunities.

It should have been mine. And now I'll lose everything.

"So we go to this Monkey House," Roland said. "Then what?"

"We find Anita," Wendy said.

"This is getting confusing," Roland said. "Who's Anita?"

"Roland, please," Wendy began, face creasing in anger. Wendy was two hours from her final dose, and if the cortisol rush was already invading her, she might become a liability. And Alexis wasn't sure she wanted more liabilities.

We learned how to deal with liabilities ten years ago. You always have to get rid of the weak link in the chain.

"Roland, I know this is hard to understand," Alexis said. "But you've just taken a drug that suppresses traumatic memories. That's why Wendy wants you to trust her."

He shook his head. "I feel more or less normal. There was… something in Cincinnati, and I had to come here."

"You didn't come here," Alexis said. "You were lured. Shepherded by Sebastian Briggs."

"You've lost me," he said. "Monkey House, Briggs, Anita. I don't know what the hell's going on."

Wendy limped to the wall, favoring her right leg. She removed a charcoal sketch pinned against the drywall with thumb tacks. She carried it to Roland, who peered at the nude figure.

"That's Anita," Wendy said.

"She was with us in the trials," Alexis said. "You, me, Wendy, and Anita. And the *real* David Underwood. Whatever happened to David?"

"Don't forget Susan," Wendy said.

Bitch. Wendy Leng had always wanted the project to fail. First she'd tried to coerce Roland, and when that didn't work, the little yellow slut had mated with Briggs. That was a violation of every ethical code in the book, and some that were unwritten.

"We don't talk about Susan," Alexis said. "No matter what. Susan didn't happen."

"Am I going to have to tie *you* up?" Roland said to Alexis.

She could feel the tension and anger gripping her face. "You'd have to carry me to the car, and the neighbors might notice. We don't need cops."

Roland shrugged. "I have a feeling they're after me for something anyway."

"Come on," Wendy said, leading the way to the door. "We have to save her."

The early-evening sunlight cast ocher and orange light into the trees. Alexis shielded her eyes against the glare. The parking lot was like an alien landscape, the windows of the cars glittering needles of fire.

"This way," Roland said, pushing past Wendy. "But one of you better know the way to the lab or we're lost."

"I do," Alexis said. She glanced at her watch. "But only for eighteen more minutes or so."

She wasn't sure how well Briggs had timed the doses. In the original trials, both Seethe and Halcyon had reaction times that varied by a couple of hours. And each subject had responded differently.

If he'd been working on the formulas for ten years, there was no telling what sort of refinements he'd made. And part of her, a sick, grasping, ambitious part, knew she should have been there.

Halcyon has evident value, but what about Seethe? Wouldn't you love to play with that one? Exploring the most primitive impulses of the brain would open up limitless avenues of research and knowledge. What would the bioethics council think of you then, when you were the one pushing the boundaries?

Fuck the council. I'd dose their asses and laugh while they Stooge-slapped each other with their journal publications.

Oh, yes, "Seethe" had been a good name for it. She could almost feel the blood boiling in her veins.

She looked at the last pill in her hand. All she had to do was get rid of Wendy and Roland, and she could have Wendy's pill to herself. It might grant her a window of opportunity to synthesize the Halcyon and perhaps break its formula.

Then it would be Alexis Morgan and not Sebastian Briggs who would change the world.

And maybe I can trick Wendy and Roland into getting rid of Briggs for me.

"Lex?" Wendy said.

Alexis pulled herself from the murderous reverie and looked down the flight of steps. Roland was already behind the wheel of a blue sedan, and Wendy was standing beside the open passenger-side door.

Time was already slipping away.

But maybe there would be a better chance later.

From the back seat, as Roland pulled onto the highway following her directions, Alexis asked Wendy for a piece of paper. "I don't remember the road names, but I can draw a map from off the highway," she said. "Then it will be up to you, Wendy. Roland and I won't be much help."

Wendy turned, her frightened eyes just at the level of the seat. "What do we do when we get there?"

"Don't worry about that," Roland said. "We'll think of something, babe."

Wendy touched his arm with affection, and it triggered a rush of feeling inside Alexis.

Mark. How could I have forgotten him? Are the drugs already changing me that much?

"Can I borrow your phone?" she asked Wendy.

"No calls," Roland said. "These people seem to be one step ahead of us, all the way. We can't trust anybody right now."

"I need to call my husband."

Roland glanced at her in the rearview mirror. "I didn't know you were married."

He'd been at the wedding. They'd all been acquaintances then, if not friends, bound by a force they couldn't define. Now Alexis understood their involuntary denial—the Halcyon had dulled their awareness, but the memory of the original trials must have hibernated deep in their unconsciousness. They were like survivors of a bloody war in which they still weren't sure which side had won.

"Mark can help us," Alexis said. "He's got sources at CRO that can—"

Roland nearly ran off the highway as he slammed on the brakes and pulled to the shoulder of NC 501. Impatient homebound commuters blared horns as they passed.

"Goddamn, Roland, you nearly killed us," Wendy said, with the bickering familiarity of a long-time couple.

But Roland was nearly over the seat, reaching for Alexis. She shrank away. The Halcyon was supposed to suppress the rage and fear, but cracks showed in Roland's face.

God, what if the compounds are merging? What if it all clashes together in a hot ball of crazy?

"CRO?" Roland said. "Who the fuck is that?"

Alexis shrank out of his reach, not trusting him. "You know. The pharmaceutical company."

"They killed her."

"Who?"

"The girl in Cincinnati." Relief and confusion battled for control of Roland's face, but neither could beat the anger that pinched and contorted it.

"Keep moving," Wendy said. "Lex is about to take her dose, and we'll lose her."

"Those guys are in on it somehow." Roland turned his attention back to the steering wheel and spun back into traffic. "Hell, it's starting to feel like everybody's in on it but us."

Mark? He couldn't.

But Alexis had images of him meeting with defense officials, lobbying the health committee, moving in mysterious orbits that were always a little too complicated to explain. She'd taken it as the dedication of a career-driven husband, but maybe her own career had clouded her perception.

And one image froze in her mind, like a still frame from a movie that summed up the entire plot and theme: Mark shaking hands with Burchfield, an ambitious eagerness in both their eyes and a smug, conspiratorial air.

She couldn't be sure when she'd seen that. It could have been after a meeting of the bioethics council or it could be simply a fantasy, but it screamed at her so insistently that it became the truth.

The bastard.

She didn't know what he'd done, but she was going to kill him.

Wendy's voice pulled her from the self-inflicted pain as she realized she'd been digging her fingernails into the flesh of her wrists hard enough to draw blood.

She looked down at the wounds and found she was able to focus.

"Two minutes until your pill," Wendy said. "You'd better give me those directions."

CHAPTER THIRTY-ONE

Mark parked half a mile from the Monkey House property, pulling the car into the concealment of the roadside pines, whose late-afternoon shadows stretched toward darkness.

He'd never been there, but he'd overhead the plans for its security system. It was one of a dozen facilities on the company books, although it had been mothballed and listed for sale since the 1980s. However, the price was too high, even for the booming Research Triangle Park, which meant no danger of a serious offer.

The revived Monkey House project had been pitched as "Burchfield's baby," which suggested only a few close allies were in the loop. But maybe Burchfield was careless in his arrogance, and Burchfield was not without enemies who would be watching his every move.

Enemies both in and out of government.

The Glock had been almost a joke, one of those little macho tokens that were supposed to make corporate executives feel like big shots. Mark had even licensed his handgun, which diminished the locker-room points at the racquet club. He'd only had it out at the range three times. It had made him uneasy to even store it in the closet, and he never thought he'd actually be concealing it, fully loaded.

He'd insisted on a newer model with an internal locking system, because he wasn't comfortable with the series of trigger safeties. Now he only hoped he didn't have to use the gun at all.

Mark had dressed in leisure wear, taking a cue from the jogger. Workout freaks could be seen just about anywhere, in all hours and types of weather, without arousing suspicion. People merely turned away with slight resentment as they touched their own soft bellies and made useless, silent vows to get themselves fit.

Mark didn't run, though. He needed to get the lay of the land first. Two compact research complexes stood to the west of the property, glassed entrances giving way to brick, windowless structures. Mark had seen dozens of them as a CRO exec, and the shiny prescription medications with inventive names often grew from well-lighted but tediously mundane operations in such featureless buildings.

To the south, the orange glow of Raleigh was just visible against the horizon, a state capital that was more sprawling than metro. Sunset brushed the top of the pine forest to the west, an area that industrial development had yet to claim.

CRO couldn't have chosen a more remote, yet easily accessible, location, which made him wonder how far back they'd been planning the need for secrecy. There was a cartoon he'd once seen of a gorilla standing amid a crowd of briefcase-toting businessmen in suits, with the slogan, "If you want to hide, hide in plain sight."

He didn't have any sort of plan besides finding Alexis and getting her out of there. He tried not to think about the fallout, but he was shocked at how little he now cared about his career at CRO.

Alexis. When in hell did you become the most important thing in my life?

The undergrowth scratched at his face, and vines that he hoped weren't poison oak whipped at his ankles. The forest canopy blocked the dying rays of the sun, which slowed his progress but helped him feel less vulnerable and exposed. He found a road of crumbling pavement that appeared to run parallel to the property, and he followed it where the walking was easier. If any vehicles approached on the access road, he would be able to hear them and hide in the woods.

A minute later, he came upon the sedan with the tinted windows parked just off the road, pulled into the weeds in a half-hearted attempt at concealment. It was a Lexus, not the kind of car someone would use for off-road exploration.

So Briggs has got company besides me.

The road widened ahead and Mark entered the woods again. Foot-high grass and small saplings thrust up through the asphalt beyond the fence, a sign that the complex had not been used much. The front gate was likely monitored, which meant he'd have to find a way through or over the fence.

At least the scrub vegetation grew right up against the wire, a sign of long neglect that meant he could probably buy enough time to find a way in. He was tugging on the bottom of the chain links when he heard the crackle of tires.

Mark ducked low and scrambled through the brush, which tore at his exposed wrists, until he found an opening in the clusters of honeysuckle vines girding the entrance. He peered through and saw a black limousine idling in front of the fenced gate, headlights cutting blue-white swathes.

He recognized the limo, even though its windows were tinted as well.

Burchfield. Checking up on his investment.

He wondered if Burchfield had shown up without an invitation. Either way, Briggs would have to let the senator in. Assuming Briggs was inside.

The question resolved itself with the hum of an electric motor and the clanking of chain as the fenced gate was tugged to one side along a slotted steel track. Mark timed the opening, counting down in the dark rather than risking his watch light.

Seventeen seconds.

The gate clanged into place and the limousine entered the grounds. Mark wasn't sure whether a monitor camera or laser had revealed the car's arrival, but he was betting on the limousine diverting attention from inside, and the limo driver—*what was his name? Something butler-sounding*—would be focused on the narrow, overgrown approach. The car was through the gate and fifty feet down the bumpy driveway when Mark made his move.

He tore through the honeysuckle, discovering it had grown over a series of long steel poles that bruised his shin. He clambered over and kept as close to the fence as possible. The gate began retracting, and he had to expose himself to run ahead of it.

He moved, ducking low, half-expecting a gunshot or a megaphone blare of warning. Instead, he hurtled through and rolled just before the gate locked back into place.

The forest inside the fence was sparser, with taller, spindly trees that made for easier progress yet offered less concealment. The meager landscaping had long since gone wild, and the asphalt lot was spider-webbed with weaving rows of tall grass and weeds. Mark wondered if maybe he shouldn't have flagged down Burchfield's limousine and rode in with the boss, but the chill that had swept over him upon seeing the limo affirmed his instinct to hide.

The road was easy to follow while still remaining in the trees, and he heard the distant echo of car doors closing. He couldn't make out the voices but there were at least two, and maybe three, men talking. He moved through the darkness as fast as he dared.

The voices had stopped, which led Mark to assume everyone was inside. Unless there were guards on the grounds.

Mark didn't think so, because of the secretive nature of the project. A show of security would have aroused suspicion both from competing pharmaceutical companies and from the government agencies Burchfield hoped to avoid.

He reached the edge of the woods and an expanse of rough lawn about twenty yards wide separated him from the building. A high band of light marked a row of windows near the top, and he estimated the facility at about an acre in size. A solitary spotlight projected from the front of the building, revealing the shadowed alcove of an entrance with a steel door. The limousine was parked near the door, and Mark saw no sign of movement.

Great. What do I do now? Knock?

He turned to sneak around back and check for additional entrances when something moved to his right.

"Looking for your jogging buddy?" came a brusque voice.

"Uh, I'm…uh…"

"Yeah, I know," the big man said, moving just out of the shadows so Mark could make out his square face and small eyes in the floodlight. His mouth sagged to one side as he spoke. "You're lost. That happens a lot around here."

"I guess this road is the way out?" The gun seemed like a stupid idea now, but still Mark debated fishing it from his waistband. In the gloom, the man probably wouldn't even notice until he already had it out.

But then what? It wasn't like Mark was going to shoot him, and he couldn't see forcing the man to let him in the building.

"Well, it would be the way out *if* you were leaving," the man said.

And then the gun was out, but it wasn't Mark's. The man pointed his gun at Mark and then waved the barrel toward the building. "If you're so curious, let's go have a tour of the place."

Mark had never been threatened with a gun before. All the movies made it seem like no big deal. You banter with the shooter, and before you know it, he drops his guard and you jump him. Mark had seen it dozens of times.

Except the cold, black eye of the gun seemed to be peering deep into his soul.

As Mark headed for the limo and the factory door, the man came close behind him and yanked the Glock out of the back of his waistband. "Careful with this. You don't want a new asshole."

"I'm a friend of Senator Burchfield's," Mark said.

"Sure you are," the man said. "And you brought the Easter Bunny and Hillary Clinton with you, didn't you?"

Mark wondered if he should have mentioned Sebastian Briggs, but Briggs was the kind of guy people didn't like to talk about.

"You're one of the people from the trials, aren't you?" the man said. "You're about the right age for it."

"Yeah," Mark said, wondering whether the lie would keep him alive or amp up the danger. Whatever happened, he figured it would get him to wherever Alexis was.

"How come you're not freaking out like the rest of them?"

"I'm freaking on the inside."

The man gave a bark of laughter and pulled out an old-fashioned key ring. He opened the door and stepped back. "Welcome to the Monkey House."

CHAPTER THIRTY-TWO

"This complicates things," Briggs said, though secretly he was pleased. If circumstances warranted, he'd synthesized enough Seethe to dose them all, one way or another.

You always have to keep an ace up your sleeve.

But Briggs had two aces and a joker stashed away. While Burchfield knew about the serum that was deliverable via injection and oral delivery, he wasn't aware that Briggs had developed a gas version as well.

The military loved chemical agents that could be dispensed from afar, because that added extra layers of plausible deniability, reduced resource risk, and always seemed more humane. After all, it wasn't the military leaders of the world who had called for the banning of mustard gas. No, it was the do-gooders and the self-righteous. And Briggs suspected those do-gooders wanted to keep their killing up close and personal.

Briggs certainly did.

And so did his little monkeys.

"What's going on down here, Briggs?" Burchfield said, glancing warily at the hulking machinery. "You promised delivery of Halcyon and a lot of people are waiting."

"I'll have it next week. The FDA already has the data on the animal testing. Once we prove the efficacy and safety in the human clinicals, we can move into formal trials. You know the drill." Briggs couldn't resist reverting to the quasi-Marine talk Burchfield loved to employ, even though Burchfield's military experience had been limited to three years in the Boy Scouts.

"And you're sure they can't trace all this back to ten years ago?" Burchfield said.

"Names have been changed because mistakes were made," Briggs said, now employing passive voice in a parody of bureaucratic doublespeak.

Burchfield's scared. An interesting development.

The fire-breathing defender of American principals was famous for his televised rhetoric and advocacy of a U.S. military presence in the Middle East. It could be the influence of the little white-haired man standing beside him, Wallace Forsyth, whose moral compass always pointed straight to God.

Forsyth's gaze was focused on the charcoal sketch of the naked Wendy Leng, his mouth puckered in distaste but his eyes exhibiting a decadent glow of hunger.

Ooh, Mr. Forsyth, the things I could do with you, given time. But I don't think we'll have much time. Besides, she's spoken for.

Now where is Mr. Kleingarten, my dim-witted insurance policy?

Briggs secretly glanced at the bank of monitors, letting his unexpected guests study the bizarre scrap-metal maze Briggs had constructed with the help of his illegal Mexican friends. From their vantage point, Burchfield and Forsyth couldn't see the monitors.

On screen, Kleingarten stood at the front door, his gun leveled at a man in running clothes. The man's back was turned to the camera.

Another agent? The partner of the man Kleingarten had murdered earlier?

On the screen, the limousine door opened and Burchfield's driver got out. Kleingarten spoke to the driver, who also had the look of a federal agent, impassive and steely-eyed.

"Senator, how many bodyguards did you bring with you?" Briggs asked.

"Just Winston, my driver," he said, approaching the bank of monitors. "What's wrong?"

"It appears I'll need to put out another place setting for our mad little tea party."

As they watched, Kleingarten shifted his gun toward the driver, who went for the inside flap of his jacket. There was a silent flash from the muzzle and Winston collapsed. The report echoed dully inside the big, open building, rattling off the steel and rotted rubber.

"Goddamn it," Burchfield said. "I told Winston to keep it holstered."

"I don't think it's Winston you need to be worried about," Briggs said.

The noise upset David Underwood, who began howling and shrieking from the depths of the building. His cell was dark, so the monitor showed only the dim greenish outlines from the infrared camera. Anita was asleep or catatonic, exhausted from her encounter with Briggs, who'd played a delicious but dastardly game of "Let's make some amateur porn" using a few toys he'd saved for the occasion.

"What's that wailing?" Burchfield said.

"Sounds like somebody opened the gates of hell and called the devil to supper," Forsyth said.

"Winston?" Burchfield shouted, filling the factory.

Kleingarten and Mark Morgan emerged from around a tall sorting machine that dangled rusty chains from its array of pulleys. Under the dim glow of the high fluorescent lights, Mark's face looked green.

"Mark!" Burchfield said, losing his characteristic poise. "What the hell are you doing here?"

Mark shrugged. "You told me to keep an eye on things."

"All these people just keep asking to be killed," Kleingarten said, his gun held down near his hip.

"Drummond," Burchfield said, with the indignant anger of a man who was never crossed. "You're supposed to stay on the perimeter."

"Well, that's what *you* were paying me to do," Kleingarten said, then nodded at Briggs. "He paid me for something else. And you can drop the 'Drummond' bit. I'm my own man now."

"What's going on here, Daniel?" Forsyth asked. The man's wrinkled hands flexed in dismay.

"Hello, Mark," Briggs said. "I guess you didn't believe me when I said your wife would probably survive."

"You can't blame me for not trusting you," Mark said. "Your goon here just killed a Secret Service agent in cold blood. That's not going to be so easy to cover up."

"Hey," Kleingarten said. "He was going for his gun. And if he wasn't, he would have sooner or later. That's just what those guys do. You better be glad you're such an amateur, or I'd be covering you up, too."

Briggs smiled. Kleingarten no doubt had a juvenile jealousy of real cops and agents, since he'd only risen as high as night watchman. But the man was behaving erratically, even for a hired killer.

Maybe he saved a little of that Seethe dose meant for Alexis. Maybe he'd wanted to see what all the fuss was about. In which case, the night might prove even more interesting than I predicted.

Ah, the scientific method. Always with the unexpected outcomes.

"Look here, Briggs," Burchfield said. "We're wrapping up Halcyon. Now."

The broken, demented wails of David Underwood provided the soundtrack to Burchfield's last power play. The five men stood in Briggs's high-tech cage, Forsyth shrinking away from the confrontation. Mark, to his credit, was keeping his wits about him. He appeared to be taking in all the equipment and hiding his amazement at the scope of the operation.

Briggs decided there was little to be gained by a power struggle, since he still needed both the senator and the killer. At least for a while.

"Senator," Briggs said. "You don't understand the full implications of our work here. As Mark no doubt told you, we're not just developing drugs to help veterans with post-traumatic stress disorder. We've discovered something far more valuable."

"Yeah," Burchfield said. "That 'rage' drug. I'll back you on that, too, of course. I'm sure I can get my friends at CRO to cough up a little more seed money. But I need something to show for their investment."

"So word's getting around," Briggs said, glancing at Mark.

"These drugs are critical to national security," the senator said. "The CIA is already taking an interest. But if we keep this among ourselves, I'm sure we'll all achieve our objectives."

"I understand your concern. A man in your position, with so much to lose. Wallowing in the base human cesspool of fear and hate and paranoia must be so alien to you. Only true sociopaths can achieve political success, because compassion and humanity are the first casualties of any war."

Burchfield's lips quivered, as if he were just now grasping the fact that he was outranked.

"What do you want me do with him?" Kleingarten said, pushing the gun into Mark's back.

"We have some extra rooms in the psych ward," Briggs said. "Make sure our guests here are comfortable."

"Damn it, Briggs," Burchfield said. "You're finished for good this time."

"Scientists never finish, they just discover new problems," Briggs said. "Try rooms three through five," he said to Kleingarten.

He fished out his key ring and handed it to Kleingarten, who took it while keeping one eye on Mark. Briggs didn't trust Kleingarten with the code for the electronic keypad. He'd use the remote-control button beside his monitors.

"Do we have to be back there with that screeching devil?" Forsyth said. "We'll all go off the deep end if we put up with that for long."

"It won't be long, Mr. Forsyth. But I suggest you pray. I suggest you pray a lot."

"That's a mighty sad suggestion, coming from the likes of you," Forsyth said.

"Your god is built on fear, so my discovery should put millions of people in touch with him eventually," Briggs said.

"You're the devil," Forsyth said.

"Thank you for the promotion, but, please, let's stay humble. There is still work to be done. Kleingarten?"

Kleingarten cocked an eyebrow, noting Briggs had used his real name. "Yeah?"

"After you've shown our guests to their rooms, please clean up the mess outside. You can park the limousine in the woods."

"Whatever he's paying, we'll double it," Burchfield bellowed, making a last play with the only weapon he had left.

Briggs waited while Kleingarten mulled the options.

Bad move, Senator. You should have offered him the job as your new bodyguard, something with prestige. A man like Kleingarten enjoys money, but it's his ego that requires feeding, not his wallet.

Briggs decided that Burchfield had just lost his vote, should the man survive the scandal—and the night—and eventually show up on a presidential ballot. The senator was simply a lousy judge of character. He should have taken a few psychology classes in college.

"You heard the man," Kleingarten said to his three captives. "Just follow the screaming and we'll be there in no time. And, you, the praying guy? You better pray he doesn't start in with 'Home on the Range.' Talk about hell."

Mark took one step toward Briggs, but Kleingarten held the gun out with a smile.

Mark visibly tensed. "Where's Alexis?"

"Don't worry. Your wife will be here soon."

"If you hurt her—"

"Please, Mark. We're all friends here."

"CRO's pulling the plug when they find out."

"You know something, Mark?" Briggs met the gaze of each of the others, so they would know his words were for all of them. "CRO, the U.S. government, the three or four shadow organizations keeping an eye on me, Al Qaeda, Mossad, and God knows who else? They want what I have. And I am the only one who has it. I'd say that puts me in the driver's seat."

"Go on," Kleingarten bellowed at them. "I got work to do. All these corpses don't hide themselves."

As the four men navigated the dim corridor, Briggs checked the monitors, the security equipment, and the several little surprises he would soon spring.

He was in the driver's seat, all right, and he was about to slam the pedal to the floor and let go of the wheel.

CHAPTER THIRTY-THREE

Roland squinted at the gate, which filled up the fat yellow beams of the headlights.

The dented yellow sign that said "No trespassing" was like a fleeting image from a long-ago dream, but it also sent off tiny warning flares in his head.

"Is this it?" he asked.

"Yeah," Wendy said. "It hasn't changed much."

"Are you sure?" Alexis said from the back seat. She'd gone quiet after taking her Halcyon dose, and Wendy had to relay directions despite the escalating effects of Seethe.

Roland glanced sideways at his estranged wife. In the dashboard lights, she glowed with a blue radiance, an ethereal and beautiful woman. He'd always loved her exotic, almond-shaped eyes and the mysterious pools of her dark, placid pupils.

Shit. Whatever this drug is, it's making me love her again. But I never stopped loving her. I just started hating myself more.

"This is where we killed Susan," Wendy said.

"I wish you'd quit saying that," Alexis said with quiet resignation.

"Susan," Roland said. "She was one of us, wasn't she?"

"Don't you find it strange that we could have loved each other after that?" Wendy said. "We are horrible, disgusting people."

Susan's death was just another dream image to Roland, but every time Wendy mentioned her, the girl's face crystallized a little more in his mind.

Her smiling, sweet, chubby face.

And then the bloody and battered thing it had become.

He pounded his fist on the steering wheel so he would have some pain as a distraction. "Now what, guys? Ram the gate like in a movie? Or do we try to find another way in?"

"He'll be expecting us," Alexis said. "That's what this is all about. He timed the doses to get us here now."

She was right. His every step had been guided from the very beginning, since he'd woken up in Cincinnati with a corpse in the bathroom. In an odd way, the idea of manipulation gave him comfort, because it probably meant he hadn't killed her.

But he could have. He was clearly capable. And probably more eager than he'd like to admit.

But that was the Seethe talking. He could almost feel the effect growing, like a sentient being slithering through his nervous system and dispensing its twisted brand of poison.

"Anita's in there," Wendy said. "One way or another, we have to go."

Roland was about to respond when the gate gave a jerk and then began retracting.

"That was easy," Roland said.

Wendy touched his arm, and a tingle raced up his flesh. He was afraid the Seethe might be exaggerating his response to her, but he welcomed the contact. No matter what happened, it was right and fitting that they were together for this.

"So, we all vote for going in?" Roland said.

“No choice,” Alexis said. “We’ll be out of pills soon. And we’re likely to have a total meltdown then. We either lose it out here or take our chances on finding some Halcyon inside.”

“You mean it gets worse? That we’re better off in there with Briggs than out here with Seethe taking control of our minds?”

“She’s a scientist,” Wendy said. “We better trust her on this.”

“We don’t know what we can trust anymore. Even each other.” He didn’t mean to say that last sentence, but he knew they’d all been thinking it.

One of the wonderful side effects of this nutty joy juice was paranoia, apparently. But maybe that wasn’t such a big discovery. After all, if this thing trimmed existence down to the bone, there was nothing left but survival instinct.

Kill or be killed.

He eased the car forward, following the broken pavement into the trees. The building revealed itself through the treetops via its high band of narrow lighted windows, and then the brick façade came into view. The sight of it sent an icy spear of recognition up Roland’s spine.

“I don’t see any other cars,” Wendy said.

“Don’t worry,” Roland said. “They’re here.”

“You think Briggs is alone with Anita?”

The question irritated Roland because it sounded almost like jealousy. It wasn’t Wendy’s fault that Briggs had seduced her while she was vulnerable. After all, she was ping-ponging on Seethe and Halcyon. Hell, people did worse things. Like commit murder.

“He’s trying to recreate the original trials,” Alexis said.

“Except he can’t do that,” Wendy said. “He’d need David Underwood and Susan Sharpe, too.”

“Nobody knows what happened to David,” Alexis said.

"David's in on this somehow," Roland said, pulling the car to a gentle stop. "It's all part of the maze, and Briggs has his rats jumping through hoops, looking for the next chunk of cheese."

"Why go to all that trouble, though?" Wendy said.

"I think we have to go in and find out," Alexis said, opening her door.

"She's the brains of the bunch," Roland said to Wendy as they watched Alexis walk toward the building entrance. "But you're the one not dulled by the Halcyon. So I'm counting on you, okay, babe?"

"I'm afraid," Wendy said.

He touched her shoulder, and before he gave it a thought, he was leaning toward her, brushing her hair from her ear, kissing her cheek. It should have been wrong, but it was the most familiar thing he'd felt in days. Maybe years.

"Roland," she whispered, and then they crushed their lips together hard, the way people who might die would do.

She tasted of raspberries and mint, but there was a metallic *whang* on her breath that Roland assumed was due to the chemicals in their bodies.

"Let's find Anita and get out of here," he said with a confidence he didn't feel.

They walked arm in arm from the car to where Alexis was waiting near the single metal door. She pointed to a dark wet spot on the pavement. "Blood," she said.

"I wonder whether it was somebody trying to get out or somebody trying to get in," Roland said, leading the way to the door.

He wasn't sure what he expected. Maybe a booby trap, maybe an ambush, maybe an avalanche of confetti and circus music and fat clowns.

The door was unlocked, more proof that Briggs was ready for them. He peeked inside the opening.

And ten years fell away in a heartbeat.

Alexis glanced around the dim, cavernous interior and its clutter of broken machinery. The high fluorescent lights cast an alien glow over the chaos, accenting the shadows beneath metal armatures, shelving, and grid work.

"It's almost exactly the same," she said as they navigated the main corridor. "But I don't remember the ceiling being so high."

Wendy dug in a pile of tractor parts and brought out a jagged length of steel pipe. She swung it in an arc before her, grunting.

"Hey, hey," Roland said. "You're going to hurt yourself."

"She's due," Alexis said. "She needs to take her next dose now."

Wendy growled as if threatened, and she backed away from them, her free hand upturned in a claw. The deterioration was sudden: one moment Wendy had been twitchy and distant, and the next she was feral.

"Here, Wendy," Roland said. "Put down the pipe and you can feel better."

Alexis was riding the Halcyon herself, now accustomed to its dulling effect. But the Seethe still stirred restlessly beneath it, as if waiting for its chance to erupt. She wondered if the two compounds were playing a Jekyll-and-Hyde tug-of-war inside their heads.

Maybe the effect was like that suffered by a cancer-ridden Alzheimer's patient who might emerge into awareness only long enough to realize how much pain he was in.

She kept to the shadows while Roland closed in on Wendy. "Come on, hon," he said, in a smooth imitation of lovey-dovey talk. "Who's my good girl?"

"Careful," Alexis said. "I think the building has triggered some memories."

"Thanks for the tip, Einstein," he said. "Like we come back here and suddenly it turns into a giant game of Candyland?"

"Don't be an asshole, Roland. I liked you better when you were flattened on Halcyon."

Alexis knew her anger was chemically induced, but as a neurochemist, she understood that all moods were the result of fluctuations in serotonin, glutamates, and dopamine. But where all the other brain researchers were still stabbing in the dark, Sebastian Briggs must have stumbled onto something so primal and obvious that she had no room to fight it.

After all, the awareness that fear existed didn't make it any less scary when the scalpel swept toward your eyeball or the shark fin appeared beside you in the ocean.

"You were the first one to hit her," Wendy said to Roland, the words squeezing out between clenched teeth.

"No, no, you're remembering it wrong," he said. He stood in place, repeating the shout he'd uttered when they'd first entered the building. "Briggs! Anita! Is anybody here?"

Under his breath, he emitted a "Goddamn it" and turned away from Wendy. Alexis wasn't sure whether he did it as a show of trust, but Wendy saw it as an opportunity and leapt for him.

Alexis opened her mouth to warn him, but he must have sensed Wendy's movement—*Holy hell, we're being reduced to animals*—and he spun to the side just in time to miss her downward swing of the pipe.

The momentum carried her arm forward and the pipe struck the concrete floor with a muted *thunk*. Wendy dropped the pipe and shook the shock from her elbow. Roland grabbed her and overpowered her, wrestling her to the floor.

"Hurry, the pill!" he said.

Alexis broke from her paralysis and yanked the vial from Wendy's pocket, removing the last pill. She pushed it into Wendy's mouth.

Wendy nearly bit her hand, but Alexis kept her palm pressed against her friend's lips until Wendy chewed and swallowed. Within seconds, her body relaxed.

Alexis kept her hand in place while she glanced at the bottle. "Roland?"

"Yeah?"

"This was yours. D. Underwood."

"A pill's a pill," he said, keeping his weight on Wendy. "They're all green."

"Briggs might have engineered specific dosage levels for each of us. That's why we each had our own labels."

"Who gives a shit? I'm not that interested in protocol at this point."

"Roland," Wendy said with a whimper.

He looked down at her. "What, babe?"

"You're hurting me."

"Sorry." He helped her sit up. "You were freaking out."

Wendy leaned forward and dry heaved, then spat. Chewed bits of medicine scattered across the floor.

Alexis glanced at the pipe, which lay about six feet to her left. Then she studied the pale angle of Roland's neck above his collar. She could have the pipe before Roland noticed.

But the bitch Wendy deserved to die, too. She'd risked them all by not taking her medicine.

Before Alexis could make a decision, a loud clapping erupted. Sebastian Briggs stepped from behind a giant stamping machine, approaching them with the same arrogance he'd always displayed. He finished his applause and said with a smile, "My volunteers have returned."

He'd changed little, physically. The only difference was the first hint of gray at his temples. He was dressed in chinos and a blue shirt with the top button undone, looking more like a day trader than a researcher.

"Roland and Wendy," he said. "The happy couple reunited."

"Where's Anita?" Roland said.

Briggs ignored him, gazing at Alexis as if to hypnotize her. "Alexis. My star pupil. I'm hearing great things about you."

"It should have been mine," she said, spit flying from her lips. "It was my fucking formula and you stole it!"

"There would have been enough glory to go around, Alexis. But you had to commit that horrible, horrible atrocity."

A warbling wail arose from somewhere in the bowels of the old factory. It resembled singing, but the sound was so forlorn and tormented that Alexis couldn't place it at first. All her attention was on Briggs and that smirk she'd always found insufferable.

Every time he'd corrected one of her mistakes, every time he'd chided her for a theory he found outlandish, every time he leaned over her shoulder and pressed against her when he was studying her cellular images—

"'Home on the Range,'" Roland said. "It's his song. You've got David here, too, don't you, you psycho son of a bitch?"

Roland tensed as if to launch himself at Briggs, but he was stopped by the researcher's chilling words. "You need me, Roland. I have the Halcyon. The *real* Halcyon, not that watered-down junk you've been taking. Without me, you turn into psychotic animals, and we all know how that ends, right?"

Roland didn't look convinced. Something clattered atop the assembly-line sorter to the left of them and a curved acrylic hood toppled to the concrete and cracked. A man crouched atop the machinery, his face obscured in the shadows.

"That's my Igor up there, so don't go playing hero," Briggs said. "He's an excellent shot."

Igor. That's what Briggs had called Alexis when she'd been selected as his graduate assistant. *We'll save the world, my little Igor,* he'd say, patting her "hump" and letting his hand linger. And she'd endured it because she had a career to consider, and Briggs was gaining notice.

Why am I just now remembering all this? Could he have developed a regimen that would have us all breaking down right here, right now?

But of course that was what Seethe was all about. A timed disintegration, a mass-market chaos, insanity prescribed and delivered on schedule. Part of Alexis had suspected it, even back then, but she was so intent on the beneficial Halcyon research, she'd overlooked the dark side.

"Oh, Alexis, I can see the disappointment on your face," Briggs said. "I believe you understand now. But I wasn't trying to steal all the credit. I was trying to protect you from the fallout."

Wendy, who'd been lethargic after taking part of the pill, stirred and said, "Where are we? Roland?"

"Right here, babe," he said, leaning down to help her stand. "It's going to be okay."

"Wendy," Briggs said. "It's really good to see you again."

Alexis noted the pathetic tremor in his voice. The schoolboy crush. It had been no secret the two had been carrying on. Back then, when Wendy was innocent and Briggs was still young and vital and charismatic, it had almost seemed normal. And the affair had lessened Briggs's fondling of Alexis, so she was grateful for the reprieve.

Now, though, it seemed like a terrible betrayal.

Seethe. It was all because of the Seethe. We wouldn't have done those things otherwise.

"Here's the deal," Roland said. "We get Anita and David, and we leave. Nobody says a word about any of this. You can go back to boiling your witch's brew and cutting livers out of rats for the rest of your life. But we're out of it."

"Roland. You don't mind if I call you Roland, if we're indulging in fantasies? You're in no position to make demands. The only two doors are locked, the retracting door has been welded shut for decades, and the only people who know we're here are already here."

"Then what do you want?" Alexis said, eyeing the pipe on the floor. The urge to grab it and smash his head came and went in waves, one moment hot and pulsing and right, and the next repulsive and impossible.

"Why, to finish the trials," Briggs said, as if amazed at the simplistic view of a student. "That's what we *all* want."

Roland clutched Wendy in a protective hug, which caused Briggs to shoot him a menacing glare. "You married out of guilt, but we know your real fear, Roland. You're scared somebody will count on you. Because you always fail them, don't you?"

Before Roland could react, Briggs shouted, "Are you ready, Mr. Kleingarten?"

"Just give the word, Doc," said the man on the sorter.

David Underwood's weird ululations were the only sound, reverberating around the hulking machinery, gaining brittleness and depth from the steel and the high glass: "Where seldom is heard…a disss…kurrr-ajin' word…and the skies are not kuh-loudeeeeeeeeee…"

Briggs took a bottle out of his pocket. "In this vial is a special version of Halcyon. One pill each. These don't last four hours. They will stave off the worst symptoms for maybe fifteen minutes, maybe twenty minutes. We don't know yet." He beamed at Alexis. "If we knew everything, we wouldn't need to experiment anymore, would we?"

"…alllll…daaaaaayyyyy," David wailed.

"So what now?" Roland said.

"We see which of you get out of here alive, just like last time," Briggs said, leaning forward and placing the vial on the floor at his feet. "Susan was the weakest ten years ago, but I suspect it will be Wendy this time."

"You fucking bastard," Roland roared, rushing forward at the same moment Alexis went for the pipe.

"Now!" Briggs shouted.

There was a click and hum as the factory went pitch-black.

Mark put his ear to the wall, but the insane man's singing drowned out any hope of hearing what was going on. He thought he heard Alexis's voice, but he couldn't be sure. Then the lights went out, and he felt along the wall to the door, trying the handle for the tenth time.

A hissing emanated from somewhere to his right, and in the dark he felt along the wall. Inches off the floor was a tiny metal grill, and air was circulating through it.

No, not just air. Something vaguely metallic and acrid. He sniffed, trying to place it.

He retreated to the far side of the room and slumped in the corner, his heart slamming against his ribs. Someone pounded on the wall to his left. Burchfield had probably made the same discovery.

Now I know how prisoners in the gas chamber feel. Except I don't know whether I go brain dead and forget who I am, or if I get lizard-brained and tear my own eyes out.

Mark yanked his shirt up, tearing buttons, and held the fabric to his face, hoping it would serve as a filter. He tried to concentrate on his breathing, but the panic caused him to forget and take huge gulps of the contaminated air.

He scrambled to the door, bumping into it hard enough to see lime-colored sparks behind his eyelids, and he wondered if he was hallucinating. He punched the door twice, and by then the acrid odor had permeated his nostrils and left residue at the base of his throat.

Shit. It's in me, whatever it is.

He grabbed the handle out of instinct, and this time it turned.

The surge of relief was stronger than his wariness, and he propelled himself into the fresher air of the hallway, even though it, too, was in darkness.

"Mark Morgan, is that you?" It was Burchfield, somewhere to his left.

"Yeah. Briggs must have used a remote control to unlock the doors. Why did he let us out?"

"Because we're free." It was a woman, and it sounded like she was still inside her cell. Mark hadn't realized there might be other captives besides the lunatic singer of "Home on the Range."

"Who are you?" Burchfield bellowed in his authoritative voice.

"Anita Mann," she said with a giggle. "Who wants to be first?"

"Where's Forsyth?" Mark called to Burchfield. The hallway had a main door, which Kleingarten had unlocked when depositing them in their cells, then locked again upon exiting; the acoustics suggested the hallway was still sealed off. The cell doors must have been sprung by remote control.

"Wallace?" Burchfield called.

"Come on, handsome," Anita said. "I have a cozy cot right here waiting. And you don't have to take turns. There's plenty for everybody."

"Nuh-nita," someone blubbered. Mark recognized the voice as the singer's.

"David?" The woman now sounded almost normal, though groggy, as if waking from a dream.

"They…killed Susan."

The woman screeched in the dark. "Shut up! Shut the fuck up! That never happened, any way you remember it."

"Mark, these people are off their rockers," Burchfield said. "Let's get the hell out of here. Wallace!"

Mark heard Burchfield scrabbling and scratching along the wall, then a metallic *ding* opposite him as a door closed.

"Goddamned," Burchfield said. "He went back into his cell."

Or maybe Briggs didn't let him out, for whatever reason. Although Mark recalled his door had a privacy lock as well.

"He's probably safer in there," Mark said, thinking the elder statesman wouldn't be much good if they had to fight or tear their way out of the hallway.

He tried to recall the layout of the hallway, but all he recalled were glimpses of the rows of doors, the low ceiling, lights inset so there were no low-hanging fixtures.

When somebody has a gun on you, you can't think about much besides that deep black barrel and whatever might come out. If I ever see that son of a bitch again, I'm going to shove that—

Terrible, red images flooded him and he shook them away.

"Okay, people," he said as calmly as he could, in the direction of David and Anita. "We're going to get out of here, but we need to work together."

He felt something warm and moist near his cheek and then she was entwining her arms around him, like a slithering, sinuous snake. Her body was fervid and her breasts were soft, her hair brushing gently across his face, and then her tongue was on his neck. "Hey, lover," she whispered, and he realized she was naked.

He tried to push her away, but her grip tightened, and then she had her legs around him in a scissors grip, the heat between her legs radiating against his crotch through his pants. Half of him wanted to slam her against the wall, to hurt her and shake her off, but another part of him pulsed in alternating bands of languid blue and brilliant yellow.

Her lips found his and he tasted the acrid chemical again.

Drugged, he recalled, but knowledge didn't diminish the insanity. He was aware of his two minds, the one that was frightened and murderous and the one that wanted to surrender to the raging lust that sprang from some primitive, disturbing depth.

He kissed back, sickened at his lust, and Burchfield's distant hammering and shouting came as if from underwater.

Then other hands were at his back, pulling, tugging, even as he pressed himself harder against Anita's exposed flesh and his hands frantically explored her curves. But there was no sensuality in his touch, only a carnal craving driven by an almost sickening desire to possess and consume.

"Luh-leave her alone!" the man grunted and stuttered as he grabbed at Mark. "Not like Suh-Susan."

"Come on, David," Anita whispered. "Plenty for all."

But David's intrusion had turned Mark's mindless lust to something else, and he turned, feeling for the man in the darkness. It was easy to grab one of his thin arms and run a punch toward the center of where he thought the man might be.

His fist landed with a dull *thud*, like hitting a sack of paste. The man wheezed and fell backward, and Mark got a sense of his victim's scrawniness as he turned toward Anita again. But she was gone, slithering somewhere along the wall, chasing whatever mad obsession had seized her next.

Burchfield ranted about how he'd be ordering an investigation, NSA, CIA, FBI, Homeland Security, and the "fucking Boy Scouts of America." He was as unhinged as Mark, who drove his fist against the wall hard enough to drive some of the madness away.

With the spark of pain, clarity descended and pushed aside the conflicting demons of lust and violence. Or maybe they were all the same demon. He could feel them up there in his brain, explosive forces ready to breach their dams and flood him once again.

Pain. That's the way to beat the Seethe.

Alexis could probably explain the chemical process, how pain was perhaps the most primitive part of the brain, less sophisticated, more essential, more basic, more *human* than fear.

But right now, he had to find her. Because if she was out there, and she was as bad off as he was, then she was in deep trouble.

And, for now, pain was his friend.

Forget Burchfield, CRO, and the FDA.

Pain was his only fucking ally.

Anita must have found Burchfield in the dark and was now working her seduction on him, and he proved less resistant than Mark. Their moaning and slobbering filled the hallway, and David, crawling on the concrete floor toward the couple, muttered the opening lines to "Home on the Range."

Mark rubbed his bleeding knuckles, reawakening the pain. He used it like a totem, a beacon of sanity in the induced madness. He guided himself along the hall, hoping he was moving in the right direction.

He tried to think of the worst pain he'd ever endured, and recalled the time one of his dental crowns had popped loose. The arteries in the teeth ran straight to the heart, he'd heard, so they were significant.

By the time he found the door, Anita was whimpering in the throes of pleasure and Burchfield was grunting, and even though Mark hadn't seen Anita, the memory in his fingertips hinted at her erotic prowess and moist potential. A tiny surge of regret and jealousy rocketed through him, but he knew it was false, and he raked his knuckles along the door hinges just to remind himself of what was real.

Pain. Pain is real. Maybe the only real thing in this world.

Then, girding himself and trying to picture Alexis's face, he peeled back his lips and drove his mouth hard into the middle hinge.

He grunted as one of his incisors broke in half, splintering up into his gum. He fell away spitting blood and broken enamel, the agony sluicing through his head like lava.

The pain consumed everything for a few moments, and he wiped the blood from his mouth. He was plenty hurt, but it consumed his mind, and he was able to remember his task.

The hallway door was open. It must have been on the same switch as the cell doors. He slipped out into the cool air of the factory and eased the door shut behind him, making sure it was locked. He couldn't withstand any more temptation.

Nor any more pain.

CHAPTER THIRTY-SIX

The party begins.

As soon as Kleingarten hit the remote switch killing the lights, Sebastian Briggs had backed away and reached for the night-vision goggles dangling from his back pocket. The facility interior wasn't in absolute darkness, since the faint urban glow imbued the high windows with gray, but the subjects were cast in the bleakest night.

The goggles had their own infrared-emitting source, however, which meant he was broadcasting an invisible beam that would reflect on objects and allow him to see even in total darkness. There were places in the maze that were designed to be closed off from all light, and he didn't want to miss an inch of the fun.

The goggles were a little clumsy, since they were strapped to his head and added a little weight, but at least his hands were free.

The trio staggered around, blinking, at their most helpless. He'd calculated correctly that Wendy was the most vulnerable to Seethe and Alexis was the most coherent. Alexis had always been astute, and he wouldn't have been surprised if she had figured out his pharmaceutical game of cat-and-mouse. But apparently the Seethe was more powerful than he'd imagined, or else she wasn't as smart as he had hoped.

She fumbled for the pipe that Wendy had dropped, and Briggs wondered if she would turn first on the others or look for him. Roland, who should have been the most confused, had the presence of mind to drop to the floor and crawl along, patting the concrete in front of him to find the vial. Wendy—

Ah, Wendy.

Moving as silently as possible, Briggs eased along the massive sorting machine that assembly-line workers had once used to piece together motors. Chains clinked farther down the corridor, and he knew Kleingarten must have made his retreat. He'd instructed the man to wait an hour, and then turn the lights back on, but he certainly didn't trust Kleingarten.

But there would be time for Kleingarten later. Right now, he had Wendy.

She had recovered a little, although she stood wobbling like a foal, blinking against the darkness. She was twenty feet away from the others, forgotten now even by her former husband.

Ah, Wendy. I have missed you.

He stood close enough to smell her. She'd shampooed with a chamomile-and-honey concoction, but it had been at least a day before, because animal sweat, tainted with a faint touch of the chemicals decomposing in her body, were her dominant odors. He didn't mind, though. He rather liked it.

His nostrils flared as he indulged again. She turned, possibly sensing his presence, and he froze in place.

"Roland?" she said.

"Stay where you are, babe," Roland said from twenty feet away. "All this junk around here, you might get hurt."

She obeyed, just like she always did. Sure, she'd been Briggs's second choice in the beginning, but she'd proven the sweetest selection because of the deeply suppressed eroticism and hunger she'd hidden even from herself. Her yearning and seeking had manifested as an artist's passion in her waking life, but Seethe had peeled away the conscious layer and exposed the carnal creature inside. Alexis would have been too much trouble, and like any good researcher, Briggs knew all windows of opportunity were brief, and he would rather indulge than match interpersonal wits.

A successful predator always knows how to pick out the easy meat.

He knelt, hoping his knees didn't pop, and he leaned closer, trying to smell the rest of her.

"Got 'em," Roland said, shaking the vial before slipping it into his pocket.

"I'm losing it over here," Alexis said, still feeling along the floor for the pipe. Her fingers brushed it, and Briggs smiled as she brought it up with the barest scrape of metal on concrete.

"We can't trust that bastard," Roland said. "Every four hours, every fifteen minutes, once in a fucking lifetime. He's just playing with us."

"I need one," Wendy said.

"Not yet," Roland said. "We need to hold out as long as we can."

"We don't have *long*." Alexis squeezed the pipe and, crouching, she moved toward Roland, trying to keep him talking. "All we have is now."

"This isn't some dipshit sixties song, Alexis," Roland said. "This is life and death."

"You ought to know about death, after what you did to Susan."

Roland turned toward the sound of her voice, the gap between them narrowing. "I didn't do anything to Susan. You were the leader, remember? Little Mrs. Briggs, right there pushing our buttons."

Alexis raised the pipe and, with a screech, rushed toward him. Briggs watched through the night-vision goggles, six inches from Wendy.

Roland flinched at the cry and rolled to the side, but he wasn't fast enough. The pipe bounced off his shoulder with a bruising *thwack*, and he grunted, "Fuck."

"Lex! You okay?" Mark shouted from the far end of the factory.

Briggs smiled in the dark.

Ah, the hero to the rescue. But a kiss won't wake this princess. No, this princess is ruling with an iron hand.

"Lex!" Mark repeated, more frantically. A stack of boxes fell over somewhere, sending a spray of small metal objects—lug nuts, rivets, ball bearings—across the floor.

Alexis swung the pipe back and forth, probably hoping to find Roland so she could deliver another blow. But Roland had learned his lesson and was keeping his mouth shut, now staggering down the corridor, his left arm hanging limp.

Briggs took the opportunity to grab Wendy's wrist and tug her in the opposite direction.

"Roland?" she whispered.

"Shh." He moved quickly, not giving her a chance to get oriented. He loved it when the monkeys were lost and confused.

Alexis banged her pipe against the hulk of a tractor frame, giving away her location. Mark would be able to find her, with a little time and patience. However, if the Seethe Briggs had dispensed through the ventilation system had done its job, Mark would have precious little of either. And surely Mark now understood the risk of exposing himself to a group of raving, murderous lunatics, but like fools throughout history, he was sticking his neck out for love and a senseless notion of duty.

Love. If only I could invent a drug for that, we'd truly have a crazy world.

"Where are we going?" Wendy whispered, as though understanding the need to be secretive. It sent a shiver of delight through Briggs. Just like old times.

What they shared wasn't love, not exactly, but it was the best thing he'd ever had. And what man wouldn't take advantage of such a situation?

"Shh." He pulled her along, the goggles revealing the turns in the heaps of scrap iron, towering stacks of rubber tires, and old wooden crates. He knew the layout well enough that he could have navigated it in his sleep.

"It's the Seethe!" Mark shouted from the far end of the facility. "It's making us freak out."

"Mark?" Alexis called, from one corridor over, though her voice echoed throughout the cavernous shell.

"Be careful!" Roland yelled. "She's gone violent!"

"I'm not violent," Alexis said, followed by the sound of scuffling feet. "Now give me those goddamned pills or I'll bash your brains in."

Upon hearing Roland call out, Wendy resisted Briggs's pull. "Roland?" she whispered. "How can you be in two places at once?"

"Because he's two people," Briggs said. "And I'm the good Roland."

Wendy wasn't convinced, and she tried to pull away, digging her fingernails into the back of Briggs's hand. He yanked her close and grabbed her hair, pulling her ear to his mouth. He didn't need to be quiet, because the others were shouting, but he knew the power of a whisper.

"This was all for you, Wendy," Briggs said. "We belong together. After CRO pays me off, we'll go away. Bermuda, the Yucatan Peninsula, New Zealand. You name it."

"No," she moaned, still resisting.

"I can fix you," he said, impatient now. "I have some Halcyon in my office."

"Let me go," she said, her body tensing as she strained to break free of his grip. He wrapped more of her long hair around his fingers and put his other hand around her throat.

"If you scream, I will hurt you very badly, and I don't want to do that," Briggs said. *Yet.*

She started to scream anyway, and he knew he'd miscalculated. More fear would only accelerate the effects of the Seethe, and she'd already crossed the line.

He squeezed her throat, choking off any sound but a faint, nasal wheezing. Through the night-vision goggles, her eyes appeared as bulging green orbs in her beautiful, heart-shaped face.

"Come on," Briggs said. "I've waited ten years for this. I know you've been waiting, too."

As he dragged her to his office, she grew limp, and he wasn't sure she was still breathing. He let go of her hair and put one arm around her slim waist, letting his hand trail across those breasts he had fantasized about for so many years. She wasn't wearing a bra.

A hundred feet away, Alexis and Mark were calling to one another, feeling their way in the dark. An occasional piece of equipment clattered to the floor. Roland must have decided to play it safe and keep his mouth shut.

Briggs had instructed Kleingarten to wait by the front door. Even though the lock wouldn't release until Briggs had keyed the command from the security console, he didn't want to take any chances. Plus the task would keep Kleingarten safely out of the way until Briggs was ready to assign him mop-up duty.

And then Briggs would dispose of him along with the rest of the trash.

He reached his office just as Alexis began shouting for Roland. "I need my pill!" she shrieked.

He'd never known she was such a bitch. But then, he'd forgotten what she was like on Seethe. He hadn't watched the video recently.

He propped Wendy in his leather swivel chair by the computer and turned her to face the rows of video monitors. "Here, my sweet, let me make you more comfortable," he said, loosening her top two buttons.

Her breasts were as pert as he remembered. He dipped to have a sample, even though the night-vision goggles cast it in an unappealing shade of muted green. Her nipple puckered in the cool air; he told himself it was because of his skill.

"I know you're anxious, but there will be time for that later," Briggs said, and she gave a distant moan in response.

He withdrew a syringe from his top drawer. He'd wanted to save it for later, but he couldn't control himself any longer. He realized he was as juiced up as any of his monkeys. Except his juice was natural.

The Seethe serum was engineered for intramuscular use, so he could stick it virtually anywhere. He moved the point of the needle over her breasts, stroking. Then he inserted it just below her collarbone. She sighed as he flooded her system.

He hit the electrical override breaker, which would prevent Kleingarten from switching on the lights if he chose to disobey Briggs's orders. He connected the battery backups, which had just enough power to run the equipment in his office.

On the top row of monitors, with the hallway camera switched to thermal imaging, he saw the orange-and-yellow outlines of Anita and Burchfield copulating on the floor, their bodies radiating heat. A smaller man, obviously David Underwood, was making a pathetic attempt to pull Burchfield from atop her, but the senator was pumping like a man possessed.

If the electorate could see him now. But no surprise there. He's been fucking Americans for years.

The final captive, Wallace Forsyth, had not left his cell, and the isolation camera showed his form huddled in the corner, apparently on his hands and knees, hands clasped in front of his bowed head.

Ah, prayer. The last refuge of the hopeless. That's what happens when you come face to face with yourself. You become your own worst nightmare.

He checked the wide-angle cameras attached to the factory ceiling, thirty feet above the floor. He zoomed in the one pointed at the rear of the building.

"Ah, that explains it," he said to Wendy. "Mark must have locked them in. Not exactly according to plan."

Because the door had a regular lock in addition to the electronic lock, Briggs couldn't open it again without doing it manually. And he wasn't going to leave his office until this was over. It would be the only safe place when the subjects degraded to their most primitive selves.

He slid the cage door into place and secured it with a hasp lock.

Then he rolled Wendy in the chair over to the monitors and faced her toward the largest screen in the middle.

"I have something I'd like you to see," he said, taking her hand. "And something to remember."

CHAPTER THIRTY-SEVEN

Mark found Alexis in the dark, though he'd cut a gash in his cheek prowling through the clutter of the factory. The pain was sharp enough to cut a swath through the clamoring fog of murder, and he ran his tongue over his shattered, throbbing tooth.

Pain is my ally.

He chanted it to himself like a mantra, fighting off the madness that threatened to engulf him.

Alexis was screeching Roland's name, her voice echoing through the high metal rafters, and all he had to do was anticipate her direction, press back into an opening, and wait, focusing on the red streak of flaming agony in his face.

When she passed, he jumped her, counting on his familiarity with her height to hit her in the right spot. He thought he was tackling her around the shoulders, but his skull thudded against something solid. He went blue-minded for a moment, and she tried to raise her arm, but he gripped hard, fighting for consciousness.

"Lex, it's me," he said. "I'm sorry, but I have to hurt you now."

He moved his mouth to her upper arm and bit hard, causing her to scream and drop whatever she was carrying. He didn't let up, but instead let his teeth dig until they stopped on bone and the coppery sweet blood painted his lips.

"Owww, Mark, you're hurting *meeee*," she moaned, trying to fling him off, but her struggles subsided as the pain took hold.

"Pain," he said wetly, pulling his mouth away. "It clears the Seethe. But you have to keep it fresh."

Taking his own advice, he slapped the spot on his skull where the metal had struck, then dug a fingernail in for good measure.

"Yeah," Alexis wheezed, relaxing in his grip. "Like rock-paper-scissors. Pain covers fear."

"And lust cuts pain," Mark said. He wasn't sure what he was talking about, but even now the twin powers of Anita's lingering touch and his wife's warm body threatened to reduce him to a slavering satyr.

"We need the Halcyon," Alexis said. "We have to find Roland."

"What if Briggs screwed with the dose? What if it's a placebo?"

"No, he wants it like ten years ago."

"When Susan Sharpe died?" Mark weighed the impact of her sudden silence before adding, "I know what happened."

"Don't say her name, Mark. Please, God, don't say her name—"

She trembled in his grip and he said, "Yeah, okay. Focus on the bite wound."

"Roland!" Alexis shouted to him in the dark. "We have to work together."

"If he's as messed up as we are, he'll be too paranoid. We'll have to find him."

"Unless he took one of the pills. Then he's okay for a little bit, though he won't remember why we're here."

"Then he'll be scared as shit anyway," Mark said, realizing he'd lost all orientation. "Have you seen Briggs?"

"Not since the lights went out. Wendy's gone, too."

"I locked the others back there. At least they're safe for now, assuming they don't rip each other's throats out."

"I'm sorry," she said.

"Me, too." He punched her in the stomach and she grunted. Her arm flew out reflexively and caught his mouth, causing a fresh eruption of blood and torment.

"Now let's find Roland before we beat each other to death," she said between gasps. "He's got three doses of Halcyon."

They held hands as they hustled down the dark corridor as fast as they dared. Mark kept his free arm out in front of them, in case they ran into one of the obscured mountains of junk.

"I see a glow over there," Mark whispered. "Along the far wall."

"Probably where Briggs is."

"We go the other way, then."

They'd only traveled about a dozen feet when Roland spoke from somewhere below them, near the floor. "Hey, you guys."

"Where are you?" Alexis whispered.

"Shh. Dr. Sunshine must have some cameras in this joint. Get down and crawl. You're not going to kill me this time, are you?"

Mark felt his wife pull him to the floor and he eased forward on his hands and knees. He had a sense of a narrow, confined space, because he could hear the muffled sounds of their breathing.

Then a small light came on, and he saw Roland's hand cupped around a cell phone. They were in a large wooden crate, reinforced with metal bars and smelling of axle grease.

"Shit," Mark said. "Did you call somebody?"

"No signal in here. But it's a light."

"Good thinking," Mark said. "That armed gorilla took mine."

"We need the pills," Alexis said. "We can't last much longer."

"I took one," Roland said. "And I'm good for maybe fifteen minutes if our zookeeper was right."

"Where's the bottle?" Alexis said.

"Not so fast. Think about it. Only two pills left, so we better have a plan. And we still have to find those other people. Is my wife here?"

"Yeah. Mark is Seething, too."

"Fuck. This your husband?"

"Yeah. He's with CRO."

"We met before," Mark said, awkwardly extending his hand. "I was at your wedding."

"I ought to kill you," Roland said, ignoring the offered shake. "Not sure why, but it sounds right."

"You'll probably get your chance," Mark said, running a finger over his broken tooth. "But Lex is the expert. Better listen to her."

Roland nodded and slid the phone into his pocket, where the light quickly died.

"Our only chance is to buy more time," Alexis said in the dark. "We can't help the others. That means one of us is going to have to take the two remaining pills."

Mark scraped his hand along the rough side of the crate until several splinters drove into his skin. "I can hold out," Mark said, though there was probably a threshold beyond which even pain wouldn't fight off the demons. He could feel them lurking back there, waiting to claim him.

"Two left," Roland said. "And I might need both of them to save Wendy."

"But you don't know enough," Alexis said. "You're already forgetting where we are."

"We're in a goddamned crate."

"Keep it down or they'll find us. We need every edge we can get. *Oww*."

Mark had clawed her shoulder, and was pleased to find his bite mark was still raw and wet. "Pain. It's the only cure."

"You guys are hurting each other?" Roland said. "Doing Briggs's job for him?"

"Two pills will buy me at least half an hour," Alexis said. "I can find where Briggs has taken Wendy."

"Wendy's here?" Roland said, apparently forgetting he'd already asked that.

"I know the layout, and I know better than anyone how Briggs's mind works. I was his Igor, remember?"

The way she said it irked Mark and made him want to hit her for real, but he couldn't trust any of his feelings. Except the feeling of pain.

"She's making sense," Mark said. "And don't forget that goon with the gun is still around."

"Goon with a gun?" Roland said in the dark.

"Lex, what if you become like him?" Mark said. "What if you take your dose and forget to take the next one?"

"What choice do we have?" she said. "Give me the vial, Roland."

There was a sigh and then a rattle in the dark, and then Alexis's mouth was near Mark's good cheek. He was afraid she was going to bite, and he cringed but didn't draw away. Instead, she kissed him. Gently.

Mark found the tender residue worked almost as well as pain at clearing his head. But tenderness wasn't something he could trust, either. Like pain, tenderness didn't last.

"I love you, honey," she whispered, giving his hand a fleeting squeeze as she scrambled out of the crate.

As her shuffling footsteps faded, Mark said, "So, Roland, have you heard of a cure called 'pain'?"

Chapter Thirty-Eight

Doc's turned all his monkeys loose.

Kleingarten had seen the security system in Briggs's office, and he knew some of the cameras were infrared and thermal imaging. It hadn't taken long to put two and two together when Briggs had explained the "lights-out" trick.

But damned if Kleingarten was going to wait by the door until it was over.

It was a little dangerous moving around all that shop junk in the dark, but he was reluctant to use the penlight on his keychain. The entire factory could be viewed via the monitors, but Kleingarten had cased them enough to know that if he clung to the left side of the main corridor, Briggs couldn't see him until he reached the end.

That's assuming he ain't busy eating Chinese.

If the Slant was the only reason for the horror show, Kleingarten could have saved Briggs the trouble. He could have picked her up right after the car crashed into the coffee shop, whisked her away while she was confused, and delivered her right to Briggs's little torture chamber. Or even nabbed her before all the noise.

But something bigger was going on than just a Looney Tunes genius playing games, and Kleingarten wanted a piece of it. Once he figured out what it was, he'd turn the tables on Briggs, gallop in like the cavalry, and rescue the senator.

Sure, he'd have to explain why he'd pretended to side with Briggs, but there was enough clusterfucking monkey business going on to keep everybody confused for the rest of their lives.

He came to the end of the corridor—he'd counted the steps ahead of time, right after Briggs had told him the plan—and debated whether he should sneak or just make a run for it. About twenty-seven steps to the right would put him on the fourth and final row, and Briggs's office was about thirty more steps. He squinted between the arms of some sort of metal drill press and observed a faint greenish glow.

So Briggs is watching him some TV.

Something heavy, what sounded like a stack of harrow disks, collapsed and fell in the middle of the factory, slamming to the floor. A man shouted in pain.

Sounds like Roland Doyle. After what he did to that woman in Cincinnati, he deserves a little punishment.

Wait. Wasn't that David Underwood who did the killing?

Aw, fuck it, Briggs must be scrambling my skull, too. Except I'm too smart for that.

Kleingarten took advantage of the distraction, knowing Briggs would check the commotion on the monitors. He crouched and hustled, his Glock in his hand. Though he believed he was the only one armed, the night had already been full of surprises, so he was ready for anything.

He hadn't had this much fun since he'd murdered the porn star's shrink.

Briggs's cage was ahead, and in the glow he made out the two forms. He didn't have to worry about Briggs seeing him on the monitors now, because the doc was busy pulling the pants off the woman in the chair.

Kleingarten wasn't one for peep shows, and he definitely didn't want to see the doctor's naked ass when he got down to business, but Kleingarten needed to see where the cameras were focused. The cage door was closed and a thick lock held it in place, and the security system controls were inside. Nobody was getting in or out of the Monkey House unless Briggs said so.

The Slant was staring ahead, eyes like marbles, though her fingernails dug into the arms of the leather chair. In the radiance of the monitors, she was blue-green instead of brown mustard.

She was already naked from the waist up, and her breasts looked like they had tiny bite marks on them, though it was hard to see in the bad light. Briggs was breathing heavily, and Kleingarten noticed some sort of harness on his head, reared back so the lenses were pointed up.

Night vision. Why the hell didn't I think of that? Must be slipping in my old age. Yep, definitely time to retire.

As he edged closer, the doc flung the woman's pants to the side and stroked the insides of her thighs. "Just like old times," Briggs said, his voice husky.

And that's when Kleingarten saw what was playing on the main monitor.

The scene was of the same factory, but it wasn't dark. He recognized Roland, Alexis, and Wendy, though they were clearly younger, leaner, and wearing filthy clothes. They were closing in on a naked woman he didn't recognize. She looked eighteen, chubby but short, maybe a hundred and ten pounds soaking wet.

And she was plenty wet. Even in black and white, Kleingarten could tell it was blood.

The chubby teen turned and tried to climb up an empty tool tree that resembled a pegboard, but her own blood caused her to slip. Roland was the first to grab her, but Wendy was right there. The camera zoomed out, and Anita stood to the side, naked and also damp with blood, her hand stroking between her legs as she watched. Wendy yanked the girl by the hair until she turned to face her attackers.

"This is why I've always loved you," Briggs murmured as he licked Wendy's legs. "A woman who can do something like that, she deserves a little scientific observation."

Kleingarten was sickened. He'd killed people, sure, but that was for money. Most of the time, anyway. To do shit like this just to get some jollies…

But he couldn't look away, as on the screen the younger versions of the Briggs monkeys grabbed the bleeding woman, Roland on one side and Wendy on the other. And as gorgeously perverted as Anita was, it was the woman approaching the victim that sent a chill up Kleingarten's spine.

Dr. Alexis Morgan, the suave, polished, educated big shot, grinned as she stood over the cowering teen. Her lips moved, obviously giving a little lecture, probably some horseshit learned from Briggs. The eyes of the three were wide, bright, and crazed, like that picture of Charles Manson where the swastika was carved in his forehead.

Alexis held a thick and pointed piece of machinery in her hand, and something dark dripped from it.

She lifted it as the teen struggled, but Roland and Wendy held the girl tight. Roland punched the girl in the kidney and the fight seemed to go out of her.

Kleingarten thought a soundtrack must have come on, because he heard the victim moaning, and then he realized it was the Slant. Briggs was doing something to her, and she loved it, because she was watching the screen and purring like a hooker on the clock.

Jesus. This Seethe is some powerful shit. Fucks you seven ways to Sunday without a rubber.

As Alexis jabbed the piece of broken metal at the teen, a blur of movement came from the left side of the screen and slammed into her, causing her to drop the weapon. Alexis and the man wrestled, and then Kleingarten recognized him as the albino monkey, David Underwood, only he was a hundred years older now.

It sounded like the Slant was having an orgasm inside the cage, and Kleingarten had had enough. He aimed his Glock between the bars at the top of Briggs's head.

Fuck. If I kill him, I won't be able to get out, and I don't know where he's keeping all his joy juice.

On the screen, Anita wallowed on top of David, laughing, and Alexis had retrieved her jagged weapon. This time the chubby teen just closed her eyes.

Everybody onscreen looked as happy as sharks at a seafood buffet, except the person about to get killed.

"Party's over, Doc," Kleingarten said.

Alexis had taken the first pill right away, and an inner voice said to go for the second one, too. But the longer she could hold out, the better.

Even if it means Mark…

Mark what?

She felt along the row of machinery. It was the assembly line where the plows were pieced together, and she could picture the rusting machinery beneath her hands. It hadn't changed in all those years, as if the junk had been left as a museum to their—

No. That didn't happen. And if you think for a second that we really killed Susan, we don't have a chance.

She heard talking on the far side of the factory, where Briggs had once kept his office. The man who'd turned out the lights was yelling at Briggs. The man was making a big mistake, but he'd find that out soon enough.

There's something I'm supposed to do.

She reached for her arm and found the throbbing wound.

Pain.

She gouged the wound and remembered Mark, her husband, waiting back there somewhere in the dark, counting on her. He'd been dosed somehow, too, even though he wasn't part of the original trials.

She felt buoyant and energetic, though she knew it was serotonin and cortisol pumping though her body, kicking adrenaline from her kidneys. The neurochemicals could so easily turn, amplified by the Seethe, but the Halcyon seemed to be suppressing the worst of the impulses. She welcomed the nullifying tug of the cocktail, maintaining an academic awareness as she rode above her own sick impulses.

She ran her hands along the equipment—the connecting pins, bolts, curved edges of blades, swivel joints, and loose steel plates with serrated edges from welding jobs. The tangle of farming equipment was knotted so tightly that she couldn't extricate any pieces, so she was forced to keep going toward the sound of the voices.

Alexis had no plan, only determination.

How many of us were there?

Mark, Roland, Wendy…

Were there others?

Susan?

"Susan?" she said aloud. "Are you here?"

She bumped into a wobbling wire-framed cage, and something heavy fell, crashing to the floor inches in front of her feet.

She scooped it up. It felt like a plow blade, about eight inches long, with a short metal tube on top where it attached to the frame.

Alexis swung it like a battle ax.

It felt goddamned good.

And familiar.

"All right, Doc, where are the keys?" the man was saying.

"Put that away, Kleingarten," Briggs said. "You kill me, you don't get anything."

"I ain't killing unless I have to."

Alexis remembered the man had a gun. Was it last night, or ten years ago? She couldn't be sure.

All she knew was that Briggs was the boss. Briggs had the pills, and she needed pills.

Pills for what?

Dr. Sebastian Briggs had something she craved. An image flashed through her mind, a memory or a fantasy. A computerized image of the compound's cellular structure.

It should have been hers. She was there. And if...whatever happened...hadn't happened, she would have joined the ranks of those who'd made revolutionary leaps in science. Pasteur, Curie, Salk. Except instead of curing diseases of the body, she'd have healed the mind.

The most broken part of the human race.

Alexis crawled under a long conveyor belt, careful not to let the plow piece drag on the concrete and give her away. Her heart thudded and the fine hair on the back of her neck prickled.

Instinct.

Despite all her study, all her research, all her books and papers and experiments, she'd not learned a thing. There was no higher mind. It always came down to kill or be killed.

And Briggs needed to die.

"You need to die," Kleingarten was saying, not twenty feet from her. "But not right now. Tell me where you keep all your bottles of witch's brew. Or is it barrels? To get a U.S. senator down here, you must have some major inventory."

Alexis peered between two oversized tractor tires, the rotted rubber mingling with the chemicals, dust, and petroleum of the factory air. Kleingarten's bulky form was between her and Briggs, silhouetted by the dim glow of high-tech equipment. When he moved one arm, the barrel of his gun glinted.

The bank of monitors spotlighted Briggs as if he were a stand-up comedian. He stood in his cage, shirt open, hair unkempt, seemingly calm despite the gun pointed at him. Behind him, Wendy was splayed in a chair, naked except for her panties circling one ankle.

The scene brought back memories of another time, but it wasn't a cage, it was a university office, a sunlit room, when Alexis had swung open the door to report on Halcyon only to find Briggs and Wendy writhing on his desk. She'd slipped out without Wendy noticing, but Briggs had heard the door and had flashed Alexis a smirk as he thrust inside his willing, moaning partner.

This could be you, that smirk had said. And Alexis had been tempted. Because that would have bought her access to his research, and the secrets would be hers.

But her anger at Briggs and disgust at Wendy shifted to something else when she saw what was playing on the monitor behind them.

Wendy and Roland held Susan's naked, bloody body.

And there was Alexis, on the screen, approaching them, snarling, face twisted, eyes glittering.

In her hand was a jagged piece of curved metal—

She squeezed the handle of the broken plow blade.

Almost like this one.

But what's happening? Susan's here now, so how could she be on TV?

"Turn it off, Doc," Kleingarten said. "It's making me want to puke."

"We learn from the mistakes of the past," Briggs said. Wendy moaned, stroking one of her breasts.

On the screen, Alexis lifted the weapon.

Under the conveyor belt, she raked the plow blade across her forearm, the searing stripe of pain bringing a moment of clarity.

Mark was right. Pain worked.

On screen, drops of blood fell from her weapon, Roland's and Wendy's faces were stretched and bright with anticipation, Susan's eyes widened as she denied what was about to happen.

It really happened.

Before the jagged metal fell, the screen exploded, and the gunshot boomed throughout the factory. Briggs shouted, and Wendy stirred in the chair but didn't get up.

I was supposed to do something.

Kill somebody.

Yeah.

She eased out from beneath the conveyor belt, took five silent steps forward as the shot's echo died away, and swung the plow hard and high. Kleingarten was fixated on Briggs and the shattered monitor, and he was likely deaf from the resonating din. Or else he'd forgotten he was trapped in a mechanical graveyard with a bunch of rampaging monkeys.

Either way, he was vulnerable, and the vulnerable always died first.

The tip of the plow dug deep into the base of his skull, just at the top of his spinal column. He barked an "Urp" and spouted a couple of gushes of blood as he pitched forward.

She hauled the blade out of him and lifted it again, to smash him and smash him—

"Lex!"

She froze, blinking and trembling. "Mark?"

"You're Seething, remember?"

Pain. Something I'm supposed to remember about pain...

She looked at the dim outline of the makeshift ax in her hand. A clot of brain and hair clung to its tip.

Then Mark had her, and she struggled to raise the ax—*He* bit *me, the motherfucker!*—and then he slapped her hard and she dropped the weapon. He grabbed her by the shoulders and shook her.

"Lex! Where's the other pill?"

"They killed Susan."

"*You* killed her, Alexis," Briggs said. "You haven't lost your magic touch."

Mark slapped her again, and she came around, not all the way, but enough to remember where she was. Mark jammed his hand in her pocket and pulled out the pill bottle, flipping the cap away.

She thought she was supposed to do something, but all she could think about was the lurid home movie Briggs had made, and how they'd all staged a murder scene.

What a weird fucking research project. Pretend to kill somebody so Briggs could measure their neurochemical activity.

Mark shoved the pill in her mouth and ordered her to swallow it.

Mark was right about the pain, so maybe he was right about this.

She swallowed, and he held her as she glanced at the cage. Briggs stood behind Wendy, who looked lost in another world, or in some twisted fantasy Briggs might have planted.

On some of the smaller video monitors, shapes moved and flitted.

More people?

"It's okay, honey," Mark whispered, holding her close. "It hurts, but it's okay. It's up to you now."

"Turn on the goddamned lights and open the door," Roland said. "Nobody else move."

He held Kleingarten's gun in his fist, and Alexis wished she'd killed him while she had the chance.

CHAPTER FORTY

Roland was sick of these fuckers.

He didn't know how many bullets the gun held, but he figured there were plenty enough for all.

He remembered everything now. Especially how that bitch Alexis had made him take the pills. Telling him forgetting was a *good* thing.

No, he'd rather feel alive, even if the truth hurt.

"Do it!" he yelled at Briggs. "I'm not like your other monkeys. I don't jump every time you slip them the banana."

"Easy, Roland," Briggs said, and Roland was pleased the doctor sounded a little scared. The smug bastard's cool was only an inch deep, about as far as his shriveled little pecker could penetrate.

Roland's finger tightened around the trigger as Wendy moaned, oblivious to everything. The sight of her sweat-slick skin confused him, and he didn't like confusion. No, he was a fucking monkey with a hard-on for revenge.

Roland fired, and Briggs's computer exploded.

"My data!" Briggs yelled.

"Open!" Roland roared as the report echoed off the concrete walls.

"Okay," Briggs said, unconsciously pulling his shirt closed as if that would offer protection from a bullet. He fished in his pocket and pulled out a key ring, digging a key into the hasp lock.

Roland swiveled the gun at the Morgans, but they were staying put, raking at each other's wounds, bleeding and crazed in the faint light.

The lock popped free and Briggs swung the door open. "Now the lights," Roland said.

He felt great, better than he had in years. Seethe was like booze and sex and cocaine rolled into one. Why the fuck was that bitch Alexis trying to keep it from them? Probably wanted it all to herself.

Probably wanted to fuck Briggs, too.

Hell, everybody else was.

Wendy.

"Turn on the lights," Roland said, not even bothering to raise his voice. As Briggs worked the switches on the security system, Roland entered the creepy cage and knelt beside Wendy's chair.

"I know what happens when you lose control," Roland said to the beautiful woman. "Hell, that's the story of my life."

Her eyelids fluttered. "Roland?"

"Yeah, babe. We're getting out of here."

"Don't do it, Roland," Alexis said. "We need Halcyon or we're going to do terrible things, and remember all of this. And what we did to Susan."

"I'll take my chances."

"You're going to lose it. You might Seethe forever."

"I've been Seething since before I was born. This is just how God made me, and that's goddamned good enough for me."

The lights began blinking on, stinging Roland's eyes. All their faces were pale. He picked up Wendy's clothes and dropped them on her lap.

"Get dressed," he said.

"What happened?" she asked.

"I'll tell you later."

"Make Briggs give us the Halcyon," Alexis said, standing outside the cage and holding her husband with fierce desperation. "You can go crazy if you want, but we still have to deal with this."

Roland felt the rage flood him, and he saw Susan's bruised and blood-spattered body, and then he imagined Alexis with a bright red hole in the middle of her forehead.

But you can't bury the past. Halcyon just helps you lie to yourself, and I already know how to do that.

But he could tell he was getting angry, so he kicked the base of Wendy's chair. He grunted in pain. He might have broken his big toe, but it felt good.

That was the trick behind it all. God invented suffering because the world had no meaning without it. And without pain, you had no need for God, because you didn't need relief. Pain served a higher purpose, maybe the *only* purpose.

And pain felt kind of good when you got used it.

At least it was always there when you needed it.

"All right, Briggs, give them their monkey juice, before I get tired of playing Mr. Nice Guy," he said, his jaws tight.

Briggs moved to an old industrial locker beneath his computer and fumbled with the key. He opened it and brought out a plastic bottle about the size of a quart jar.

"That other stuff, too," Roland said, loving his pain. "The Seethe."

Briggs brought out a pint of clear liquid in a glass jar.

"That's *all*?" Alexis said.

"He's got to have more," Mark said. "He promised Burchfield enough Seethe to dose an army."

"You think this is easy?" Briggs said. "You, better than anybody, Alexis, should know you don't just cook up this stuff in a bathtub like a meth redneck." He lifted his hand to indicate the equipment in his office. "Look what I've had to work with. And now my data's destroyed. I'll have to reconstruct it from memory."

"I think you're holding out," Roland said. "And I don't give a shit who ends up with it, as long as it isn't you, and as long as you never put any more of it into Wendy."

"He's got more," Mark said.

"CRO can shove it up their asses," Roland said, forcing himself to focus on Wendy, who was struggling to slide one slim leg into her pants. "Now, give me the key to the front door and open the gate, and if I have to come back here, I'm going to be a little unhappy."

His heart felt like a bottomless black hole. But that was okay. It was deep enough to swallow anything.

He took the key from Briggs and put his free arm around Wendy. "Come on, babe."

They limped a few steps in the direction of the main entrance, Roland walking backwards. He debated locking the three people in Briggs's cage, and his money would be on Alexis to be the last one standing. That was one cunning bitch.

"Look out!" Alexis yelled, and he dodged on instinct.

Briggs was a blur of movement, and the glass jar hit Roland's shoulder and bounced to the floor, shattering, its liquid seeping out and soaking into the concrete. Roland pulled the trigger twice before he even thought about it.

Briggs gave a grin, winked at Wendy, and then he collapsed. The shirt hadn't stopped bullets after all.

The plastic bottle busted open as Briggs dropped it, and dozens of green pills rolled across the floor. One crunched under Roland's foot as he escorted Wendy past the rusting equipment.

He thought about collecting a few pills, but decided he'd rather take his chances with madness rather than the sick brain candy of Dr. Sebastian Briggs.

"Did you kill somebody?" Wendy murmured.

"Maybe," he said. "I don't remember."

One thing he *did* remember. He sure as hell wasn't David Underwood.

CHAPTER FORTY-ONE

Alexis frantically gathered the pills as they rolled across the floor.

She couldn't believe this was all the Halcyon Briggs had manufactured. She fought an urge to kick his sorry corpse.

"My head's clearing a little," Mark said. "But my tooth is killing me."

"The gas has lower efficacy than the other forms. You'll make it."

"Yes, Dr. Morgan."

"Help me pick up these pills."

"I have to let the others out first. If they haven't eaten each other's livers, that is."

"That's not funny." She glanced at the bloody plow blade.

"How are you doing? Is the Halcyon working?"

"Barely enough." *You fucker. You'll probably tell CRO everything. And all this could be mine.*

"You look okay. I can leave you alone for a minute, huh?"

"Sure."

As Mark jogged off, she retrieved the plastic bottle and began dropping pills in it—*tick tick tick.*

She wondered how long the Seethe would run through her system without the Halcyon suppressing it. It could be hours, or it could be days—or maybe the rest of her life. As far as she could tell, she was the only one who'd been injected with the serum form, though God only knew what David Underwood had gone through or how long he'd been imprisoned in the Monkey House.

Briggs probably had a backup hard drive somewhere. And he'd probably been too paranoid to move data off-site, so it would be here somewhere.

She glanced at his face and the blank eyes staring past the world. Then again, secrets to Seethe and Halcyon might be locked in the dead vault of his brain.

Her eyes kept going to the plow blade and she recalled how it had felt driving the tip through Kleingarten's skull. She'd never felt so alive and powerful. And she could have that feeling a long time, if she cracked the formula.

Fear is its own kind of pleasure. Up there, it all gets cross-wired.

A few of the pills had rolled into the pool of Sebastian Briggs's blood. She fished them out, wiping them one by one, and slipped them into her pocket. She'd retrieved most of the pills by the time the others returned.

Anita stood between Burchfield and an unsettled Wallace Forsyth. Mark was supporting a pale skeleton she recognized as David.

"You killed Susan," David said, upon recognizing her.

Alexis glanced at the blade. As the Halcyon eased, she didn't want this transitional feeling to end—that cliff edge of awareness, the black abyss on one side and the peaceful plateau of forgetfulness on the other.

Two kinds of oblivion.

No choice, really.

"No," she said. "She died of fright."

Anita nodded, closing a couple of buttons on her blouse with shaking fingers. "Yuh…yeah. It was a fake experiment, David. It was make-believe."

Burchfield looked subdued and embarrassed. He cleared his throat and attempted to sound authoritative, but he failed. "This is official property of the U.S. government, Dr. Morgan."

"Shut up, Senator," Mark said, pointing to the monitor bank. "The cameras recorded your behavior. Fox News will love it."

"Are you threatening me, Morgan?"

"Just playing by your rules."

"Where is it?" Wallace Forsyth said in his tremulous, hoarse voice. He sounded a century old. "Where's the Seethe?"

It's mine, you bastard, and you better put the fear of God in you, or I'll get there first.

She reached for the plow, but there was a green pill beside it. She pinched it and slipped it into her mouth as Mark moved toward her.

"Don't!" he yelled. "You don't know if it's Seethe or Halcyon!"

She swallowed as he jammed his fingers between her lips. She wanted to bite him, but she decided she'd hurt him enough.

Restraint. Must be coming down.

Mark yanked the bottle of pills from her.

She glanced at the blade again.

Ah, shit. I love this man.

CHAPTER FORTY-TWO

They'd dressed their wounds as best they could, using Briggs's emergency first-aid kit. Alexis's arm was the worst, and as Mark cleaned it with water and a gauze pad, she made little growling noises that scared him. He only hoped the pain was enough to keep her tamed.

His tooth was still throbbing, sending colossal waves of pain through his jaw, but he clung to its rhythm like a boat riding out swells.

"This has to be worked out between CRO and the government," Burchfield was saying, although no one was listening to him. Anita was tending to David, who was slumped in the leather chair.

"Alexis," Forsyth said. "The Lord spoke to me back there in the dark. The devil is in them pills. And I don't think they can be trusted with either corporations or governments."

"That's why we're keeping them," Mark said.

"We're all on the same team," Burchfield said. "And if what I experienced is any indication, Briggs was onto a winner."

"No," Mark said. "The Seethe is gone. I looked around, and unless he had off-site storage, that jar was all he was able to synthesize."

"Briggs didn't go anywhere without our knowledge," Burchfield said. "We've tracked him with GPS since the beginning. Picking you up at the airport was the only time he's been out in three weeks."

Mark pointed to the wet blotch in the concrete, where the liquid fear had mingled with old oil stains and Kleingarten's blood. "Good luck cutting that up and isolating it, because that's all we have left."

"I'm back, honey," Alexis said. "But you'll have to tell me what happened."

Her eyes almost looked normal. Still, there was something in them that inspired him to nudge the bloody plow blade away with his foot.

"Give us the Halcyon, then," Burchfield said. "That's an order, in the name of national security."

"These people need it," Mark said, waving at Alexis, David, and Anita. "We don't know how long the Seethe will last."

"Just one pill," Burchfield said, glancing around the floor to see if Alexis had missed any. "We can analyze it."

"A drop of the devil's blood is enough to pollute the whole ocean, Daniel," Forsyth said. "Nobody should have to see what I saw in my head."

"If there's a hell, that's the only place it could exist," Alexis said.

Mark was relieved to hear her sounding like her old self. Hopefully, there would be no permanent damage.

Still, she was capable of murder. Whether that was an instinct, or a deep, essential part of her personality, was for the shrinks to decide. Or maybe God.

"Here's the deal, Senator. You pull strings and get all this covered up." Mark nodded at Anita and David. "They take the

Halcyon as long as they need it. And when my wife is confident they're all normal again, you get what's left."

Mark had no intention of letting anyone have those pills. Not the government, not CRO, not Forsyth, not even his wife. No one could be trusted with the power to change people's minds. There was no "better living with chemistry," only the lying and the dying.

"All right," Burchfield said, somewhat wary but probably recognizing he had little bargaining power besides brute force, and his hired muscle was currently a cold, stiffening corpse. "We've got four dead. An industrial accident with limited exposure should work. CRO will have to sacrifice the property, though, because we'll have to turn it into an EPA brownfield site."

"Why should we believe you?" Alexis said. "What if you called in the CIA and had then search for the formulas? What if this stuff is too addictive and you find you can't resist?"

Burchfield glanced over the damaged monitors and equipment as if measuring the evidence that might implicate him in the conspiracy. "Things happened here that are best forgotten. I have my enemies, too. We're all in the same lifeboat on this."

"Fine," Mark said. CRO's board of directors would squeal, but given the possible collateral damage, they would hold their tongues and take it. Not that Mark gave a damn. He was finished with CRO, one way or another.

"She killed Susan," David said, his mind apparently stuck on one track.

Anita stroked his hair and began singing in a soft, angelic voice. "Home...home on the range...where the deer and the antelope play..."

David joined in, wailing in his atonal style, but he was smiling.

Fuck, Mark thought. *So that's the bottom on Seethe and Halcyon.*

An elevator that goes up and down until the cables snap.

I hope you don't get there, Lex.

He kissed her. "Better get you to a doctor."

"Your face is a mess," she said. "That tooth looks like it hurts."

"Yeah," he said. "The things you do for love."

She touched his face, and she was placid, gorgeous, determined, the same woman he'd married. She must have already forgotten the worst. "And I'd do anything for you."

"I believe it."

She nodded. "I wonder how Roland's doing."

"He seems like he can take of himself."

"He's Seething, honey. All bets are off."

"Yeah." He himself was married to a lunatic serial killer. The odds were lousy, but he was all in.

Chapter Forty-Three

"Where are we going?" Wendy asked.

Her head was resting on his shoulder, and despite the chemical stink and the lingering factory smell, Roland liked it. She belonged there.

"Anywhere away from hell counts as heaven," he said. He had to use little tricks to keep himself focused, jabbing at his wounds or biting his lip until it bled. He kept one hand on the wheel and the other curled in a fist.

Once, when the image of Briggs slobbering on Wendy's naked thighs flashed, he'd wanted to pull over, drag her by her hair, and beat her brains out.

But he got over it.

That's what you do when you love somebody. You get over it.

"You feeling okay, babe?" he said, kissing the top of her head.

"Better. But it all seems like a dream."

"We've got a different dream now."

"There at the last...in the cage..."

"Forget it."

"Briggs wanted me to remember something—"

"Forget it."

She snuggled closer, and she was warm. He was on I-40 and the midnight traffic was sparse, mostly truckers. He couldn't help but wonder what might be stored away in the long trailers, hidden from view, and how many other potions might be getting shipped around the world.

"I'm glad you came back," she said.

"Well, I didn't have much choice."

The gun was jammed in his waistband, and he liked the feeling of power there. It was new and strange, something like control. But he knew control was an illusion.

A memory flashed of digging through the wallet in Cincinnati and looking for photos of David's family. He wasn't sure if the memory was real or imagined, but it had been driven by some deeper impulse. Or maybe something beyond him, a god that might have knitted itself back into existence from the lost, gray vapor.

He remembered. That was good. He had a chance.

"We never really talked about having kids," Roland said.

"We haven't talked about a lot of things," Wendy said.

"Maybe we ought to change that. The talking, I mean."

She turned to him and her lips were close. "Remember that time in the park, when you picked those roses for me, and that park attendant came running over and yelling?"

He didn't remember, but he laughed a little and said, "Yeah. That was something."

"I still have those roses, pressed between the pages of the Manet book you gave me. You know I love my Manet."

That was funny, because he'd bought her a book of Gaugin, but maybe one weird French painter was as good as another when it came to storing keepsakes.

He smiled. If he could remember a name like "Gaugin," then maybe his brain wasn't too full of holes. He'd piece it together eventually.

He turned his face to kiss her.

"You love Manet, and I love you," he said. "Looks like we're in for a hell of a ride."

One day at a time, they said in his recovery program. But sometimes it was a second at a time, because fear only needed the blink of an eye. Everything else took longer.

He headed west, away from the sunrise and false hopes and bottled nightmares, and toward the endless road of memories that awaited them.

THE END

About the Author

Scott Nicholson is author of more than a dozen novels and seventy short stories, as well as six screenplays, four children's books, and three comic book series. His novel *The Red Church* was a finalist for the Bram Stoker Award and an alternate selection of the Mystery Guild. He also has collaborated with bestselling author J.R. Rain on several paranormal novels. He has served with the Mystery Writers of America, the Horror Writers Association, and International Thriller Writers. A former journalist, radio broadcaster, and musician, Nicholson won three North Carolina Press Association awards. To learn more about him, check out his website at www.hauntedcomputer.com.